THE CAFÉ AT
SEASHELL
COVE

ALSO BY KAREN CLARKE

Being Brooke Simmons
My Future Husband
Put a Spell on You
The Beachside Sweet Shop
The Beachside Flower Stall
The Beachside Christmas

A HEART-WARMING LAUGH-OUT-LOUD ROMANTIC COMEDY

THE CAFÉ AT SEASHELL COVE

Karen Clarke

Bookouture

Published by Bookouture in 2018

An imprint of StoryFire Ltd.

Carmelite House
50 Victoria Embankment
London EC4Y 0DZ

www.bookouture.com

ISBN: 978-1-78681-367-1
eBook ISBN: 978-1-78681-366-4

To Tim, with all my love

Chapter 1

I'd known my early return would come as a surprise to my parents. What I hadn't anticipated, on stepping into the brightly lit living room, was the sight of my mother's breasts in all their naked glory.

'Cassie!' She goggled at me over the back of the sofa, as guilty as a teenager, while I tried to snap my jaw shut.

'What... are you... please tell me you're having a hot flush and that's why you've taken your top off.' I clamped a hand over my eyes to block out the sight of her rumpled hair and fiery cheeks. Not to mention her naked breasts.

'I'm not menopausal,' she huffed, as if I'd just returned from a longish walk and interrupted her favourite TV programme.

'Of course you are. You're fifty-eight,' I argued. 'It's simple biology.'

She gave an exasperated tut, which wasn't the sound I'd imagined her making on seeing her beloved daughter return to the fold. On the journey down, I'd shaped a scene where tears of joy and perhaps a bit of crying featured, considering she hadn't seen me for nearly a year. (Skyping didn't count.)

'We weren't expecting you until tomorrow, love.' Dad's voice was accompanied by the sound of a zipper, and I let out a quiet moan. Glancing through my fingers, I was treated to an eyeful of his greying chest hair, as well as his receding head hair.

'For god's sake, you two.' I turned my back, reaching for the dimmer switch to reduce the overhead glare, listening to them scrabble about for discarded clothing. It was bad enough that they'd copulated twice before, to conceive my brother and me, but faced with the evidence that they were still 'at it', nearly thirty years later, was a bit much on an empty stomach. 'It's barely seven thirty,' I grumbled.

'You should have phoned.' Mum sounded reasonable, and I turned, relieved to see she'd put her top back on. 'We would have postponed our lovemaking—'

'LA-LA-LA-LA-LA LA-LA-LA-LA-LA-LA,' I sang, childishly jamming my fingers in my ears, while my parents exchanged coy smiles, and Dad pulled on his ancient Garfield T-shirt, flattening his hair to his scalp. He'd started going grey in his thirties, and at fifty-nine was a shade that Mum called Silver Fox.

'You should be pleased your parents still find each other physically attractive and like a cuddle before dinner,' he said, when I'd unblocked my ears, with the merry twinkle that made people instantly warm to him. 'Shouldn't she, Lydia?'

'I've no objection to you cuddling,' I said. 'It's'—I flapped my hand—'the groping I can't cope with.'

In response, Dad lunged for Mum while making kissy noises, causing her to let out a girlish squeal. 'Stop it, Ed!' She pretended to bat him away, and I wondered whether I'd fallen asleep on the train from London to Devon and was, in fact, dreaming.

It would explain the slightly surreal feel the day had taken on, which had begun with me standing on a packed Tube train that morning, sleep-deprived after another uncomfortable night on Nina's sofa bed, reminded of a different morning, two months earlier: the morning I'd met Adam Conway. Finding myself sardined against a tall, dark-haired man, who'd smelt like the interior of a leather-seated car, I'd taken the unusual step of acting on Nina's advice to 'be more proactive in the man department', by slipping a business card into his jacket pocket with a pithy 'Call me, some time', accompanied by a flirty eye-twinkle (which might have come across like a nervous tic, because of being tired and rubbish at flirting). Unfortunately, my watch strap had snagged on his pocket flap, causing his head to jerk down and his dark-chocolate eyes to rest on me with a glimmer of amusement.

'Are you trying to distract me while you steal my wallet?' he'd queried, his gaze sweeping over my unremarkable work suit, carefully made-up face (copied from a popular beauty guru on YouTube), and strands of hair escaping my never-perfected topknot. 'Because I don't carry a wallet in my pocket.'

'Only old men carry wallets,' I'd managed, my cheeks hotter than molten lava, before freeing myself and leaving the train two stops too early, wondering why I couldn't have apologised like a normal person instead of blurting out something that probably wasn't true. What did I know about wallets?

I'd almost fainted when he called to ask me out to dinner, certain I was punching way above my weight. But although his job in investment banking was as far as you could get from the frivolous world of event planning, I felt like I'd managed to impress him. It had been a shame that our hectic work schedules meant we'd only been on a handful of dates before I was fired, and that I'd probably never see him again.

'Oh, Cassie, I'm so glad you're here!' Mum finally sprang off the sofa, fluffing up her curls as she came over to enfold me in a tight, floral-scented hug that prompted a prickling feeling behind my eyelids.

'Nice to see you, too,' I acknowledged, trying not to squeeze too tightly in case she was alerted to the fact that something was wrong.

Dad joined in, his strong arms encircling us both as he pressed a clumsy kiss beside my ear. As usual, he smelt of Right Guard anti-perspirant, undercut with coffee beans, and I snuggled in a bit closer. 'Good to have you back for a bit, love.'

'Sorry to interrupt your petting session,' I mumbled. It dawned on me that they might not even want me home, but I swiftly dismissed the thought. They'd been asking when I was going to visit for a while now.

'So, how are you?' Mum released me at last, her wide, grey eyes searching my face with a gratifying intensity, as if she'd forgotten what I looked like. 'You seem tired, but that's probably to be expected with your lifestyle.'

Oh god, not the 'lifestyle' comment, already. She was convinced I'd spent the last few years mingling with celebrities and aristocracy (and I might have played up to that image, just a little bit), but while it was true that I'd booked my fair share of them for awards shows, festivals and fundraisers, it had been through their representatives. I hadn't been hanging out with Meghan Markle, or swapping recipes with Mary Berry. I'd been too busy making sure everything ran like clockwork, before crashing into bed at 3 a.m., worried about sleeping through my alarm. 'I've been on trains for most of the day, and didn't sleep much last night,' I said, while Dad leaned over and grabbed the TV remote, muting a guest on *The One Show* who was riding a unicycle.

'Who on earth watches this rubbish?' He tutted, and I refrained from pointing out that he and Mum certainly hadn't been. He turned back to me with a look of concern on his solid, kind-looking face. 'I could have collected you from Dartmouth. How did you get here?'

'Taxi,' I said, not adding that I'd walked the last half-mile, after instructing the driver to drop me off. Despite my overstuffed suitcase and weighty rucksack, I'd been desperate for a glimpse of the water at Seashell Cove, where diamonds of sunlight twinkled off the sea. At least, they did in my imagination.

Unfortunately, despite a mild start to April, fog had rolled in off the sea, obscuring the view, and I'd ended up keeping my head down while my aching feet directed me past the colourful sprawl of houses and shops that made up the small village, until I was standing outside our achingly familiar, stone-fronted house, marvelling at how gut-wrenchingly good it felt to be back. I'd reminded myself that, as far as my parents knew, I'd left my demanding, high-flying job with a generous severance package, and was taking a much-needed holiday to plan the next stage of my career. They didn't need to know I'd been fired after a series of cock-ups, and had so far failed to find another job.

A memory of my boss Carlotta's furious face flashed in front my eyes, still managing to convey rage despite being stuffed with fillers, and although I blinked the image away I couldn't prevent a blast of remembered humiliation.

'Cassie?' Dad's blue eyes were suddenly too close to mine, like a doctor checking my pupils were dilating properly. 'Are you OK, love?' he said, urgently. 'You look frightened.'

'Still getting over the sight of you two half dressed.' I forced a grin, knowing I was taking it too far, but unable to tell them the truth. 'I wouldn't say no to a cuppa.'

'That's my girl.' His face cleared and he gave my shoulder a squeeze. 'It's not as if I've been making drinks all day.'

'Ah, yes, sorry.' I remembered Mum and Dad would have been on their feet at the café for hours. 'I'll make it, if you like.'

'You'll do no such thing.' Dad gripped my other shoulder and frowned at my topknot, as if he'd just spotted it wasn't my natural colour. 'What shade is that, love?'

'Plumberry, according to the stylist.' I self-consciously fingered my heaped-up hair while my parents rearranged their faces and murmured 'lovely'.

'Very executive,' said Mum, before I could mention that I was planning to let it grow back to Normal Brown. Not the most memorable of reinventions, but I'd never really liked the purply shade and still started whenever I caught sight of my reflection.

'It suits you,' she added, tucking a strand behind my ear. 'It makes your eyes look almost silver.'

'Sounds a bit creepy.' Mum had never coloured her hair, which was mostly still a rich chestnut colour, with just a few strands of grey running through. She'd always been comfortable with her appearance.

'There's food, if you're hungry,' said Dad, rubbing his hands together.

'Yes, please, I'm starving. I haven't eaten since breakfast.'

'No wonder you look so skinny.' Mum scoped my outline. 'You've definitely lost weight.'

'Too busy for regular mealtimes,' I said, which had been true before I lost my job. Since then, I'd lost my appetite a bit.

'I'm afraid it's only casserole.' Dad's smile spasmed into a grimace. 'Probably not what you're used to.'

He made it sound as if I ate at Michelin-starred restaurants every night, just because the team I'd worked with had once been invited to a charity bash at The Ivy.

'Casserole sounds lovely.' I sniffed the air. 'Smells good, too.'

As Dad exited the room, Mum helped me remove my rucksack, which felt as if it had moulded to my back.

'What on earth's in there?' she said, as it crashed to the floor. I felt as if I might float off without it.

'Just books and stuff.' I rotated my shoulders to loosen them, but they hadn't been loose for at least three years and weren't about to start easing up now. 'I'm hoping to do some reading while I'm here. Work stuff, you know?'

'Oh, of course,' Mum said, with the slightly reverential air that overtook my parents whenever my 'career' was mentioned – as if I was a brain surgeon or firefighter. They'd made no secret of how proud they were of their 'brilliantly clever' daughter, and 'talented, semi-famous' son. Rob, my younger brother, was the keyboard player in a three-man band called X-Y-Zed, which a critic in the *Daily Mirror* had described as 'cinematic and slightly sinister'.

'You don't want to stay around here like we had to,' Mum and Dad had drilled into us during our teens. Neither of them had siblings and both had taken care of their mothers, growing up: Mum, because her mother had been sick, while Nan had leaned heavily on Dad, because his father was always having affairs and leaving her. 'You're clever enough to do whatever you like with your lives.' Mum had spoken as though running a café was akin to road-sweeping, though I knew for a fact she loved it. Dad had bought the café at Seashell Cove when I was eleven, after being made redundant from his banking job in Dartmouth, with a decent enough pay-off to afford him a change of profession. He'd relished his new role, and Mum had thrown in her job as a school secretary to help him run it.

'Your job makes what we do seem so ordinary!' she'd exclaimed during our last call, and I'd only just stopped myself from blurting out that a petting-zoo party for 100 six-year-olds had gone terribly wrong: the animals had pooed everywhere, the Shetland pony had been a biter, the goat had eaten the vegan birthday cake, and the parents were threatening to sue.

It was supposed to have been Carlotta's event, but she'd booked herself on a health retreat in Thailand, to prepare for a televised awards ceremony, and handed it to me, as no one else was available. Exhausted after a night spent trying to reorganise accommodation for a hen party in Paris, thanks to a burst water pipe, I'd stepped outside to take a call from the frantic client, and returned to find the petting-zoo party had gone to hell. It didn't help that, keen to impress Carlotta, I'd insisted on overseeing the event on my own – a decision that had spectacularly backfired.

'Why don't you put your feet up?' Mum said, tugging my coat off and gesturing across the comfortably cluttered room, which still had a stencilled vine-leaf pattern on the ceiling from a thwarted 'makeover' attempt. But, as tempted as I was to sink into the old springy sofa, I had the feeling that if I sat down I might never get up again.

'I think I'll take my stuff up to my room and get settled in.'

Mum's mouth curved into a smile. 'I can hardly believe you're both back.'

'Both?' I glanced at her soft, round face, which was an older version of mine. I used to long for high cheekbones and a regal profile, instead of a snub nose and too-wide eyes, and for people to think of me as 'striking' rather than 'trustworthy', but at least I could look forward to being described as 'youthful' in my fifties. 'What do you mean, both?'

Mum's eyes crinkled. 'Rob's home, too.'

'What? Why didn't you say so?'

'It's only been a week,' she began, but I'd already kicked off my trainers and pelted upstairs. Without knocking, I flung open Rob's bedroom door and stuck my head round.

The room was empty.

'He's out,' Mum said, from the top of the stairs. 'If he'd known you'd be here tonight, I'm sure he'd have stayed in.'

'Oh.' Deflated, I closed the door on the explosion of clothes and bags I'd glimpsed inside. I hadn't seen my brother for ages – apart from some YouTube footage of him falling offstage during a gig in Berlin, in front of a roaring crowd. 'How come he's not at Bossy Emma's?'

'She decided they needed some space,' Mum said, not without a note of vindication. None of us had particularly warmed to his girlfriend, with her micro-managing ways. We couldn't understand why he'd hooked up with her, when he could have had his pick of girls. Emma was the sister of a friend he'd met at university before he formed the band, and they'd got together properly a couple of years ago on one of his rare visits home. 'As if she hasn't had enough space, with him away on the road.'

'Poor Rob,' I said, though I doubted he'd be single for long if the split turned out to be permanent. Although electronic dance music wasn't completely mainstream, X-Y-Zed had plenty of fans.

'Dinner's ready,' Dad sang from the hallway.

'Coming!' Mum and I carolled back, as I shoved open the door to my bedroom and looked greedily around the comfortingly familiar space. It wasn't a shrine to my childhood, thank goodness, as I'd let my school friend Tilly practise her interior-design skills on it before she moved to Canada, but the double bed with the padded velvet headboard was the same, and so was the wardrobe with the wonky door, and my teddy bear, Mr Rabbit, still resided on the bookshelf.

'I always forget how green it is,' I said to Mum, who was hovering at my elbow. Tilly had been going for a botanical theme, with fern-patterned fabrics and shades of moss and mint paint, but the effect was a bit 'pea soup'.

'She did get carried away,' Mum said with a chuckle. 'I spoke to your nan on the phone earlier,' she added. 'She can't wait to see you.'

'I can't wait to see her,' I admitted. 'Is she still with Marcus?'

'Ancient history.' Mum did an eye-roll. 'He was a fussy eater, apparently. You know how Nan loves her food.'

'Poor Marcus.' Thinking of Nan brought me almost to the verge of tears. It was only now I was home that I was beginning to realise how much I'd missed it.

'We don't see her very much these days,' Mum said with forced brightness. She was very attached to Nan, having lost her own mother in her thirties, swiftly followed by her father. 'She's so wrapped up in her hobbies.' Ah, Nan's hobbies. They were legendary. 'Still, she must do what makes her happy.'

'So, how come Rob's back?'

'Oh, you can talk about it to him tomorrow.' Mum's smile was radiant now. 'Do you know how long you'll be staying?' She was still clutching my coat, like an old-fashioned maid, and I took it from her and flung it onto my bed, resisting the urge to throw myself after it and snuggle into the duvet.

'Not sure yet,' I said, switching to my breezy, professional tone. 'It depends how things work out.'

'I know you've left your job, but you will be going back to London, won't you? Or, maybe New York?' I had gone on a bit about New York, but it had been so exciting to be there, even though it had only been for a month and I'd been working most of the time. 'I mean, that's where all your contacts are, surely?'

'W-e-e-e-ll—' I began.

'I'm surprised you wanted to come here for a holiday, instead of going travelling,' she continued.

'I *am* travelling.' I spread my hands in a *tah-dah* gesture. 'I've travelled from London to here.'

Her smile quivered. 'Yes, but... we can't compete with, say, Singapore or Japan.'

'Japan?' I gawped at her. 'Why on earth would I want to go to Japan?'

Her lips pressed together. 'I... I don't know, love.'

'Look,' I said, with a bravado I was far from feeling, considering I currently had nothing to go back to in London. 'I wanted to see you all, it's as simple as that, and I'm going to arrange some events while I'm here to keep my hand in.' At least, that was my plan. 'And to start building my portfolio.' A suitably high-flying word I knew she would like.

'Don't you have one already?'

'A new one,' I said, thinking quickly. 'Of events organised solely by me.'

'Events around here?'

'People have them, don't they?' I accompanied the words with a light little laugh that came out more like a cough.

Mum gave me a funny look. 'Well, yes, but they don't need people to *organise* them, they just get on and do it themselves. They don't want to *pay* someone to do it.' She made it sound like the silliest idea, ever.

'Well, I'll just have to persuade them otherwise, won't I?' I said, while Dad clattered plates downstairs in a clear attempt to hurry us along.

'But why, when there's no need?'

This was turning out to be tougher than I'd expected. 'Actually, I've an ulterior motive,' I said, deciding it was as good a time as any to mention the idea I'd had on the way over, to kick-start my new future. 'I'm going to help you and Dad put the café on the map.'

Chapter 2

Emerging from a fog of sleep the following morning, I marvelled afresh at how comfy my mattress was, and how peaceful my surroundings. No Nina, crashing around in her kitchen, or singing loudly in the shower, as if to prove a point.

I'd got along well with Nina at work, where she was senior events coordinator. When she'd realised I was good at taking orders, eager to learn, and didn't mind the long hours, she'd taken me under her wing. But, apart from the odd drink after work, and a few confessional sessions over some wine and a takeaway, we weren't exactly best mates. She'd always stressed the importance of maintaining a professional relationship – even if she hadn't always stuck to it.

She'd offered me her sofa bed when I decided not to renew the lease on my flat, and had let me store my things in her basement, but hadn't wanted me there too long because she'd started dating her personal trainer, and having an unemployed house guest wasn't conducive to romance.

'Do you really want to stay in event planning?' she'd asked one evening, while I was scouring job sites on my laptop in my bathrobe, and she was painting her nails a deathly shade of blue. 'Maybe it's time for a change.'

Panic had caught hold of me. After all the hours I'd put in at Five Star, and the skills I'd learned, how could I even think about giving it up? I was only a few years into the glittering career I'd planned after completing a management course at college and moving to London with a friend on a wave of optimism. The first couple of years had been thrillingly chaotic, brimming with excitement, even if the jobs I'd ended up doing mostly involved waiting on tables, or making the tea at some fancy agency. At weekends, we'd wander around art galleries and museums, and visit pubs and clubs in the evenings, and it was only when it began to sink in that my career hadn't exactly started that some of the sparkle vanished. Then, my friend Trudy had landed a job at Five Star and persuaded Carlotta to take me on to chase up bookings and liaise with suppliers. Even though Trudy had left soon after, following her new boyfriend to Italy, I'd grabbed the opportunity with both hands. I was determined to make my mark in the world of event planning and relieved I was finally on my way to becoming the successful businesswoman I'd assured my family I would be. It had never occurred to me to give it up – even with a boss as difficult as Carlotta, who seemed increasingly annoyed by my attempts to rise from the ranks of assistant to… something more than an assistant. But now my plans had been cut short, thanks to a hungry goat and a grumpy Shetland pony. Event planning was a competitive market, and as I'd been fired with no chance of securing a reference from Carlotta (apart from a character assassination) I was struggling to get even as far as an interview. Going solo seemed to be my only option, but with nothing to show for my time at Five Star I was fighting a losing battle, and with nowhere to live I'd had no choice but to come home.

I'd decided early on not to tell my family the real reason I was back. Much better to subtly set the wheels of my new future in motion, before returning to London with a portfolio of events I could show to prospective clients. In no time at all, I'd have a list of bookings, my own little army of staff, and perhaps a nice apartment near a park or some gardens. My parents would be even prouder if I had my own business, and would probably end up seeing more of me in the long run. There'd been no time to visit them for more than a flying visit at Christmas over the last few years, and on their occasional forays into London they'd ended up visiting the tourist spots on their own, because work had been so crazy that I'd had to be available all the time.

Sighing now, I thrust off my duvet and swung my legs out of bed. It felt odd to be up so late. I normally set two alarms to make sure I was awake at five thirty, ready to email suppliers and check out venues, before grabbing coffee for Carlotta on the way to the office.

I picked up Mr Rabbit, who looked rather doleful, and gave him a reassuring kiss, then wandered downstairs in my pyjamas, pausing to look at the photos lining the wall. There were several of Rob and me in school uniform, with missing front teeth; a couple of us on the beach at Seashell Cove, exploring the rock pools, sand clinging to our skinny legs; and a recent one of Rob onstage, playing his keyboard with one hand. My gaze skimmed over a selfie my parents had framed of me at an event in New York, surrounded by people in Bollywood fancy dress. I was grinning manically, despite battling a forty-eight-hour headache, and I remembered I'd had to remove a faulty lighting box that had started billowing smoke, before anyone noticed. Someone had noticed, though, and had reported it to Carlotta, who'd given me my first warning.

I wondered whether Rob was still in bed. I hadn't heard him come in the night before, but I'd been so tired after dinner I'd barely been able to keep my eyes open, and could only summon one face-splitting yawn after another when Mum had attempted to probe me about what I'd meant by 'putting the café on the map'.

'You'll see,' I'd managed, attempting an enigmatic smile as another yawn broke out, and, to my relief, Dad had suggested I take myself to bed with a mug of tea. I hadn't argued, and had quickly succumbed to the merciful pull of sleep.

The kitchen was deserted, but there was a note on the table in Mum's loopy handwriting:

Take it easy, sweetheart, you're obviously worn out! Come down to the café when you're ready, if you've got time, and if you want to!! Or pop and see your nan, or go for a walk and blow the cobwebs away! Plenty of food, so help yourself, you could do with putting on a few pounds!! Plenty of hot water, if you'd like a bath. I'll be back to cook dinner, so see you later!!!

She'd gone a bit overboard on the exclamation marks and I had the sense that my mum in particular was behaving as though a celebrity had come to visit. Imagining her disappointment if she knew why I was home, it suddenly became imperative that I start planning my future, and my thoughts turned to the café.

On my last visit home, I'd gathered that business wasn't too good, and yesterday it had occurred to me on the train that it shouldn't be too hard to re-launch an old-fashioned café in south Devon. Not when I'd helped to arrange lavish corporate affairs, and the wedding of a minor soap star. It would be a perfect opportunity to network and, once word spread, job offers would start flooding in. Maybe I could persuade a local magazine or newspaper to run a feature, and I could subtly mention I'd worked at Five Star... without going into too much detail.

On a sea of enthusiasm, I set about breaking eggs into a pan.

'Rob!' I called from the foot of the stairs, impatient to see him and start trading stories now we were under the same roof for the first time in ages. 'Rob?'

Even before I ran up to check, I knew he wasn't there. Judging by the state of his bed, he'd been wrestling a giant squid all night. Dejected, I returned to the kitchen. Had I really imagined us eating around the table like we had as kids? That Mum and Dad would have asked one of their staff to open the café, so they didn't have to rush in? Then I remembered, I hadn't been due home until today, so of course they wouldn't have made plans.

'Get a grip, Maitland,' I ordered, in a sergeant-major voice, rescuing the eggs before they burnt. Once I'd eaten, I stood for a while at the window overlooking the sunny garden, where the old swing and slide set were rusting away at the bottom, then went to retrieve my laptop from my bedroom to make a 'to do' list. No time like the present, as Carlotta used to say, with a tight-lipped smile that never reached her eyes.

1. Order in some specialist teas and coffees.

Dad fancied himself as a coffee connoisseur, because his grand-mother had been French and had introduced him to espresso at an unnaturally early age – according to Nan, he'd be bouncing off the walls for hours after a visit there, and once stayed awake for nearly forty-eight hours – but he'd been stocking the same brand at the café for years.

I remembered a company that Five Star had dealt with in the past, and logged on to their website. I selected several varieties from around the globe, adding some unusual teas for good measure. A taster session at the café – or 'cupping' as it was known – would make a perfect first event.

Having racked my brains for more ideas, I decided it might be sensible to take a look at the café with fresh eyes, and clapped my laptop shut with a sense of relief.

After a quick shower, I dragged my hair into a ponytail and pulled on a slouchy pink top and blue jeans, happy not to be wearing my usual monochromatic work outfit, designed to look 'professional, but to blend in'.

Outside, spring had returned, bathing the street in pleasantly warm sunshine. On the other side of the street, Sid Turner was buffing his old blue Ford outside his house, and threw me a friendly wave as I came out.

'Visiting your mum and dad?' he called, as if there might be another reason for me being in their house.

'I thought it was about time.' I crossed the road in a confident fashion befitting a woman too busy to pop home often.

The wrinkles of his face lifted into a smile. 'Still not got a car?' he asked, patting the Ford's bonnet as if it was a beloved pet. 'I can still remember your dad teaching you to drive, and you kangarooing down the road.'

I smiled and shook my head. 'No need, in London.' It struck me that I'd have to get a car – providing I could remember how to drive – if I was going to stay in Devon. 'I just hop on the Underground.'

'Rather you than me.' He shook his head, probably imagining worse things happening on Tube trains than being ignored by your fellow passengers. 'I'm surprised you haven't got a driver, what with you doing so well.' Mum had obviously been extolling my virtues, but my salary – while generous by Devon standards – had hardly extended to being carted around the city by a uniformed chauffeur. 'Hey, do you remember when you and your friends formed a girl band?' With a throaty chuckle, he folded his polishing cloth into the pocket of his faded corduroys. 'What was it you called yourselves?'

'Legal Mystics,' I said right away, still proud of the name I'd come up with. 'It was an anagram of Meg, Tilly and Cass.'

'That's it.' Sid chuckled again. 'You did that show for everyone in your mum and dad's back garden, do you remember?'

'Hard to forget,' I said drily. We'd thought we were so edgy, channelling our favourite band All Saints in combat trousers, teeny vest tops and chunky trainers. The summer we turned fifteen, we'd been in possession of a wild and soaring confidence that even a lack of talent couldn't dent, and had wowed our family and neighbours with a well-choreographed performance. Rob had accompanied us on his electronic keyboard, risking the mockery of his mates. I wondered what Meg and Tilly were doing now. We'd met at secondary school in Kingsbridge, drawn there from our respective villages – Meg from Salcombe and Tilly from Ivybridge – and had bonded during a fire drill on the first day, when Tilly offered Meg and me some chewing gum (immediately confiscated).

'And now it's your brother who's in a band, not that his music's my cup of tea. I prefer a bit of rock and roll,' said Sid, clearly hungry for company. I guessed his wife was visiting her sister in Scotland, which she'd done every April for as long as I could remember. 'Performing all over the world,' he went on, sucking in a breath. 'I don't know how your parents coped with the pair of you off goodness knows where from such a young age.'

'Not that young.' My smile faded. 'They wanted us to be independent.'

'Of course they did.' Sid's rheumy eyes grew big, as if worried he'd said something wrong. 'They're very proud of you both,' he added, turning back to his gleaming car, and bending to polish the bumper with the sleeve of his shirt. 'I'd better let you get on.'

A little unnerved at being so hastily dismissed, I said goodbye and headed for the lane behind the sloping row of colourful houses that led to the cove; a shortcut Rob and I used to take as children to avoid the longer walk through the village.

As I finally emerged onto the coastal path, a smile leapt to my face. There was *so* much space. When I was in London, Seashell Cove had shrunk in my memory to a tiny, twinkling jewel, when in reality there was so much of everything – sky, sea… clean air.

The stretch of sand in the cove was as butterscotch golden as I'd remembered, and the sea a perfect, shimmering turquoise. Waves lapped the shore where the curve of the headland hugged the beach and I stood and listened, until my heart was beating in perfect synchronicity. It was hard to imagine that the area had once had a reputation for smuggling, and for plundering ships that had been wrecked on the jutting rocks on the other side of the headland. Today, it looked holiday-brochure perfect.

I switched my gaze to the café nestled on top of the headland, surrounded by a white picket fence, the light dancing off its whitewashed walls… *Hang on!* There hadn't been a white picket fence the last time I'd looked, and the exterior hadn't been quite that white. Had the windows – wide and deep to make the most of the view – always been as sparkly? And where had those tables outside come from, with navy and white parasols offering shade from the sun? They looked a lot smarter than the bench tables, worn and scarred by the elements, which had been a fixture for as long as I could remember.

Hurrying now, I almost tripped along the path, suddenly too warm in my jeans and slouchy top, wishing that I'd worn a vest underneath so I could take the top off.

Growing closer to the café, I was surprised to see that the tables outside were crowded with customers. As far as I remembered, the café only got this busy at the weekends, and even then the regulars had been more inclined to sit inside, even when it was sunny, probably so used to the view that it barely registered.

A couple of customers had laptops and looked to be working, which couldn't be right. Mum and Dad didn't agree with anything but the most basic technology at the café, insisting it was a place for people to escape to, not for 'laptop lingerers'. I'd suggested more than once that they get Wi-Fi installed, to compete with the chain cafés springing up everywhere, and Dad had told me, with a sorrowful look, that I 'didn't get it'.

'Old-fashioned charm, that's what our customers want.'

'There's old-fashioned and there's pre-war,' I'd grumbled, concerned that their reluctance to move with the times might one day spell the end of their business, but from the look of it they'd taken my words on board.

As I made my way to the entrance, I noticed one customer sketching the view on an artist's pad, and a group of women discussing a book they'd read. *A book group? At Maitland's Café?* Feeling destabilised, I pushed open the door and stepped inside. At least in here nothing would have changed.

My eyes swung round and my mouth fell open.

I couldn't have been more wrong.

Everything had changed.

Chapter 3

'Cassie, you're here!' Mum couldn't have looked more surprised if Catherine Zeta-Jones had pitched up at the café and demanded two cream buns. 'I thought you'd be having a lie-in,' she added, as I made my way to the new, mosaic-tiled counter, gazing around as though I'd landed on Mars.

Where were the dark-wood tables and chairs left by the previous owners? The red-and-white checked tablecloths; the ancient clock that never told the right time; the faded, signed picture on the wall of Frank Sinatra (he was rumoured to have visited, once) and the green and mustard linoleum that had been held together in places with gaffer tape? Even the gingham curtains, which had graced the bottom half of the windows for about a century, had disappeared. That's why the windows looked extra big and sparkly.

'Wha… what's happened?' I managed, eyes darting from the array of delectable- looking cakes, cookies and pillowy scones, nestling beneath glass domes, to a gleaming, state-of-the-art coffee machine behind the counter, and rows of cheerful cups and saucers arranged on fancy shelving edged with bunting. There was even a new machine for dispensing hot water, and the chipped old sink – where the tap used to drip – had been replaced by a shiny white one with a fancy, chrome-fronted fridge underneath. In place of the leaking metal teapots were an assortment of chubby earthenware pots in cheerful colours, and the eclectic mix of old teaspoons had been exchanged for a gleaming set that matched.

'So, what do you think?' Mum was eyeing my reaction with a mixture of suppressed excitement and apprehension. 'Do you like it?'

I turned once more to scan the interior, though it was hard to take in when the place was so busy, the noise level only just tolerable. 'It looks… bigger,' I managed. It was true. The whisper-of-lemon paintwork, sand-coloured floorboards, and ocean-shaded fabrics covering the scattered cushions had brought the outdoors in. The wall behind the counter had been stripped back to warm brick, while the brightly tiled counter lent an almost tropical feel. 'Where's all the old stuff?' I murmured, eyeing the pale-wood tables and chairs. 'They were practically antiques.'

'They're the same ones.' Mum pointed eagerly to the nearest table, where an elderly man was doing a newspaper crossword, while his younger, female companion scanned her iPhone. 'They've all been sanded down and smartened up. I had no idea they could look so good.'

'Those are new.' I nodded to a couple of leather tub chairs in the corner, where a pair of mothers in almost identical narrow-legged jeans and floaty-sleeved tops were sipping drinks with their toddlers on their laps, as if sitting in their own living rooms.

'They came from a junk shop,' said Mum. 'The chairs, not the customers.' She laughed at her little joke. 'They've been repurposed. Or upcycled. One or the other. The chairs, not the—'

'Customers,' I finished. *How had this even happened without me knowing?* 'It must have cost a fortune.'

'Not really, the leather was in good condition—'

'I mean the whole thing.' I turned to look at her. She'd always been proud of the business, but her face was as shiny as if it had won an award.

'We thought it would be a good investment,' she said. 'We had some savings and your nan chipped in. You know how keen she is to get rid of her money.'

'She could always buy me a house,' I said, only half joking. Nan was pretty well off, thanks to some shrewd investments my grandfather had made in his lifetime, and had no qualms about spending the money now he was dead, on account of him being a cheating bastard. Her words, not mine.

'I'm sure you can afford a house whenever you want, with all the money you've been making, and then there's the severance package you mentioned. I imagine that's quite substantial.' Mum's smile was comfortable. She was just stating the truth, based on what she knew about my life. Or, thought she knew.

'Well, it looks amazing.' Deciding to ignore her comment, my eyes roved round once more, spotting details like the overhead lighting, which no longer consisted of old-fashioned floral shades and low-watt bulbs, but dangling glass pendants, and a row of upside-down cups in saucers above the counter.

'They're playful, don't you think?' Mum said, seeing me looking, sounding as if she was quoting someone else.

'They certainly look like they're having fun.' I felt a bit mean when her smile dipped. 'Honestly, Mum, it looks brilliant. I like the new menu, too.' I nodded at the board, where a list of drinks and 'cake of the day' (Earl Grey and blackberry) were chalked out in fancy script. It was a far cry from Dad's illegible scrawl, but then customers had never needed to look at a menu as they'd tended to know what they wanted – a cup of coffee or a pot of tea and a toasted teacake, or a slice of whichever cake Mum had baked the night before. Usually fruit, or lemon drizzle.

'Flat white?' I said, shaking my head as I read. 'Since when?'

'It's just a milky coffee really.' Mum lowered her voice as though people might walk out if they overheard. 'But the newer clientele likes to think they're getting something modern.'

I hid a smile at her use of the word 'modern', which only revealed her lovely, old-fashioned core. 'Did you write it out?'

'What?' Mum turned her head to look. 'Oh, no, that was Danny. He did the new sign outside, too. Quite a dab hand at the signwriting. We're still called Maitland's though, we'd never change that, it's our name.' She looked suddenly stricken, as though I'd suggested otherwise, but my mind had snagged on one word.

'Danny?'

'Danny Fleetwood.' Mum was all smiles again. 'Apparently, you were at the same school for a while. He remembers you.'

'Does he?' My heart gave an odd little throb. 'He was a bit of an idiot, back then.'

Danny and I had shared art classes in our final year, but, although talented, he'd been too laid back to put in much effort, and too aware of his own good looks and the effect they'd had for my liking. He'd unexpectedly asked me out once, and when I'd told him loftily that he'd need to do more than scrawl, *Will you be at the leavers' party on Saturday?* on his canvas, he'd said, 'Meet me there and I'll win you over,' and had given me a sparkly-eyed grin. Only, when I'd arrived he wasn't there, and I'd felt stupid for even agreeing to meet him... for secretly looking forward to it. Clearly, he'd loved the chase more than he'd wanted the prize.

The last sighting I'd had of Danny, he was chatting to a girl outside as I was leaving.

I'd made sure he didn't see me, and within days he'd slipped from my mind.

'He's definitely not an idiot.' Mum's voice broke in, her tone of reproof channelling heat to my cheeks. 'He did a very good job.'

'Well, obviously he's grown up now.' Though probably not much if he was still hanging around south Devon, painting signs. 'I didn't notice the sign outside,' I added, but Mum had shifted along to serve a customer.

A small queue was building, and people seemed content to wait for a table to become vacant. A smiley young waitress in a turquoise, short-sleeved shirt, which matched the ones Mum and Dad were wearing, was clearing up, while Dad was in deep conversation with a customer I recognised as my old geography teacher from Kingsbridge Academy, Mr Flatley – or Lord of the Dance, as we used to call him.

Dad hadn't noticed me come in, and was still deep in conversation, so I looked around again, letting the changes sink in, while Mum dealt with the waiting customers. Part of me was shell-shocked by the transformation – it was so different to the café I remembered, sitting out the back with my colouring book on rainy Saturday mornings with Rob, while Mum and Dad were working – but I could see it was a massive improvement, and just the shot in the arm the place had needed – except *I'd* wanted to do it. Well, not the nitty-gritty, but the organising of it.

'You can't have done this all on your own,' I said, when Mum had taken the final customer's order and passed over two cups of frothy coffee and a plate of chocolate cookies. 'Did you get someone in?'

'It was Tilly,' she said, pouring a cup of tea the way I liked it – strong with a splash of milk. A middle-aged member of staff I didn't know sidled behind the counter and started taking orders, as if Mum had summoned her telepathically. 'Thanks, Gwen,' she said.

'Tilly? Tilly Campbell?' I said at the same time. 'My old school friend Tilly, who decorated my bedroom?'

'The one and the same,' Mum confirmed, eyes flicking around to check nothing needed her attention. 'Hasn't she done a wonderful job?'

My brain whirled. 'But Tilly and her family moved to Canada years ago,' I said. 'That's why we lost touch.'

'Oh, she's been back a while.' Mum gave a casual shrug. 'She's still doing a bit of interior design when the fancy takes her, and she does walking tours around the coastal paths. She'll be in later. The cafe's a stop-off point, it's on TripAdvisor.' Not seeming to notice I was stumped for words, Mum carried on, 'Meg works here now, did I tell you?'

'What?' I gawped. 'Meg Larson?' As if I knew loads of Megs.

Mum nodded, smiling over my shoulder as she threw a wave to a leaving customer. 'She needed another job when her hours were reduced at the bakery, so does a few afternoons here, as well as supplying the cakes.'

I had a sudden, lurching recollection of Mum coyly mentioning a new member of staff, during one of our calls last year, but I'd been busy sourcing a 'haunted' castle for a Halloween bash and hadn't really taken it in.

My gaze dropped to the nearest glass dome, beneath which a two-tier cake squatted, oozing lashings of buttercream. 'Meg made this?' Mum nodded. 'Wow.' She'd always liked baking, even when we were at school – had even talked about owning her own bakery one day. 'Meg *works* here?'

'Like I just said.' Mum did a little head-wobble, indicating I was being a bit slow on the uptake. 'You know she's worked at the bakery here for ages.'

'I did not know that.'

'Are you OK, Cassie?'

I brushed away an image of Legal Mystics belting out 'Never Ever' in my parents' back garden that burnished summer, almost fifteen years ago. 'I'm fine,' I said, not sure that I was. 'It's just a bit "school reunion" all of a sudden, that's all.'

'I told her you were coming to visit,' Mum said. *Visit.* It sounded so... temporary. 'She'll be thrilled to see you.'

I wasn't so sure. We'd drifted apart after Tilly's father uprooted his family to Canada, where his parents lived. Meg had been wrapped up in her boyfriend Sam, and hadn't had much time for anyone else.

'How come I didn't know *any* of this?'

'Oh, well, you were always so busy,' Mum said, vigorously wiping down the counter. 'I didn't think you'd be that interested in our little redecoration.'

I noticed a muscle flexing in her upper arm as she wiped the surfaces. Wiping was probably good exercise, but you'd have to alternate arms to get even results. 'Of course I'd have been interested.' I tried not to sound hurt. 'Why wouldn't I have been interested?'

'Oh, Cassie, you've got so much going on in your life, and you were in New York when we started. It was just a tiny project, it didn't take long at all. We were only closed for a week, would you believe?' She stopped wiping and smiled at me. 'When you mentioned putting the café on the map,' she said, 'I was going to tell you then that we'd made some... *changes.* But your dad and I thought it would be a lovely surprise if you came and saw for yourself.'

'It's certainly that.' I took a deep slurp of tea, which almost emptied my cup. They really were too small.

'You get a couple of refills,' Mum said, topping it up, and a guilty flush travelled over my face. 'So...' She paused. 'Is it modern enough?'

From the look on her face it was clearly a rhetorical question, but I'd just noticed, with a flash of relief, that they were still using the same brand of coffee they'd used for years. 'Well, actually,' I said, in my perkiest voice, 'it's perfect. All you need now are a few events to boost business, and I've already made a start by ordering some unusual coffees and teas for a tasting session. We did one for a start-up café in Berlin last year, and it went down really well.'

Mum's smile became fixed. Her Stepford smile, I used to call it. She pulled it on like a mask when hearing something she was unsure of, but didn't want anyone to know. 'Did you hear that, Ed?'

'What's that?' Dad materialised, and slung his arm around my shoulder. 'Thought you'd be relaxing, Cassie.' He planted a kiss on my hair. 'Isn't that why you're home?'

'She's ordered some fancy teas and coffees for an event. Here.' Mum's eyes skated between the two of us.

'Oh?' Dad's mouth started smiling too. 'I'm not sure that's necessary, love,' he said, scratching under his clean-shaven chin. 'Our customers seem very happy with what we're offering.'

Tension cramped my chest. I wasn't about to give up before I'd even started. 'They won't know until they've tried,' I said, with the 'fake it 'til you make it' air of confidence that Nina had instilled in me when I started at Five Star. She'd been a big fan of sayings and inspirational quotes. 'Like I said, I've already placed an order.'

'Well, I think it's a terrific idea.' Mum's smile grew brave. 'Cassie knows what she's talking about,' she said to Dad, and they nodded in tandem. 'She can do this sort of thing in her sleep, can't you, love?'

At times, it had felt like I had. 'I have some other event ideas, too,' I said. 'They'll definitely help fill the place up.'

Mum and Dad glanced at each other, then at the tables all filled with chattering customers, and out to the terrace, also heaving with people.

'If you think we need to.' Mum's smile was straining at the edges.

'We've been turning people away just lately,' Dad said, the corners of his mouth quivering slightly. 'We've got some excellent reviews on TripAdvisor, especially now we've got Wi-Fi.'

'I suggested that ages ago.'

'Did you?' He looked surprised. 'Tilly thought it would help business, and it seems to be working, though I don't really approve, as you know.'

'Right.' So, they'd listened to Tilly, but not to me. Then again, it sounded as if Tilly had been around a lot more than I had. I wondered why she'd come back, and how come she'd been in Seashell Cove, and whether she was back living in Ivybridge.

'I'm not sure we need any more changes, love,' Dad said.

For god's sake. How could I become a self-employed event planner if I had no events to plan? 'Well, you definitely need some pictures on the walls.' I was grasping at straws, but Mum leapt on my words.

'Oh, yes, we didn't get round to that,' she said with gusto. 'We meant to sort it out, but you're right, those walls look far too bare, and we didn't want to put Frank Sinatra back up; he'd got a bit stained.'

'I could arrange for some local artists to display their work.' Some of the tension lifted from my muscles. Art was something I *did* know a bit about – even if I'd decided against studying it further after my A levels. 'They could sell their paintings, which would benefit the artists too. Like in a gallery.'

'Ooh, that's brilliant,' Mum gushed, clearly glad there was something she could get on board with. 'What a super idea!'

'There's lots more where that came from.' I tapped my temple, hoping they wouldn't ask what.

'Like what?' Dad crossed his arms and looked at me with such mingled fascination and respect that I immediately felt like a fraud.

'Well, er, there are lots of things I could organise that would attract new customers and keep business ticking over, or even take things to a whole new level of... business,' I floundered. 'I could spread them over a week perhaps, to maximise interest, sort of like an entertainment blitz.' The thought was taking hold. 'Perhaps we could have a music night—'

'We close at six,' Mum interjected, her hand shooting across the counter to grasp Dad's arm. 'We need our together time in the evenings.'

Dad jiggled his eyebrows at her.

Ugh. 'Of course you do,' I said. 'But it wouldn't hurt to stay open until ten for a few nights, and if it's a success perhaps you could roll it out permanently, say one night a week.' I felt a bolt of excitement. 'It would be great in the summer. You'd be quite the place to hang out,' I said, attempting a twenties flapper tone and twirling a pretend pearl necklace.

'Ten o'clock?' Mum looked aghast. 'But what about our Monday quiz nights at the Smugglers Inn?'

'Ooh, we could have a quiz night here,' I said.

'We don't want to compete with the pub. Bill wouldn't like it.'

'What about board games then?'

'Board games?' The smiling had stopped as Dad screwed up his nose. 'Bit old-fangled.' Said the man who'd only recently got the hang of texting, and still used paper maps to navigate, if the well-thumbed stack in the kitchen was anything to go by.

'It'll be a novelty.' I tried to squash my impatience. 'It doesn't have to be board games, but I can think of lots of other things.'

Dad squared his shoulders. 'I suppose we could at least give it a try.' He looked to Mum for confirmation.

She nodded. 'I'm up for it,' she said, her smile slightly glazed. 'If Cassie thinks it's a good idea, who are we to argue?'

'Good point,' agreed Dad, and they exchanged a look I couldn't place.

'Great!' I did a little handclap. 'I'll put something on social media about it. I take it you've updated the website?' I'd have bet my life that they hadn't even considered it.

'Oh, Rob's sorted that out,' said Mum. 'He's done a wonderful job.'

As if on cue, my brother's head darted round the side door behind the counter. 'Sandra!' he said, grinning broadly. 'I thought I heard your fishwife tones.'

'Rob, you little shit!' I shot round to give him a hug, not caring that he still used the version of Cassandra that made me sound like a 1970s secretary. 'Good to see you, you prat.' I noticed he'd given up contact lenses in favour of his old, square-framed glasses, and seemed to have reverted to his student uniform of loose jeans, battered sneakers and a plaid shirt over a faded T-shirt.

I reached up to ruffle his untidy hair, which was the same curly brown style as Mum's, and he grabbed my arm and twisted it up my back.

'Ow, gerroff!' I broke free and punched his bicep.

'AHH that hurt!' He clutched his arm and pretended to cry, then straightened. 'Gotchya,' he said.

'No, you didn't, I knew you were pretending.'

'It's like you're both still twelve,' said Dad behind us.

'For goodness sake, you two,' added Mum with a tut. They joined the pair of us in the little passageway, which was still reassuringly old-fashioned and smelt of teabags, and it felt so good to be back in the bosom of my family that I burst into noisy tears.

Chapter 4

'Cassie, what on earth's wrong?'

Mum's shocked voice quickly brought my crying under control. 'Oh, nothing, sorry,' I sniffed, accepting a tentative hug as I wiped my sleeve across my face. 'Just got a bit of a headache, that's all.'

'Here,' Dad said gruffly, stuffing a paper napkin into my hand. 'Blow your nose.'

I managed a high, embarrassed laugh as I obliged. 'I feel like I'm six again.'

'You never cried when you were six,' Rob pointed out, even though he'd been a year younger and couldn't possibly remember. 'You never cry.'

'She cried on her seventh birthday,' Mum reminded him. 'Remember… when you snapped the arms off Kimberly?'

'Only because she wouldn't let me play with her.' Rob sounded defensive, even after all these years. 'She was too possessive with those Power Rangers.'

'And I cried when Tufty died.' I'd loved that hamster, but it was true that I hadn't been prone to tears as a child. I'd never had cause to be.

As I dabbed my eyes, Mum flashed me a knowing look that suggested she'd worked something out. 'It's that boyfriend of yours, isn't it?' she said. 'You've broken up, am I right?' *Oh god, they still think I'm seeing Adam.* 'Is he the real reason you've come home?'

'Ah, yes, the amazing Adam,' said Rob in a film-announcer voice. 'We never did get to meet him, did we?'

'It was… complicated.' I blew my nose again while I tried to find the right words.

Rob lifted a faux-sympathetic eyebrow. 'Was he a figment of your imagination?'

'Don't be stupid,' I snapped.

'Ed, tell him to stop teasing Cassie,' said Mum.

'Leave your sister alone, Robert.' Dad sounded uncomfortable, as he always had on the rare occasions he'd been called upon to tell us off. 'You can see she's upset about the break-up.'

'I'm not upset,' I said, though I was hardly jumping for joy either. 'We weren't really compatible, that's all.'

'But why?' Mum's forehead creased. 'He sounded so nice from what you told us, and was certainly very handsome' – she gave Rob a warning look – 'judging by that photo on your phone you texted me.' The one where I'd pretended to be reading a message while we were waiting to be seated in a busy Italian restaurant. I'd secretly snapped Adam standing behind me, smiling at the approaching maître d, his face deeply tanned by the golden glow of the lighting, his teeth gleaming white. 'He looked like a young George Clooney.'

'Still not over your obsession with Clooney?' Rob grinned. 'You do know he's married with kids now?'

Mum ignored him. 'So, what happened, Cassie? We were looking forward to meeting him one day.'

'It… it just wasn't working out.' My mind flitted back to us laughing over plates of linguine. I couldn't even remember what we'd been laughing at, I'd been so spaced out with tiredness, but I'd liked the feeling of something new unfolding, and the way he'd looked at me over his wine glass, as though he felt it too.

'Did you put work first again?' Mum's hesitant voice punctured the memory.

'Something like that.' It was the reason I'd given before, to explain why I wasn't in a relationship before meeting Adam. I'd been so focused on carving out a career I hadn't had time to cultivate a love life. 'We... wanted different things,' I said, aware I was talking in clichés. It was easier than explaining that I hadn't been able to face telling Adam I'd been fired, and him finding out that I wasn't quite the success story I'd led him to believe, and that after a hasty text exchange along the lines of: *It's not you, it's me* and *Can't we at least talk about it?* and *I haven't got time for a relationship*, I'd blocked his number and told myself it was for the best.

'Well, it's his loss,' said Dad. 'One day, you'll meet a man who won't be threatened by your power.' He made me sound like Wonder Woman. 'Someone you're on an equal footing with, like me and your mum.' He gave her a schmaltzy smile, and I remembered his oft-told story of how Mum had walked into the bank where he used to work, and had liked his smile so much she'd come back the following day and asked him out, and they'd been inseparable ever since. Feeling sniffy again I tried to pull myself together. Any crying I'd done over the past couple of years had been limited to tears of relief in the toilets after pulling off a successful event, while everyone else was celebrating.

'At least you'll always have your career,' Mum said kindly. 'You had so much ambition, even when you were young,' she went on, while I shoved the damp paper napkin up my sleeve, and a hank of hair off my forehead. 'We knew you'd be a success at whatever you put your mind to.'

They were nodding in admiration – even Rob, who'd taken X-Y-Zed on tour last year, reached number two in the download charts, and been nominated for a music award.

'Not as successful at Roberto,' I said in a jovial voice, hoping to distract them from my blotchy face. 'No one's ever asked me to sign their bare buttocks in permanent marker.'

'Oh Christ, don't remind me.' Rob whipped off his glasses and pushed the heels of his hands into his eyes, as if to block out the memory. 'One of the many, many reasons I'm glad I've given it up.'

I'd been on the verge of suggesting to Rob that we take a walk on the beach to catch up, while Mum and Dad were working, but the words jammed in my throat. 'What?' I looked from him to Mum, to Dad. Why were they smiling benignly? 'Given it up?' I echoed.

'Yeah.' He replaced his glasses and scratched the back of his head. 'I've quit the band. Finally accepted that a life on the road's not for me.' *What?* 'Emma gave me an ultimatum,' he continued with a sheepish grin. 'To start being honest with myself, or we're over. That's why I'm at home at the moment, instead of at hers.' He lifted a shoulder. 'Soon as she said it, it was obvious.'

'What was?' I felt dizzy, as if my blood pressure had dipped.

'That I never really wanted to be in a band, I just got carried away, and then suddenly we were doing well and it seemed like I couldn't just stop.'

'I thought you loved being on the road.'

'Hated it.' Rob shuddered. He looked younger, now I thought about it. His shoulders weren't hunched, like they usually were, as if a great weight had rolled off them, and he wasn't ghoulishly pale. The gauntness I'd noticed the last time I'd seen him – and assumed was part of the 'musician' look he'd refined – had gone. In fact, he looked better than I'd seen him in ages, despite his unstylish clothes.

'So, you're giving it up, just like that?' I clicked my fingers, a flare of something like jealousy bubbling up. Or maybe it was indigestion from the eggs I'd eaten for breakfast. 'The thing you've been doing since leaving university?'

'Yep.' He nodded, his eyebrows flipping up. 'Don't know why I didn't decide a lot sooner,' he said. 'It's all down to Ems.' I wondered whether Bossy Emma had put the idea of leaving the band into his head.

'I didn't realise that's why she'd thrown you out.' Mum sounded as if she admired Bossy Emma, all of a sudden. 'Good for her.'

'But… you *love* being in a band,' I persisted, as if saying it would make it true. 'You were always messing about on your keyboard, composing tunes.'

'Exactly.' He jabbed a finger at me. 'It was always meant to be a hobby.'

'Hobby?'

'Computers are really my thing.'

'For god's sake,' I muttered. '*Computers?*' It was true he'd had something of the geek about him once he'd reached his teens. He was never off the second-hand computer Dad had caved in and bought him one Christmas, but even when he'd pursued it at university, I assumed it was because he'd thought he ought to, just like I'd decided to drop art (my favourite subject at school) in favour of a management course, because I knew it would lead to a profitable career. 'I thought music was your *thing*.' I sounded brittle, but no one seemed to notice.

'It was OK when I wasn't doing it for a living. It was even exciting for a bit, then it became like this massive pressure.' Rob stabbed his temples to demonstrate his head being full. 'I was breaking out in spots and drinking too much.' I thought of the footage of him falling off stage in Germany and felt bad that I'd found it funny.

'I didn't know,' I said quietly.

'Alcohol kills your short-term memory.' His tone became conversational. 'After a session, there'd be chunks of time missing. And it doesn't help anxiety, it makes it worse in the long run,' he continued. 'It wasn't good for my health.'

'No, of course not.' He sounded as if he'd been in therapy for a decade, and while I was pleased he'd had some valuable insights he felt able to discuss, I couldn't help feeling as if I was standing on quicksand.

'My biggest worry about throwing it in was these guys.' He cast a look at Mum and Dad, their eyes big pools of love and understanding. 'I didn't want to let them down, when they were so proud of me.'

'We'll always be proud of you, son.' Dad fist-bumped Rob with easy familiarity. It was obvious they'd had the 'big' conversation already and had come to terms with it all.

'What about the rest of the band?' I said. 'Won't they be hacked off?'

'Nah, they were glad to see the back of me,' he said. 'They've already replaced me with Gnasher's brother Dom, and he's gone down a storm.'

'But I never even got to see you on your European tour. I was too busy.'

He looked at me with soulful eyes that were just like Dad's. 'No, you didn't,' he said, wrapping his arms across his chest. 'Even Mum and Dad managed a weekend in Barcelona, and they don't even like electronica.'

'We *loved* it!' Mum protested.

'She got a migraine for the first time ever,' Dad said, almost proudly.

'I know, you told me.' Mum had sent me some wobbly phone-video footage of X-Y-Zed playing in a gigantic nightclub called Razzmatazz, where apparently '*Bananarama once played!!*' She'd swung the phone round to herself, and her eyes had looked in danger of popping out of their sockets. It had felt like looking at someone else's family – one I barely recognised. I'd resolved to make the effort to visit, but had been too busy organising a masquerade ball for a politician's wife and couldn't get away.

'So, what are you going to do now then?' I said to Rob. A light frown ruffled Mum's forehead and I tried to moderate my tone. 'Unless you're taking a year off, or something.' A year off sounded blissful. I wished I could afford one.

Rob was shaking his head. 'Remember my mate Nick, Emma's brother?' I gave a terse nod. 'Well, he teaches now at the university in Dartmouth. They're looking for a permanent IT tutor from September, so I've started a fast-track teaching course.' He nudged his glasses further up his nose with his finger and gave a satisfied grin. 'It's a suburban life for me now, hopefully with Emma, when she realises I'm serious.' He assumed a grave expression. 'It's down to you to fly the success flag for the Maitland family.' He mimed waving a flag and pretended to bash me over the head with it. 'You're the high-flier now, Sandra.'

'Don't call me that.' I felt like crying again, but didn't know why. It wasn't that I didn't want my brother to be happy. Perhaps I couldn't accept that he would rather sit at a computer than travel the world playing his synthesised music to appreciative fans. 'And, anyway, Mum and Dad are the real success story,' I said, trying to ignore a clutch of dread in my chest. I'd come close to having panic attacks in the past, more recently since losing my job, and discovering things had radically changed on the home front wasn't helping. 'It's hard to keep a business going for as long as they have.'

'Silly,' Mum said, without a hint of false modesty. To her, what they did for a living came as naturally as breathing. 'None of us could do what *you* do, Cassie.'

I'm not doing it any more. The words were on the tip of my tongue, but I gulped them down and focused on the sounds drifting from the café: cups clinking on saucers, a burst of laughter, the whir of the coffee grinder and hiss of the steamer. 'You probably could if you put your mind to it,' I said. 'It's not rocket science.'

The noise from the café amplified as the door was pushed open, and the woman Mum had called Gwen appeared, short and stout-waisted, her face like a thundercloud.

'Could someone 'elp me, please, it's like Piccadilly bleedin' Circus out 'ere,' she said, in a strong Cockney accent, nodding a curt greeting at me. 'Sorry to interrupt.'

'Of course,' Mum said, looking horrified to have been caught slacking. 'Sorry,' she added to me with a little grimace.

Dad patted my arm. 'Take it easy, love,' he said, before disappearing after Gwen.

'Why don't you come and have a bite to eat while you wait for Tilly?' Mum suggested.

'Or, come through to the office and I'll show you the new website I've put together.' Rob extended an arm like a magician, but I shook my head. My mind was reeling with too much new information and I needed to be on my own for a while to absorb it.

'I think I'll go and see Nan, if you don't mind.'

'Good idea.' Mum nodded, approvingly.

'Good luck with that,' Rob said, when Mum had fled after Dad. 'She'll probably rope you into her latest fad.'

'Which is?'

He tapped the side of his nose. 'I'll let you have the pleasure of finding out for yourself.' He made scared eyes. 'May the Force be with you.'

Chapter 5

Scared of the runaway thoughts flying around my head, I attempted to do some mindfulness as I left the café, by pinning my gaze to the view. '*Looking at beauty in the world is the first step of purifying the mind.*' Nina had texted me Amit Ray's words once, when I'd told her I was having trouble sleeping.

The sandy beach was mostly studded with parents and pre-school toddlers, and a group of visiting students pulling off footwear and racing to the water's edge, shouts and laughter floating on the air.

I remembered the days when Rob and I had the place to ourselves, and would take it in turns to bury each other on the beach. I could still remember the cool, heavy weight on my arms and legs, and how implicitly I'd trusted Rob not to bury me completely – even after he asked once if it was possible to 'breathe through sand'.

Instantly, his face popped into my head, and his expression as he'd talked about leaving the band. I began walking more briskly, trying to banish the image. Nan lived on the north side of the village, and normally the walk would have been long enough to clear my head, but today it wasn't working. Every footstep seemed to loosen more questions, until my brain felt as if it was rattling with them, and my breathing sounded laboured. It was a relief to finally reach her bungalow, with its mottled brown roof and pillar-box red front door. At least here nothing had changed, apart from more ivy creeping around the trunk of the sycamore tree in the front garden, where I used to believe fairies lived.

Nan had found a new lease of life after my grandfather's death, five years ago. Finally freed from her role as 'wronged wife' her first hobby had been renovating the bungalow. She was particularly proud of the conservatory she'd had built on the back, where she loved to sit in the evenings with a glass of wine – when she wasn't watching films on her fifty-inch television.

'I'm watching Netflix and chilling tonight,' she'd said the last time we'd spoken, adding with a low-pitched chuckle, 'and, yes, I do know what that means.' I'd actually felt envious. My grandmother's love life had been in a lot better shape than mine.

I knocked briskly on the front door before pushing it open, mindful of the sight that had greeted me at home the evening before.

'Hi, Nan, it's Cassandra!'

Nan always called people by their full name, much to Dad's annoyance. 'Edmund sounds so old-fashioned,' he still protested, like a schoolboy.

'You should be proud to be named after a famous mountaineer,' Nan always argued. 'Plenty of famous and well-respected men were called Edmund.'

We hadn't been able to name any.

As I entered the kitchen, my jaw dropped for the second time that day. There were boxes everywhere, stuffed with books, crockery, pans, linen and the glass ornaments Nan had collected over the years, most of them bought by me for birthdays and Christmas. There was hardly anything left on her 'vintage' oak dresser, and all the surfaces were empty, apart from a pan on the stove.

Had I interrupted a burglary? It was highly unlikely robbers would arrive with cardboard boxes to magic away their loot – or that they'd be interested in Nan's cookery books, which weren't old enough to be valuable – and there couldn't be any demand for novelty salt-and-pepper pots shaped like the Queen and a corgi.

Aware that I'd alerted possible intruders to my presence, I grabbed a bread knife from one of the boxes and crept into the hallway, picturing a pair of masked burglars frozen mid-spree, waiting to cosh me over the head with the one of Nan's heavy doorstops.

The normally pristine hallway was also cluttered with boxes and bags and I recognised one of Nan's favourite blouses billowing out, as well as a stylish winter coat she'd once let me borrow. My breath caught in my throat. Was she moving? Surely Mum and Dad would have mentioned it?

Heart walloping my ribcage, I tiptoed through to the low-ceilinged living room, where I was greeted by a similar scene: boxes and bags stuffed with cushions, more books, and even the expensive cashmere throw that Mum had bought when Nan revamped the bungalow, which was usually draped along the back of her cream leather sofa. The fireside rug was rolled up and stacked in one corner, leaving the waxed floorboards bare, and the dining chairs were stacked on top of the table.

Maybe she was having a belated and very extensive, spring clean. It wouldn't be like Nan, who had 'more interesting things to do than move dust about', and although I was no expert on cleaning I was certain you didn't need to take down every picture. Where was the photo of me as a toddler, cuddling a cross-looking dog (no one knew whose it was) and the picture of her with her mother, who'd been a 'great beauty' in her day?

'Nan?' My voice sounded more querulous than I'd have liked, but as I squeezed around the boxes, heading for the conservatory, I saw her coming in from the back garden.

'Cassandra, sweetheart, you're here!' she cried, and I barely had time to put down the knife, and register that there was something different about her, before I was pulled into a hug as soft as a feather-bed. 'Look at you,' she said, releasing me to arm's length to study my face. 'Pretty as a picture.'

'Hardly,' I said, automatically. 'Look at *you*.' I stepped back to take her in, temporarily lost for words.

'What do you think?' She rotated slowly, arms outstretched.

I continued staring. There'd always been something of the duchess about Nan, with her taste for elegant clothes and her silvery hair, which she kept swept off her face in a silver clasp. Her upright bearing made her appear taller than she was, and my friends used to admire her snazzy outfits, which she'd credited with being half-French, despite having lived in Devon for most of her life.

There was nothing stylish about her appearance today. Her normally immaculate hair was hanging in a plait down the middle of her back, and the shapeless garment she was wearing reached her ankles and looked to be made of sacking. Clearly making the most of the warm weather, her feet were bare, and her face – normally made up with bronze eyeshadow to complement her blue eyes, and with her trademark 'tawny' lipstick (red was for 'ladies of the night') – was make-up free, giving her the appearance of a mole that had appeared from underground. Her eyes seemed much smaller and, although her face was remarkably unlined for a seventy-eight-year-old (which she put down to always wearing a hat in the sun), it looked less vibrant, like a faded photograph.

An icy finger touched my heart. 'Nan, what's wrong?' I gripped her fingers, noticing the knotty veins on the backs of her hands, and that her nails were unvarnished for the first time I could remember, with a rim of dirt underneath. 'Are you ill?'

'What?' Her eyebrows (so pale, she must have been drawing them in for years) rose in alarm. 'Of course I'm not ill, *ma chère fille!*' she said in the exaggerated French accent that drove Dad mad. 'I'm winding down, that's all.'

'I don't understand what's happening.'

'All of this?' She wafted a slender arm around, scowling at one of the boxes as though it had sworn at her. 'I read this wonderful article in a magazine by a Japanese lady called the Decluttering Queen, when I was at the dentist's last week,' she said. 'Apparently, holding on to clutter is holding on to the past and, to feel free, you must let it go.' Her eyelids closed in a parody of bliss. 'I'm releasing the past, Cassandra, readying myself for the next life.'

Ignoring the last bit, I said, 'But, Nan, decluttering means sorting out some stuff for the charity shop, not getting rid of everything you own.' I nudged a box containing her sewing machine with my foot. 'You love your sewing machine.'

'There'll be no need for it, where I'm going.'

'Stop it, Nan, you're not going anywhere.' I plucked a silky top, decorated with pearls, from one of the bags. 'Didn't Mum buy you this?'

Her eyes fluttered open. 'I've made myself some bamboo robes, that's all I'll need from now on.' She fingered the shapeless fabric she was wearing, which looked like the only thing it should hold was shopping. 'Natural fibres,' she said. 'I thought I'd become environmentally friendly while I'm at it.'

I groaned silently. 'Where's the watch we got you for your seventieth birthday?'

She glanced at the ghost of a watchstrap around her wrist. 'I don't need to know what the time is, I can tell by the sun.'

I glanced behind her. At least the froth of plants and exotic flowers in her beloved conservatory hadn't budged. 'What about when it's raining?'

'I'm just saying, Cassandra, that I'm no longer tied by time.'

Her overly patient tone was that of someone recently converted to a cult – or maybe someone who was losing their grip on reality.

I focused my gaze more sharply on her face. 'Nan, what year is it? Who's the Prime Minister?'

The lines on her forehead concertinaed. 'I'm not losing my mind,' she said, wagging a ringless finger. Nan had always worn rings, though she'd kept her wedding finger bare since my grandfather died, declaring her marriage null and void despite all her 'best efforts'. 'In fact, I've never been clearer about how I'd like to live out my final years.'

'Nan, stop saying things like that.'

'It's OK,' she said, with a noble and enigmatic air. 'I've come to terms with it.' She cast her eyes around and gave a satisfied nod, and I got the feeling this fad was a lot more serious than previous ones – even learning to play the banjo, which had gone beyond the point of reasonableness and had left her with a permanently weak wrist. 'Possessions shackle you to the past, and there's been enough shackling in this family,' she went on, regally. 'I just wish I'd unshackled myself from my cheating husband a lot sooner, instead of waiting for death to finally unshackle us.'

'Nan, stop saying unshackle.'

'I kept your father shackled for far too long.' She flexed her jaw. 'You've no idea how guilty and ashamed I am that we put him through what we did, Cassandra.'

'I do, because you've mentioned it once or twice, but—'

'The least I can do now is make sure I'm not a burden in my old age because, as fit as I am' – she flexed her arm for me to squeeze the wiry muscles – 'it won't last for ever, and I want to be as healthy as possible as I face the end.' She paused for dramatic effect. 'I'm growing my own vegetables and living off the land and freeing my mind to embrace this *nouveau chapitre*.' Another chin-tilted pause. 'New chapter,' she clarified.

'Yes, I got that, Nan.'

'When the time comes, I plan to slip quietly away in my sleep—'

'I don't think it works like that.'

'—and to be buried in the grounds. Your father won't even need to arrange a funeral.'

'Oh, Nan.' I wanted to contradict her; to tell her that of *course* Dad would want to arrange her funeral, and that we didn't even want to think about her dying, but I could see she genuinely believed she was doing Dad a big favour. I knew she felt dreadful that she'd relied on him so much when he was young – to mediate between her and his father – and I supposed this was her way of trying to alleviate the guilt. 'You can't get rid of these photo albums.' Spotting several of them in one of the unopened boxes, I tugged one out and began flipping through the pages. 'Dad might want to keep some of these.' My gaze landed on a photo of him astride a big motorbike, my grandfather holding the handlebars to keep it steady. Dad must have been about ten, his bony knees protruding from a pair of khaki shorts, smiling proudly up at his beaming father.

'Give that to me.' Nan snatched the album and flung it across the room like a Frisbee. 'I should have burnt the pictures of that cheating *cheval*.'

I had a feeling she'd meant dog, not horse, but it didn't seem right to correct her. 'Nan, you're not being fair,' I said. My grandfather had undoubtedly been a terrible husband, but he'd been a good granddad and father; something that had conflicted Dad terribly. 'You can't wipe him from history, it's not fair to Dad.'

'It's my stuff,' said Nan, her stubborn streak rearing its head. 'If I want to get rid of it all, I will. It'll save Edmund having to do it when I'm gone.'

I sighed. 'Mum told me they hardly see you these days.'

'They hardly see you either,' she said, with a trace of reproach. 'But they don't complain about that.'

'I live in London and have a very demanding job,' I pointed out, aware with a stab of panic that neither statement was true. 'I can't get home as much as I'd like, but you're only a mile away.'

'Well, Lydia should be glad I'm not the sort of mother-in-law who's always on the doorstep.'

'You know she thinks the world of you, Nan, especially not having a mum of her own.'

Nan's face softened. 'I think the world of her too, Cassandra, but I will not be a burden.'

I closed my eyes, briefly. 'Do Mum and Dad know about all this?'

'They're happy for me to do whatever I want, you know what they're like,' she said, doing another twirl to take in the box-scattered room. 'They're pleased I've got my own interests and that they don't have to entertain me all the time. That I'm not a—'

'Burden.' I blew out another sigh. I was clearly wasting my breath. 'What does your… boyfriend think?' She was bound to have a new one on the go. She'd been making up for lost time since becoming a widow, like a child let loose in a sweet shop.

'I'm done with men.' She waved a hand, dismissing the entire gender. 'I'm celibate from now on.'

Wishing I hadn't asked, I looked at the boxes and bags. 'Where's it all going to go?'

I wouldn't have put it past her to have booked a removal van or a skip, and was wondering whether I could persuade her to wait a week or two in case she changed her mind, when she said, 'Danny's booked some storage.' A smile lifted her face. 'He's been a godsend,' she went on. 'He's been helping me in the garden too, with my allotment. He's cleared a space where I can meditate.'

'Danny?' I said. 'Danny Fleetwood?'

Her smile broadened. 'Weren't you at school with him?'

'Yes,' I said, briefly wishing I was still at Nina's, job-surfing and watching re-runs of *Criminal Minds*.

'Come and see what we've done.' Before I'd had a chance to sort through my scattered thoughts, Nan had taken my hand and was leading me through the conservatory with a casual, 'All these plants are going, they take too much looking after,' and out into the wide, hedge-bordered garden, which had been partly transformed into an allotment, with what looked like a wigwam in the middle, twined with leaves.

'I'll have potatoes, carrots, radishes and cabbages, which I'll turn into soup every day *n'est ce pas*?' Even I knew that last bit didn't make any sense. 'And I'm going to get some chickens for eggs, and to fatten up for Christmas – if I'm still here. Much better for body and soul to eat organically. I'll know exactly what I'm eating, because I'll know what *they've* been eating.'

I knew I ought to be protesting against this outrageous plan – surely she wasn't planning to slaughter birds for food – but my eyes were drawn to a figure stooped over a spade at the end of the garden, his open shirt covering a broad back. He straightened, as if sensing my gaze, and wiped his arm across his forehead.

'Cassie Maitland?' The flash of his teeth was dazzling as he broke into a grin. 'Is that really you?'

And then he was striding towards me and all I could think was, Oh my god, he's gorgeous.

Chapter 6

'It's definitely you, I'd know those eyes anywhere.' Danny came to a halt on the grass in front of me, rugged and casually groomed, a delighted smile on his face. *Where had those cheekbones come from?* 'My schoolboy crush, no less.' He pressed a palm to his heart, his eyes sparkling. They were a greenish-blue colour. *Just like the ocean.*

My smile was lasting a lot longer than I'd meant it to, and my heart appeared to have hiccups. 'Danny Fleetwood, as I live and breathe.' I had no idea why I'd adopted an Irish accent, or why a flood of warmth had shocked my body into life. Probably the surprise of seeing him after all this time. He was taller than I remembered, with a suggestion of strength in the width of his shoulders, and his chest – from what I could see – was tanned and well-muscled beneath a downy fuzz of hair. 'You should button your shirt, you'll catch a chill.' I'd intended to sound wry to disguise the effect he was having, but unfortunately my breathing had gone haywire and I sounded as if I was planning to rip his shirt off. 'At least you don't wax your chest,' I added, wondering where all my saliva had gone. My tongue was making an unattractive clicking noise against the roof of my mouth. 'Or, maybe you do, I wouldn't know, men do wax a lot more these days, it's called male grooming.'

'You seem very interested in the topic.' The width of Danny's grin suggested he was enjoying every second of seeing me squirm. 'For the record, I've never waxed any part of my body and never will. Apart from the pain involved, I believe we were born with body hair for a reason.'

'Yes, it's to keep us warm, and to act as a barrier against infection,' said Nan, reminding us she was there, watching our exchange with open curiosity. 'I was seeing a GP for a while,' she added, by way of an explanation. 'I stopped shaving my bits a while ago.'

Catching Danny's look of amused horror, I quickly asked him, 'What are you doing here?'

'Helping this lovely lady get back to nature,' he said, raising an imaginary hat to Nan. 'The allotment's doing well, and I've just finished constructing a composting toilet behind the shed.'

I looked at her, appalled. 'Please tell me you're not going outside, when you've got a perfectly functioning toilet indoors?' Nan merely raised her eyebrows. 'How has clearing out your wardrobe led to this?'

'I told you, I want to be kind to the environment,' she said. 'I saw a television programme about it.'

'Seeing it on TV doesn't mean it's a good idea.' I was glad to have a new focus for my jumbled feelings. 'Didn't you read an article at the dentist's?'

'I did, *ma chérie*, and then I watched a documentary about how we're damaging the planet and it spoke to my soul.'

'But weeing in your garden won't make any difference, Nan. It's not like getting rid of all the plastic from the sea.'

'No, but every little helps.' She was infuriatingly calm, as though she'd been given a sedative. 'Marcus helped me to research it before I ended our relationship,' she said. 'He's not cut out for living the simple life. And by simple life, I mean being self-sufficient. That man practically lives on ready-meals. Tesco's bangers and mash, to be precise, and you should see all the packaging they use.'

I looked at Danny, who was studying the patch of grass around his boot-clad feet and rubbing the back of his neck. His hair had lightened over the years to a warm, golden-brown shade of toffee or caramel, and he wore it longer than he had at high school, when most of the boys favoured buzz-cuts. 'Do you think you should be encouraging her?' I said.

When he raised his eyes to mine, my breathing faltered again. 'I'm sure you know perfectly well that Sylvia has a mind of her own.' He was still smiling, but some of his sparkle had gone, and it struck me that I was bringing the mood down yet again.

'Sorry,' I said to Nan, who graciously bowed her head. 'It's just a lot to take in.'

A cloud passed over the sun, and a pair of pigeons clattered out of the hedge, making me jump. I fixed my gaze on a giant bee hovering over a spray of pink flowers that had somehow survived Nan's cull. Presumably they were allowed to stay as they'd grown outside. Their scent mingled with oil paint, wood chips and something like warm skin, which seemed to be emanating from Danny, making it even harder to think clearly. I was glad when Nan broke the silence by saying, 'I'll go and fetch you both a drink.'

'Good idea,' I said, gratefully.

'Lovely,' said Danny at the same time. 'Ma throat's as dry as a country road in a heatwave.'

His Texan accent was a lot more successful than my Irish one, reminding me that he'd had a gift for mimicry at school, particularly the Geordie twang of our art teacher, Miss Finch. As if remembering too, he gave me a crooked smile that sent a blast of desire rocketing through me. *It's Danny Fleetwood* I reminded myself, in the sternest voice I could summon (which sounded a lot like Carlotta's). Danny

Fleetwood who'd once invited me to a school leavers' party and had promptly stood me up. Probably an early indicator of future behaviour. A man who probably went into flirt mode with every female he met. A man who spent his days sign-writing and making outdoor toilets, which wasn't a proper job. If he hadn't settled on a career by now, he probably never would, and I doubted he was financially stable.

Not like Adam, whose salary could have supported a Third World country.

'You didn't do anything with your art, then?' I said, at the same time that Danny said, 'Your hair's a different colour.'

'It's Plumberry.' The words were laced with a hefty dose of defiance and I wondered why I was behaving as if I'd never spoken to a good-looking member of the opposite sex before. Adam had been (was) extremely handsome, albeit in a more textbook way; square-jawed and clean-shaven, with a rugby-player's physique from early-morning gym sessions, and intensely dark brown eyes. 'A mixture of plums and berries,' I added, as if more explanation was required.

Danny tilted his head, squinting his eyes as the sun reappeared. 'I'd say it was more Ribena.'

'Ha, ha.'

'I happen to like Ribena,' he said.

Not sure what to do with my hands – more used to clutching an iPad to look things up, or my work phone so I could take calls at all hours of the day or night – I stuck them in the pouch at the front of my top and moistened my lips with my tongue. 'I'm thinking of growing it out,' I said, as he appeared to be waiting for an explanation. 'It's not really me.' Why had I told him that? 'It fitted with my image, I suppose.' I wished he'd stop looking at me like that. As if he'd dug up a Roman coin and was trying to work out its value.

'What image was that, then?'

'I'm in event management.' I couldn't quite summon the requisite enthusiasm, so it came out sounding as interesting as filing legal documents. 'With a big company based in London. At least, I was.'

'Yes, your mum told me.' He bashed his spade into the ground and leaned on the handle, so his face was close to mine. He had a grazing of stubble around the lower half of his face, and I wondered whether he was growing a beard, or just too lazy to shave. 'And you reckon purple hair's essential for planning events?'

'It's not purple, it's—'

'Blueberryplumble. I get it.' A grin lifted his well-drawn lips. *Stop looking at his lips.* 'Your parents are insanely proud of you, you know.'

'Tell me about it.'

He straightened. 'They certainly told *me* all about it.'

I grimaced, trying to hold his gaze and not think about my stupid hair colour. 'Sorry about that.'

'I could hardly connect the woman they were describing with the girl I shared art classes with.' His eyes gleamed and widened. 'The girl who sketched a not-very-flattering caricature of Miss Finch when she was supposed to be doing a self portrait.'

'I didn't like looking at myself.' Embarrassed, I glanced down to see I looked pregnant with my hands bunched in my pouch, so I snatched them out and folded my arms instead. Why hadn't I brought my bag so I could fiddle about with it, like normal women? 'Anyway, she liked my drawing.'

'Exactly,' said Danny, one finger stabbing the air. 'So how come you ended up planning all these a-MAZING' – his impression of Mum was uncanny – 'events for high-profile clients, instead of doing something arty?'

'How come you're digging gardens?' I shot back, unwilling to enter into a defence of my choice of career with Danny Fleetwood, of all people. 'You were pretty good, too, as I recall.'

'Ah, so you *did* notice me?'

His teasing grin sent all my blood to my face. 'Hard not to when you were constantly messing about. Sometimes, all you did was flick paint at your canvas, and pretend you were the next Jackson Pollock.'

'Still got a good grade though, didn't I?'

'So did I.'

'I know,' he said with a slow nod. 'Because you were really good.'

His words produced a warm glow in the pit of my stomach. My temperature gauge was all over the place. 'I liked painting, that was all,' I said. 'I didn't want to take it any further.' I remembered Rob's words from earlier, about his music. If I *had* pursued art, I'd probably hate it now, like he'd gone off music. 'And, anyway, I wasn't *that* good.'

If I'd been half hoping Danny would disagree, I was disappointed. 'Sign-writing's a form of art,' he pointed out.

'It's writing with paint.' I was being horribly unfair, but couldn't seem to stop myself carrying on. 'And isn't it a dying trade? Most shops use vinyl lettering these days.' I'd picked up that nugget from a feature I'd read online about the urban art scene in London. I might not paint or draw any more, but I liked reading about people who did.

Danny pretended to look hurt – or maybe he really was. 'It's a bit more than writing with paint,' he said. 'There's been a revival. Businesses like the personal touch, something bespoke. Like your parents, for instance.'

'How did you end up at the café?' Embarrassment was making me blunt. 'Nothing better to do?'

'Christ, you're grumpier than I remember.' He swung back and held his arm out, as if to ward off an attack. 'Tilly Campbell recommended me, do you remember her?'

'Of course I do.'

'I bumped into her when I came back from Spain.'

'You've been to Spain?'

'Don't sound so surprised.' His smile was bright with mischief. 'I haven't been holed up in my bedroom for the past ten years, playing with my Gameboy. And that's not a euphemism.'

I didn't want to think about him doing anything in his bedroom, but found I was picturing him lounging on a revolving (*why?*) king-sized bed in his pants, and had to work hard to overcome a powerful blush.

'I spent a year over there, honing my trades,' he said. 'Lived with a Señorita for a while, but it didn't work out.'

'Thanks for that update.'

'Listen, while you're around we should have a drink and catch up properly,' he said, as if I hadn't just been unnecessarily sarcastic. 'I'm not seeing anyone at the moment, if that's what's bothering you.'

'Why would that bother me?' I said. 'I don't care whether or not you're seeing anyone.'

'Are *you* seeing anyone?'

'Maybe.' It was hard to understand why he was still smiling that stupidly sexy smile, which he probably practised in front of a mirror, when my body language was anything but inviting. My mind volleyed to Adam's face. He had a lovely smile, too, which showcased his perfectly aligned teeth. 'Does it matter if I am?'

'It might do, if I want to win you over,' he said. 'I don't want to be treading on anyone's toes.'

For a second, I felt as if I was falling. 'Why would you want to win me over?' *Especially when you couldn't be bothered the last time.* The words didn't make it to my lips. 'You're not even my type.'

He threw back his head and laughed. 'I've thought about you sometimes, over the years,' he said, bringing his gaze back to mine. 'Wondered how you were doing.'

He'd probably said the same thing to Tilly, who I imagined was still about ten times more his type than I ever would be. 'Funny, because I haven't thought about you at all,' I said. 'We can't have spent more than two days together, tops. In a classroom with other people, years ago. Where you mostly made fun of our teacher behind her back.'

'Listen, about the leavers' party that night,' he said, his eyes scrunching, as if suddenly remembering he hadn't bothered to turn up. 'I had a good reason for not being there. I really wanted to let you know, but couldn't find you, and—'

'You had a better offer,' I chipped in, remembering the girl I'd seen him with, who'd looked a lot like Jennifer Hartwell from what I'd made out, and everyone knew that boys couldn't resist her. 'It's fine, it's all in the past and, anyway, I got off with Lenny Jamieson.' Everyone had known of Lenny Jamieson's heart-throb status, and with his habit of choosing a lucky recipient every week to 'go out with' it wasn't unfeasible that it could have been my turn.

'Really?' His smile didn't falter.

'Yes, really. We spent most of the night snogging.'

He teased the spade out of the ground and hoisted it over one shoulder, looking every inch a seasoned gardener, down to his mud-encrusted boots. 'Well, maybe it's time I made it up to you,' he said.

'*What?*

'Let me win you over properly this time.'

I had no idea why my heart was flipping about like a fish. 'Isn't there anything better to do around here?'

Before he could answer, Nan returned, carrying a mug in each hand, her robe flapping dangerously around her ankles, and I experienced another little shock at how different she looked. 'Here you are,' she said, handing us each a drink.

'What is it?' I peered inside, preparing myself for something home-made and herbal, probably featuring dandelion leaves, which I'd have to force down to be polite.

'Tap water,' she said. 'I know you're probably used to drinking it out of bottles, but – as you've already pointed out – all that plastic's incredibly bad for the environment.'

'I'm not actually, I just... you were gone for a while, that's all, I thought you were...' *Leaving us alone together.* 'Making something... else.' I watched Danny's throat ripple as he guzzled his drink in one go. 'You usually drink coffee.'

'No more, unless it's decaf and fair trade,' Nan said. 'Plus, I'm cleansing at the moment, purifying my body.'

Unable to cope with the image this presented, I gulped some water then handed the mug back. 'Listen, Nan, I'll let you get on,' I said. 'I just wanted to pop by and say hi.'

'You should join me for a meditation session some time.' She grasped my hand. 'You seem very tense, Cassandra.'

'I'm fine.' I laughed lightly to prove it, aware I must look anything but, with my shiny red face and a pulse twitching beneath my right eye. 'I've got lots of plans for while I'm here.' I sensed Danny listening and tried to stay focused on Nan. 'I'm arranging some events for the café.'

'You work too hard, *chérie*.' She squeezed my hand, a smile creasing her eyes. 'What are these events?'

'I'll keep you posted.'

'That means she doesn't know,' said Danny.

I rounded on him. 'It means mind your own business.' I sounded more like a truculent teenager than the career woman I was striving to be. 'What are *your* plans?'

He grinned. 'Well, I was planning to carry on doing a bit of this and that, as usual, but now I have a new challenge to look forward to.'

'That's right.' Although his words had been directed at me, Nan had misunderstood. 'He's trying to find me a *jeune coq.*'

'Beg pardon?' said Danny.

'She means cockerel.' I frowned at Nan. 'It's French.'

'Ah, yes.' Danny gave me a stagey wink. 'Looks like I've got two challenges on my hands.'

I could hardly say, 'I don't want to be a challenge,' with Nan listening. Instead, I said, 'I've really got to go,' and glanced at my watch as if I had a vital appointment. 'I'll speak to you soon, Nan.'

I turned and hurried away on legs that felt strangely wonky, aware of their eyes on my back and trying not to wonder whether they'd talk about me.

I'd thought coming home would be a port in a storm – a chance to regroup and start over – but, if anything, I felt more unsettled than I had when I'd lost my job.

Chapter 7

I spent the afternoon skulking around my parents' house like a conva-
lescent, reacquainting myself with the past – hardly anything had been
thrown out or replaced since the 1990s – and ended up in a chair in
the garden with an old *Harry Potter* from my bookshelf.

'What are you doing out there?' Mum called from the patio doorway
what felt like just minutes later, yanking me away from Hogwarts.

'Just relaxing, like you suggested.' I waggled my book at her and
she came over, still wearing her café uniform, her face pink from her
exertions.

'I thought you'd be reading one of your business books,' she said,
eyebrows rising. I thought guiltily of my unpacked rucksack in my
bedroom, mostly stuffed with sketch pads and the clothes I hadn't been
able to fit in my suitcase. 'That won't help your career.'

I dragged on a smile. 'Maybe my career will involve witchcraft
and wizardry in future.' I flourished the book like a magic wand
and she gamely looked down at her outfit with a look of exaggerated
astonishment.

'Cinderella *shall* go to the ball!' she cried, pressing her palms to
her cheeks.

I smiled properly, pleased she was being playful. 'And you don't even
have to cook dinner,' I said, feeling generous. 'I'll do it.'

'Don't be silly.' Her expression reverted to 'my daughter's so special and clever she shouldn't be allowed to do normal things'. 'Mind you, I don't cook every night any more,' she admitted. 'Sometimes, your dad and I just have a sandwich when we get in, so we have the evening free to—'

'Please don't say what I think you're going to say.'

'I wasn't going to mention making love, Cassie.'

'Oh god, you said it.'

She batted a hand at me. 'I was going to say, do whatever we like.'

'And now your offspring are home, cramping your style.'

'Oh, no, not at all, it's lovely having you to stay.' She sounded genuinely horrified I might think otherwise. 'We want to make the most of you both, because Rob will soon be back with Emma, by the sound of things, and you'll be off goodness knows where.'

My nerve-endings pinged. Her words implied an end date to my visit, which meant I shouldn't be reading in the garden – I should be getting on with organising my future. 'And I'm very happy to cook dinner for you,' Mum continued. 'I ordered some parmesan and rosemary stuffed chicken breasts from the butcher's specially.'

'Sounds… lovely,' I said. 'But I'd have been happy with fish fingers and oven chips.' It had been my favourite dinner as a child.

'Oh, no.' Mum's forehead crimped. 'We can't feed you frozen food when you're used to eating out at fancy restaurants.'

'For god's sake, Mum, I don't eat out every night,' I said, unable to smooth out a snap. My fine-dining experiences had been few and far between, and I was no stranger to beans on toast for dinner. 'I'm perfectly happy to eat whatever you've got in the fridge. Stop treating me like minor royalty.'

'I'm not.' I saw the hurt in her eyes and wished I hadn't said it. 'We just want you to have a nice visit,' she said.

There was the 'V' word again. 'Thanks, Mum,' I said humbly. 'I'm sure I will. Have a nice visit, I mean.'

She smiled. 'I hope so, love.' She sounded so doubtful I got up and gave her a hug, glad when she relaxed against me. 'Silly muffin,' she said, patting my back before pulling away and turning back to the house. 'Did you go to your nan's?'

'Yes. Have you seen what she's been up to?' Glad of the change of subject, I followed her indoors. 'She's going environmentally friendly and throwing out all her stuff.'

'So I gather,' Mum said, entering the kitchen and looking around as if she'd never seen it before. 'Danny suggested putting her things in storage, but if she wants to downsize, it's really up to her.' My heart stuttered at the mention of his name. 'He's been a godsend, actually.' That was the word Nan had used. 'Did you see him while you were there?' Mum retrieved a tray of plumped up chicken breasts from the fridge and placed it on the counter. 'He's been doing her gardening for a while.'

'He's a proper jack of all trades.' There was a bit of an edge to my voice, and seeing that Mum was about to protest, I added, 'He's making her an outdoor toilet, did you know?'

I'd hoped it would elicit a stronger reaction than a chuckle.

'Mum! He shouldn't be encouraging her.'

'It's one of her fads, and if she's happy we're happy, though it's a shame she doesn't have much time for us any more.' As Mum rinsed her hands at the sink, I noticed how worn they looked from constantly washing them at the café over the years. She never remembered to rub in the moisturising creams that Rob and I bought her, despite requesting a new one every birthday. They were lined up on the windowsills in virtually every room. 'Remember when she wanted to learn to fly a plane?'

'I certainly do.' Nan had booked some lessons at a flying school in Umberleigh, but turned out to be horribly airsick.

'And then there were the Tibetan bowls,' Mum reminded me, switching the oven on. 'Part of her musical phase.'

'Oh god, that was awful,' I said, groaning. I'd been helping to arrange a charity fun run when Mum had sent me a recording of a noise like discordant church bells, accompanied by a low droning sound, which turned out to be Nan, bashing a series of different shaped bowls with a wooden spoon and humming under her breath.

'I blame that man she was seeing,' said Mum. 'What was his name?'

'Gregory, I think.' It had been hard to keep up with Nan's boyfriends. 'She met him at the garden centre.'

'That's right.' Mum shoved the tray of chicken into the oven and set the timer. 'What your grandfather would make of it all, I've no idea.'

'He couldn't complain after the way he used to carry on.' I plucked an overripe pear from the fruit bowl and bit into it. 'And anyway, I think this is more than a fad.' Blocking out all talk of her dying, I thought of Nan's make-up-free face, and how knowledgeable she'd seemed about what she needed to make her new lifestyle work. 'Maybe this is what she's been looking for since Grandpa died.'

'Well, good for her, I guess,' Mum said, her smile in place as she took some carrots from the fridge and emptied out a bag of potatoes. 'Mashed or roasted?'

'Both?'

'Good girl.' She gave a satisfied nod, seeming to forget I was supposedly used to eating more exotic fare. 'I think you should stay here until you've at least got your boobs and hips back.'

'In that case, I'd better restrict my calories so I can stay longer,' I said jokily.

'You'll do no such thing.' Misunderstanding, Mum flashed me an old-fashioned look that made me want to hug her again. 'I hope you haven't been comparing yourself with those underwear models on Instagram.'

'Do you mean Victoria's Secret?'

'If they're the ones that hardly eat so that they can parade about in their skimpies, then yes,' she said. 'One of them contacted Rob, you know. Said she was a fan of his music.'

'Blimey.' *And he'd rather live in Seashell Cove, and train to teach IT?* 'What do you think of him giving up the band?' I was genuinely curious. She and Dad had got so much vicarious pleasure from having a semi-famous son, just as I'd enjoyed having a brother whose music had been played on the radio. OK, so it wasn't our kind of music, but that hadn't stopped me from downloading it onto my phone, or my parents from proudly displaying the CDs alongside Bananarama (Mum's favourite), The Eagles, and Nina Simone.

'I think it's brave to recognise when you're on the wrong path and to step off and do something different,' she said, in a way that suggested she was parroting Rob, after he'd been brainwashed by Bossy Emma. 'At least he's experienced… *life*.' She emphasised the word to demonstrate its vast mysteries – as if she had no hope of experiencing it herself. 'He wouldn't have done that if he'd stayed around here for the past seven years.'

'He might not have started drinking either,' I said. For some reason, Danny Fleetwood's smiling face burst into my head. 'He might have been happier.'

'Of *course* he wouldn't.' Mum spoke with more bite than usual. 'He'd always have wondered what might have been.'

I studied her back as she peeled potatoes with more force than seemed strictly necessary. 'I suppose you're right.' I finished my pear and pulled a pan from the cupboard for the potatoes. 'Experience is the teacher of all things.' It was something I'd heard Carlotta say once, in an unusually reflective mood.

'*Exactly*,' Mum said. 'And he *chose* to do it, we didn't force him. You know we wanted you both to do whatever made you happy.' She looked at me over her shoulder. 'You're happy with your life, aren't you, Cassie?' There was such a ray of hope in her eyes I couldn't bear to extinguish it.

'Course I am.' I managed to say it with conviction, glad when a beaming smile transformed her face. *I will be, once I've sorted out my career*, I added silently, in order to keep my expression pleasantly relaxed. *In the meantime, I'm happy to be crunching this deliciously sweet, raw carrot.*

'Put that down,' Mum instructed, tapping my hand with the potato peeler, and, keen to hold onto a sense of normality, I took another bite, knowing she'd warn me affectionately that I'd 'spoil my appetite' like she used to, when talks about experiencing The Big Wide World hadn't been a part of her vocabulary.

'You'll spoil your appetite,' she said, and looked puzzled when I burst out laughing and squashed a kiss on her cheek. 'Maybe you could set the table,' she said, flushing with pleasure. 'If you don't mind.'

Dinner was a jolly affair, mostly because Rob was so enthused about his course, and with proving himself to Bossy Emma, that he kept up a flow of conversation, which Mum and Dad responded to with bright-eyed eagerness, and partly because I kept deflecting questions about my life in London. I came up with memories from the past: 'Remember when Dad got fed up with losing at Scrabble and made us keep playing until he won?', and random compliments: 'Your hair looks extra bouncy, Mum, what conditioner are you using?', and I teased

Rob about becoming a teacher: 'You can always resort to playing your keyboard if you're rubbish.'

'Is there someone staying in your flat while you're here?' Mum said, catching me out over a plate of cheese and crackers. I'd neglected to tell them I no longer had a place to live, and hadn't yet invented a plausible reason why.

'I'm, erm, between accommodation at the moment and have been staying with a friend.' It wasn't exactly a lie. 'My lease was up, so I've decided to... look for something else.'

'Shame things didn't work out with Adam. You could have moved in together.' Mum paused, as if imagining the pair of us snuggled together on a sofa – or maybe she was wondering whether she should have said it, considering Adam and I were no longer together.

'What about buying your own place?' Dad said, and the idea that they believed that my salary could in any way stretch to a mortgage was so incredible that I swallowed a crumb the wrong way and had a coughing fit. 'Rob's looking to buy, aren't you, son?' Dad seamlessly moved on as I shoved Rob for slapping me deliberately hard on the back.

He nodded. 'Music royalties,' he said, to my unasked, watery-eyed question. 'Got a bit of a nest egg.'

'Do you know where that saying came from?' I said, desperate to drag us away from the subject of housing. 'It originated in the fourteenth century when people would put a real or china egg into a hen's nest to encourage her to lay more eggs.' After once overhearing a client ask what it meant, I'd speedily looked it up so that I could wow her with my brilliance.

'Bit silly, when you think about it,' Rob said, straight-faced. 'It's not like the hen could buy anything with her eggs.'

By bedtime, I was so exhausted that even when Rob re-enacted my least favourite childhood memory by bursting out of my wardrobe to 'make me jump', I could barely muster a scream.

'You're no fun any more, Sandra.'

'Piss off,' I managed drowsily, but fell asleep smiling, and dreamt I was watching a documentary, in which Nan was flying an aeroplane over a field where a shirtless Danny Fleetwood was digging a grave.

I woke the next morning full of purpose. Striking out on my own meant being in charge of my own destiny, setting my own hours, and being free to take on my own staff. I'd learn from Carlotta's mistakes by being a kind and encouraging employer, dispensing wisdom, and not treating them like underlings.

Indulging a vision of my future self as the sort of person featured in magazines as 'one to watch', I drank the coffee Mum had left by my bed and, once everyone had left the house, I whirled into action. After showering, I dressed more smartly than the previous day, in a pair of tapered black trousers and a dove-grey blouse, a pair of black lace-up brogues completing the outfit. I disguised my purplish hair by fashioning a wide hairband from a scarf that I found hanging on the back of my bedroom door, and was tucking into a power breakfast of bacon, eggs and French toast, when the teas and coffees I'd ordered by next-day delivery turned up.

'Smells good,' said the courier, with a hungry look, as I signed for the boxes. 'Can't remember the last time I ate bacon. The wife says it's as bad as smoking.'

'Only if you eat twenty rashers a day,' I joked, my mood still riding high, gratified when he laughed all the way back to his van.

I opened the boxes and began pulling out fancy packages and reading the labels, knowing I'd need some rudimentary knowledge of the products before the tasting session.

There was a Nicaraguan blend of coffee beans with *complex flavours of hazelnut, cloves, and a tantalising hint of citrus.* Should coffee taste of citrus? And what about the Kenyan coffee, crafted from prized peaberries—*a particular type of coffee bean, formed when the two seeds of a berry fuse into a single tiny oval.* I'd never heard of a peaberry and was certain none of the café's customers would have either, but part of the fun would be trying them.

Dreamtime tea came in a lavender tin, and boasted a rich, malty rooibos for the base that was *blended with flavours of apricots, creamy vanilla and a spoonful of honey for good measure.* Sounded more like a cake recipe. *Whole chunks of apple make for a moreish midnight feast…* It was obviously to aid a restful night's sleep, but could be marketed as 'relaxing', while the Ceylon Orange Pekoe tea, with its *brisk taste* and *long, wiry leaves,* was bound to invite discussion.

A wave of excitement pulsed through me as I imagined word spreading about the café's exquisite new beverages – until I remembered I had no way of getting the stock to Seashell Cove unless I carried it there. It was possible, in a couple of trips – the boxes weren't exactly heavy – but not very practical, or professional.

I dithered over whether to call the café and ask either Mum or Dad to come and get me, but it was hardly fitting to be relying on my parents for a lift, and I didn't fancy turning up in a taxi, which might give the impression I was throwing my money around – money I could no longer claim back on expenses. There was a bus that meandered down to Seashell Cove every couple of hours, but I couldn't quite see myself hopping on public transport.

In the end, I called Nan.

'Is Sir Lancelot still in the garage?' It was the name she'd given the old Morris Minor that she'd had for as long as I could remember and which, these days, was probably considered vintage.

'Where else would he be, *ma bichette*?' I smiled at the endearment – *my little doe* – which Nan had used when I was a child. 'I don't drive much, since my shoulder popped out.'

'Popped out?'

'When I was learning judo last year,' she said. 'It's not been the same since I threw my opponent down.'

I shook my head. Luckily, that fad hadn't lasted long. 'I've got some stuff to take to the café and don't have a car,' I said.

'*Ma chérie*, of course you can borrow him. It's such a shame he's tucked away out of sight, he must be desperate for some fresh air.' She'd always referred to her beloved car as though it were human, much to my grandfather's embarrassment. He'd preferred his sporty Mazda, and had refused to even sit in Sir Lancelot. 'He doesn't have power steering, I'm afraid, and he's a bit of a gas guzzler, which of course is terrible for the environment.'

'I'll take my chances,' I said. 'I'm not even sure I can remember how to drive.' It wasn't strictly true. On my flying visit home last Christmas, I'd ended up driving Mum and Dad back from the Smugglers Inn after their team won the quiz night, because they'd drunk too much mulled wine, but before I could tell her that I'd walk down and get it, Nan was already speaking.

'Don't worry, Cassandra,' she said. 'Danny can drive it over and take you there.'

Chapter 8

'You didn't have to do this.'

'Are you kidding?' Danny patted Sir Lancelot's sage-green flank before opening the boot so that I could place my cargo inside. 'I couldn't miss a chance to drive this ancient beauty.' He nodded in a friendly fashion to Sid Turner, who was out on the road with his eyes on stalks at the sight of a genuine classic – albeit it one a bit rusty around the wheel arches.

'If you need her buffing up, give me a shout,' he called, brandishing his cloth as if he'd like to bolt over there and then.

'I will, and it's actually a he,' I replied, feeling foolish, trying not to look at Danny as I ducked under his arm and into the passenger seat. I was suddenly glad that I'd made an effort with my outfit. The contrast with his grass-stained jeans and loose T-shirt somehow served to heighten the different directions our lives had taken, and placed me on firmer ground. His untidy hair was sweeping his collar, and his stubble was more pronounced than it had been yesterday. *Definitely growing a beard.*

As he fired the car into life, he flashed me a wicked grin. 'Like what you see?' he said, jiggling his eyebrows.

Annoyed at being caught looking, I turned to look out of the window, hoping my face was hot because of the sun blazing through the windscreen.

'Just so you know,' I said starchily, 'I'm not looking for a relationship.' Better to get it out of the way. Just because I'd had a weird chemical reaction to seeing him for the first time in years, and he'd gone out of his way to try to charm me, didn't mean I was willing to play his 'win you over' game – because I was certain that's all it was to him: a game. 'I'm totally focused on starting a new phase of my career.'

'All work and no play?' He sucked in a breath. 'You know what they say about that.'

'That I'll build a successful business and, in a few years, have enough money to do whatever I want?'

He chuckled as he released the handbrake and drove down the road, his broad hands resting lightly on the old-fashioned steering wheel. 'So, you're motivated by money?'

'Just watch where you're going.' I didn't want a conversation about what motivated me. 'We can't all pick and choose what we want to do.'

'I think you'll find that we can.'

'Maybe, if you're living off a trust fund.'

His roar of laughter indicated that nothing could be further from the truth, and I realised that, despite us having shared a year of art classes, I knew nothing about his background. 'I'm just not driven by cash,' he said, when he'd sobered up. 'It's more important to me that I'm happy with how I spend my time every day.'

'Doing this and that?'

'Exactly.' He glanced at me sideways. 'Each of my jobs fulfils a different need.'

'How many do you have?'

'Needs, or jobs?'

I let the silence swell.

'Please yourself,' he said, cranking down the window and poking his elbow out. 'I've got three jobs.'

'*Three?*'

'Sign-writing, gardening and cooking.'

'You cook?' I wasn't sure why that was so surprising, except that his soil-engrained hands didn't look like they should be handling sausages, or whatever he specialised in. 'I'm a chef at The Brook in Kingsbridge,' he said, naming a popular and classy restaurant. 'Only a few nights a week, mind you. I wouldn't want to do it full time.'

'A chef,' I repeated, adjusting my impression of him. 'Where did that come from?'

He jerked a shoulder. 'I used to go fishing with my dad after...' He paused. 'Anything we caught, he'd cook. It sparked an interest.'

'Right,' I said, picturing a tousle-haired boy bent over a flaming grill. 'I like seafood.'

'That's good, because I was going to invite you to the restaurant one evening next week, and I do a mean cod with chorizo.'

My heart was doing silly things again, so I focused my gaze on the shiny, wooden dashboard, thinking how different it was to Adam's Alfa Romeo with its red leather seats and state-of-the-art sound system. 'I probably won't have time.'

'I'm sure you can spare a couple of hours,' he said, turning the car down the curvy road that led to the café. In the distance, the sun was shimmering off the sea and the sand looked almost white. 'Never get tired of that view,' he added, pulling the car into the only available space in the tiny car park.

'Do you live locally?' I hadn't meant to ask, but it just slipped out.

'I do,' he said.

'Did you always?' I hadn't meant to ask that either. 'Only, I don't really remember you from before that last year or so at school.'

'No, we lived all over the place when I was a kid, because my dad was in the army.' His fingers drummed the steering wheel. 'We settled in Kingsbridge after he was… after he left. I was thirteen, fourteen. I live there again, now,' he said. 'Nice house, not too far from the restaurant.'

'Your own?' Remembering what Dad had said, I realised how little chance there was at the moment of me ever buying my own place.

'My sister's, actually. I rent her attic room.'

'Ah.' I hadn't meant to convey disapproval – or maybe I had. Either way, he made the face of a scolding teacher and wagged a finger at me. 'Don't judge me, Cassie Maitland.'

My face reddened. 'I wasn't.'

'You'll like her,' he said, dropping the act. 'Louise, my sister, I mean. Most people do.'

'I've already told you, I'm—'

'Not looking for a relationship.' He gave me the benefit of his smile. 'It's OK, I get it.'

'Good.' I snapped my seat belt off, ignoring a tiny stab of disappointment.

'But that's only because I haven't won you over, yet.'

I decided to ignore the comment. I didn't want to encourage him. 'Thanks for the lift,' I said politely, getting out of the car.

He leapt out too, a smile still hovering, and I wondered whether he ever looked pissed off. 'Do you want a hand?'

'I'm good, thanks,' I said, retrieving my boxes from the boot.

'I would come in with you, but I'm installing a water butt for Sylvia today.' It was odd, hearing him refer to Nan by her name. 'For collecting rainwater,' he clarified.

'That's fine,' I said. 'I'm here on business, anyway.'

'Clearly.' He tipped his head at the boxes. 'You can tell me all about it over our meal at The Brook.'

I felt my scarf slip forward, but my hands were full and I couldn't do anything about it. 'There's nothing to tell,' I said, tilting my head back.

'Well, that can't be true.' He looked at me for a long moment, while the breeze lifted his hair, and although I tried to look away, my gaze seemed stuck to his annoyingly attractive face. 'See you soon, Cassie.'

As he walked away, I called after him, 'Aren't you taking the car?'

He turned. 'Sylvia said to leave it with you, otherwise I'd have given you a lift in my van.'

'But... how are you getting back?'

He jabbed a finger at his feet and a little march on the spot. 'On these,' he said. 'It's not far.'

'Sure you don't want a cup of tea, first?' *Damn. Why had I said that?*

Expecting him to accept smugly, I was stung when he shook his head and said, 'Cheers, but I'd better get back,' and strode off with a merry wave.

'Suit yourself,' I muttered, dragging my eyes away from his departing back. 'I was only being polite.'

Not wanting to draw attention to myself by taking my boxes through the café, I put them down and reached for the back door, just as it swung open.

'Oh, it's you,' said Gwen, as I reeled aside to avoid being smashed in the face. 'You shouldn't stand there, mate, it's dangerous.'

'I was about to come in,' I protested, wondering how she'd come by a job at the café. Maureen, who'd worked there for years, had been much nicer, like a friendly aunt. In fact, everyone had called her Auntie. 'You should have checked there was no one here.'

'There isn't, usually.' She drew a packet of chewing gum out of her trousers' pocket. 'Want some?' She held out the pack and shrugged when I shook my head. 'Don't blame you, mate,' she said. ''Orrible stuff, but better than smoking twenty cigs a day.'

'Definitely,' I said, remembering the choking fits when Meg, Tilly and I had tried to start smoking, luckily without success.

'You're the wonder girl, then?' She looked me up and down, with about as much pleasure as someone finding dog poo on their shoe.

'Sorry?'

'The one with the brilliant life we're all supposed to admire.'

'I—'

'I lived and worked in London for fifteen years,' she butted in. 'It 'ain't all it's cracked up to be.'

'I didn't say it was.'

'Anyone would think you'd split the atom, the way your parents carry on.'

Who did she think she was? 'I'm not responsible for what they say about me when I'm not here,' I said, face flaming. 'And, anyway, you don't have to listen to them.'

She moved her chewing gum around her teeth and pressed her back to the sun-warmed wall of the café. With her meaty build and military haircut, she could have been a bouncer. Her upper arms strained at the cuffs of her top, and her small, brown eyes probed me from under heavy brows. ''Ard *not* to listen,' she said. 'They're always bragging abart you and your brother, like no one else's kids 'ave ever done anythink interesting.'

Oh god, it did sound a bit over the top. My annoyance gave way to embarrassment. 'Well, I'm… I'm sorry if you've been offended by it,' I said. 'They are ridiculously proud of us, I'm afraid.'

She moved an eyebrow. 'S'pose it's not your fault,' she said when the gum had completed another circuit of her mouth. 'I'd probably feel the same if I'd spawned a couple of kids, but it just feels like it's a bit too good to be true, if you know wha' I mean?'

Sadly, I did. Unnerved by her knowing stare, worried my face was giving something away, I bent to pick up my boxes. Appearing to lose interest, Gwen inclined her face to the sun and shut her eyes. Grabbing the opportunity, I slipped into the passageway of the café, trying to claw back my earlier high spirits.

'Cassie, sweetheart!' Dad emerged from the little storeroom-cum-pantry with a giant box of teabags in his hands. 'Meg was just asking whether you were going to drop by.'

I almost dropped my boxes. 'She's here, now?'

'She doesn't start work for a couple of hours, but came in early hoping you'd pop in.'

'Right.' I'd probably met hundreds of people since leaving Seashell Cove, but my stomach was doing somersaults at the thought of seeing Meg again. We hadn't stayed in touch, after all, and probably had nothing in common any more.

'Tilly's here, too.'

'What?'

'She's leading one of her coastal walks in a while, but is dying to see you.' *Shit.* I wasn't sure I was up to this. What if, like Gwen, they'd got so sick of hearing about how successful I was, they hated me on sight? They might even be hatching a plan to bring me down a peg or two. Or, to have a go at me for not reaching out sooner. I hadn't so much as looked them up on Facebook, but, then again, they hadn't reached out to me either.

'I suppose it won't do any harm to say hello.' I hadn't realised I'd said it out loud until the smile dropped off Dad's face.

'Harm?' His brow furrowed. 'They can't wait to hear about everything you've achieved.'

They'd already have heard, if Gwen was to be believed. Still, I could always play things down – which wouldn't be hard, considering there wasn't much to play up to at the moment.

'I've brought the new teas and coffees,' I said, trying to buy some time. 'Would you like to have a look?' I shuffled past Dad and placed the boxes on the polished tiles, but when I straightened he was peering past me through the open back door.

'Is that Sir Lancelot?'

'Nan said I could borrow him.'

'At least she hasn't got rid of him yet.' His face clouded over. 'I don't know why she's so hell bent on wiping out the past.'

'She's not,' I reassured him, even though that's exactly what Nan seemed to be doing. 'She's minimising, that's all.'

He brightened. 'Maybe she'll be over it soon, like with the lace-making, and the hill-walking, and learning Mandarin.'

I hesitated. 'I expect you're right,' I said, guessing it was what he wanted to hear.

'Come on, then.' He jerked his head for me to follow him. 'Your audience awaits.'

'But…' I gestured helplessly at my boxes.

'We'll look at those later,' he said, and I had no choice but to trot after him, pushing my scarf off my forehead to avoid looking like a pirate.

The café was a bustle of chatter and laughter, with Mum in her favourite position behind the counter, slicing a generous portion of cake for a customer.

'Here's our favourite daughter,' she said, as Dad joined her and started refilling the tea caddies. He winked at me, as if to say 'prepare yourself'.

'This is Cassie,' Mum said to the customer, who smiled politely at me. 'She was an event manager for a big company in London called Five Star.' The words emerged in a rush, as if she wanted to impart as much information as possible. 'They have a New York branch as well, which Cassie helped to set up last year, and she was responsible for bringing in some really high-profile clients.' *Oh god, Mum, stop it*, I willed, but she was on a roll. 'She was practically running the company, but has left now, to set up her own business, and she's going to be putting on some events for us here, at the café.'

'Sounds impressive,' the woman said, eyeing me with respect. 'I wish my daughter hadn't dropped out of university.' She looked weary all of a sudden. 'She's been dithering about at home ever since, living off the bank of Mum and Dad.'

I wanted to say something comforting, but Mum was speaking again, while Dad was distracted by a man requesting his bill.

'We encouraged our two to be independent from an early age,' Mum was saying. 'We wanted them to experience life away from here, to not feel tied to the place where they grew up.' She turned gooey eyes on me. 'They've certainly done us more than proud.'

Bloody hell, was she always like this? I tried to catch the woman's gaze to signal that I was, in fact, human, with faults, but she'd taken her cake and was moving away, her shoulders drooping underneath her coat. Poor woman. She'd come in to enjoy some home-made cake, and had received an unwanted side order of smug parent.

'What did you say all that for?'

Mum blinked at my tone, the pleasure fleeing her face. 'What do you mean, love?'

But the effort required to explain seemed too enormous. 'It was a bit much, that's all,' I said. 'I'm hardly Oprah Winfrey.'

It was a rubbish comparison, but luckily – or unluckily – Gwen returned at that moment, radiating bad temper. 'Yes?' she barked at the man behind me, as if I wasn't there.

'A buttered scone and a latte, please.' He didn't seem to mind her brusque manner and I edged away and left them to it, fluttering a wave at Mum to show her I was fine.

'Out there,' Dad mouthed, poking his pen in the direction of the terrace. Through the window I caught sight of the back of someone's head, and knew in some primitive way that it was Meg. Part of me wanted to turn and run – to leave the past where it was, haloed in a golden haze of sunshine – but, as if sensing I was there, she turned and met my eye and it was too late.

I stiffened my spine and made my way outside.

Chapter 9

Two pairs of eyes tracked my approach to the table furthest away, and I grew clumsy under their scrutiny, jogging the elbow of a man about to sip some coffee, causing it to slosh onto his putty-coloured trousers.

'I'm so sorry,' I said, snatching a napkin off the table and thrusting it into his lap, dismayed to see a dark stain seeping across his crotch. 'I hope it wasn't too hot.'

He thrust back his chair and stood up. 'Leave it,' he ordered in an American accent. 'I'll put cold water on it in the rest room.'

He stalked off, leaving behind a tight-lipped woman, who I assumed was his wife, studiously avoiding my eye as she cradled a fluffy white dog.

'Maitland, you always were a clumsy mare.'

I turned in the direction of the voice, which I instantly recognised as belonging to Tilly Campbell. Forgetting my nerves I hurried over, a smile breaking out on my face. 'I can't believe you're both here,' I said, watching as first Tilly, then Meg, stood up to greet me. For a moment, we didn't speak, weighing each other up in the way of people who hadn't seen one another for years, assessing what had changed.

Meg still looked as though she'd just walked through a meadow, with her soft, wavy, honey-blonde hair and English rose complexion. In a short-sleeved, floral-print dress that flared out from her hips, she'd clearly stopped worrying about her (invisible) back-fat and embraced her gorgeous curves, and learnt to enhance her baby-blue eyes with make-up.

By contrast, Tilly was still all angles; tall, with sloping shoulders, and penetrating green eyes in an elfin face. Her fine dark hair was cropped short, showing off her incredible cheekbones, and she could have passed as a student in a stripy shirt, skinny jeans and faded red sneakers.

'I can't believe that the first time we see you in years, you're groping some bloke underneath the table.' Her eyes danced with amusement and affection, and my answering laugh was watery with rising emotion.

'I can't believe that Legal Mystics are finally back together,' said Meg, and suddenly we were hugging and laughing and saying, 'It's been too long,' and 'You look fantastic,' all at the same time, and I knew it was going to be all right.

'So, how come you're both here?' I said, finally pulling out a chair and positioning myself between them, while the young waitress placed a pot of tea and a plate of chocolate-chip cookies on the table. 'From your mum,' she said shyly, before scooting away.

'We were hoping to see you, you idiot.' Meg grinned as she poured the tea, her face bright with feeling. The sun sparked off a selection of jewels nestling on her ring finger, and catching my look, she said, 'Oh yes, I'm getting married next year.'

'That's amazing!' I'd have put bets on Meg being the first of us to get married. 'Congratulations.'

'To Sam,' she added, before I could ask who the lucky man was.

'Sam from school?' That wasn't exactly surprising, either. Even at sixteen they'd been inseparable, to the exclusion of everyone else.

'The one and only,' said Tilly, pretending to stifle a yawn.

'He's not boring,' Meg protested, just like she had in the beginning, when Tilly and I used to tease her about his love of fishing and collection of cycling magazines. 'We actually broke up for a while, while Sam was at university, but got back together six years ago.'

'Like a fairy tale,' said Tilly, doing a moony face. 'They've got a house together and everything.'

'You're still in Salcombe?'

'Of course, where else?' Tilly answered for her. 'You know what a home bird she is.'

Meg gave her a fondly indulgent smile and, even though our paths hadn't crossed since leaving school, I felt a pang that they'd been catching up without me.

'What about you?' I asked Tilly.

'Young, free and single.' Her soft, wide mouth tilted up. 'I'm not a nun, or anything, I go on dates, when I can be bothered, but I can't imagine settling down. Not for years, anyway.'

It was somehow typical of Tilly, who'd always been more interested in reading, or redecorating her bedroom during the holidays, than hanging out with boys.

'How come you're back in the UK?' I reached for a cookie and broke it in half. 'I thought you'd settled in Canada.'

She shrugged and picked up her mug, which looked small in her long, slender fingers. 'After my grandparents died, my parents wanted to come home,' she said simply. 'Dad had a house built in Ivybridge, not far from where we used to live, so I'm there at the moment.' I remembered her father had been – and presumably still was – an architect. 'Thought I'd look up Meg, because I knew she'd still be around, and here we are.'

'But what about your life in Vancouver?'

'You know Tilly,' Meg said, helping herself to a cookie and taking a delicate bite. 'She always goes with the flow.'

That was true. *So laid back she's practically horizontal*, Dad used to say.

'I always thought I'd come back one day.'

'Not so different from Meg, then,' I said, smiling.

She looked about to protest, then subsided with a laugh. 'I guess not.'

We looked out over the cove and fell silent for a moment, taking in the vista of unbroken blue sky and twinkling sea, offset by the deep green grass carpeting the headland.

'Remember when we used to lie on towels on the beach, and plan our futures?' said Tilly.

'I do.' There was a wistful edge to Meg's voice. 'I wanted to run my own bakery one day.'

'God, that's right,' I said, memories rearing up. 'And Tilly thought she'd be living on a barge.'

'I've no idea why.' Her bemused expression triggered giggles. 'I wanted to be an Olympic swimmer, too.'

'You were a strong swimmer,' I said, remembering. 'We could never keep up.'

Meg turned to me, eyes shining. 'You always said you'd end up living in London, and you are,' she said. 'You couldn't wait to get away.'

'I know.' Back then, only London had represented the future my parents had insisted Rob and I were entitled to – the one it would be virtually impossible to achieve if we'd stayed in Seashell Cove. 'Well, I'm not there at the moment,' I added lightly, and before they could probe, I turned quickly to Tilly. 'You didn't have a career in Vancouver?'

'I'll never be a career girl.' She sank back in her chair, catching crumbs in her hand as she took a big bite of cookie. 'Anyway, I can do my job anywhere.'

'When it suits you,' said Meg, throwing me a conspiratorial look that made my heart soar. I'd missed this, I realised. The three of us had been as close as sisters once, and I'd taken them completely for granted. 'You always liked to do as little as possible,' she added.

Tilly's lips twisted into a modest smile. 'Wouldn't want to over-stretch myself by having a proper job.'

I smiled, but something in Meg's face told me Tilly's words had hit a sore spot. I supposed it was OK for Tilly. She'd never wanted for anything. Her parents were well off and could afford to support her, whereas Meg had been raised by a single mum and probably had to work hard for every penny. Tilly was ten years younger than her sister, and had been thoroughly spoilt by her parents, to the point where it was a miracle she'd turned out to be as unaffected as she was.

'I hear you're working at the café,' I said, switching my attention back to Meg.

She nodded. 'My hours at the bakery were cut, so I only work mornings now. Business isn't so good.' Her smile flickered, and I wondered if she was remembering her dream of running her own. 'Anyway, I gave the café a call on the off-chance, and your mum offered me a job.'

'Did you make these?' I waggled my cookie at her.

'I did.' She blushed softly. 'What do you think?'

'Delicious,' I said. 'No wonder this place is full.'

'I like it.' Her smile was warm and genuine. 'Your parents are lovely to work for.'

'What's with Gwen?' I lowered my voice in case she was loitering somewhere. 'She was really rude to me earlier, and she looks like she could hurt someone.'

Meg giggled, revealing the tiny gap between her front teeth. 'She's fine,' she said. 'Well, she's not, but the customers love her, for some reason. She's Maureen's cousin, and got the job after Maureen retired.'

'Ah.'

'She doesn't give much away, but Maureen told your mum that Gwen had been through a bad break-up with her husband when she lived in London, and she lost her job and wanted a fresh start.'

I could relate to the fresh start bit. And losing a job.

'Don't your parents keep you up to date with what's going on here?' asked Tilly, finishing the last cookie in two bites. She appeared to still eat like a ravenous horse, without ever gaining weight.

'They're more interested in what I've been doing,' I said. 'They can't get enough of my stories.' My mood dipped slightly. The truth was, I'd enjoyed telling my stories, knowing they always got a good reaction. Like the time someone fell off a party boat, and had to be rescued by police divers. Sometimes, I'd even embellish the stories for effect.

'When I was helping with the café makeover, they talked about you a lot,' said Tilly, emphasising 'a lot'.

'And yet, you're still happy to see me.'

They both laughed.

'They think I'm too busy to be bothered by what's going on here, or that I won't find it interesting.' A bubble of shame floated up. Whenever I'd phoned, I hadn't always got around to asking about home, or I'd had to break off to take a work call or deal with some 'emergency'. No wonder they thought I wasn't interested.

Meg and Tilly leant forward with intent expressions.

'Your life sounds amazing, Cassie.' Meg sighed passionately, her eyes twice their usual size. 'I was so jealous when I heard how well you're doing.' If it had been anyone else I'd have assumed she was taking the mickey, but Meg wasn't like that. 'No wonder you haven't been back in I don't know how long.'

'I didn't get much time off,' I started to say, but Tilly interrupted.

'Didn't you meet Kanye West?' There was a twinkle of wonder in her eyes. 'Is he as, you know, off-the-wall, shall we say, as he seems?'

'I only really saw him from a distance, at a charity auction in New York,' I admitted. A very long distance. On a television screen. In my room. I'd been too ill to attend the auction, after coming down with a chest infection on the back of the worst cold I'd ever had. 'He seemed OK.'

'Were North and Saint with him?' Meg spoke eagerly, as though she was familiar with the family. 'Sam's a Kardashian fan,' she added, which almost caused Tilly to choke on her tea.

'He didn't have the children with him,' I confirmed. At least that much was true.

'And you had an amazing apartment over there?' Meg seemed as hungry for details as my family.

'I shared a place in Manhattan with my colleague Nina and a couple of staff from the American office while we were there.' The couple had indulged in frequent and noisy sex, meaning I'd spent what little free time I'd had walking the streets, as Nina was seeing a lawyer at the time who kept whisking her out for meals. She'd put on a stone while we were there. 'It overlooked the Hudson River.'

'Wow,' Meg breathed, and I just knew she was picturing the place where Monica from *Friends* had lived, imagining me with a Ross-type character, and Nina looking like Jennifer Aniston. She'd been obsessed with *Friends* back in the day. I'd been surprised when she started seeing Sam, with his fair-haired, boyish good looks, when she'd once declared Joey Tribbiani to be her ideal man. 'And you have a place in London?'

'I did,' I said, dabbing my finger into the cookie crumbs on my plate, wondering how much to tell them. 'I just moved out, actually.'

'What was it like?' I knew Tilly would be far more interested in my room dimensions, colour schemes, and lighting than whether or not I'd lived with anyone.

'Small,' I said, honestly. In fact, it had been quite nice – what the estate agent had called 'a hidden gem' set off a roaring main road full of betting and charity shops, but calm and cosy inside, and a big step up from the house that Trudy and I had shared with a DJ, and a fashion student who could never afford her share of the rent. 'And expensive.'

'Obviously. It's London,' said Meg. 'But you must earn a fortune, doing what you do.' She'd never been embarrassed to talk about money – unlike me.

I noticed her squinting her eyes in the sunshine. 'Do you want to swap seats?' I indicated the parasol, keen to move away from my financial status and life in London. 'It's nice and shady here.'

'I'm fine.' She scooched her chair closer to mine. 'You must know loads of people,' she said, as if she spent her days in isolation. 'Living in the city.'

'I… suppose so.' I'd *met* lots of people, but wouldn't have said I *knew* them.

'It's got to be more exciting than here.' Although Tilly made a dead-eyed face, I got the impression she was perfectly happy where she was, and I suddenly couldn't bear for either of them to know how uncertain my future was. Or that I'd been fired from my 'amazing' job. And they definitely didn't need to hear about the pockets of loneliness I'd felt whenever I'd had time to examine my life and the things I didn't have – a partner, children, or close friends. I'd never made it to Italy to stay with Trudy, despite repeated invitations, and with our old connections broken we'd gradually lost touch. Apart from Nina, there hadn't been time to form any new friendships, and ours hadn't been the sort to involve wild laughter, gossip, swapping clothes and singing. 'It *is* exciting,' I said with a forced note of determination. 'But I'd gone as far as I could at Five Star and it's time for a change now.'

'Isn't it risky, striking out on your own when you were doing so well?' Meg said, and I didn't know whether to be admiring or annoyed that she'd thought to ask.

'To be honest, I'm looking forward to the challenge.' The back of my neck was growing hotter by the second. 'And there's a lot to be said for being a big fish in a smaller pond.'

'Ooh, a small pond, are we?' Tilly put on a la-di-da voice. 'You do talk quite posh now.'

'I had to lose the accent,' I said, remembering how Carlotta used to make fun of it when I started at Five Star. 'I learnt to en-un-ci-ate properly.'

'If you hang around long enough, you'll soon be talking like us again,' said Meg.

'How come you don't have a Canadian accent?' I asked Tilly, desperate to divert the spotlight away from me.

She shrugged. 'I guess I'm a Devon girl through and through.'

Or maybe she had a stronger sense of her own identity than I did. The thought was oddly depressing.

'You look the part, too.' Meg eyed my hair and outfit, seeming unwilling to move on. 'I love your top.'

'Thought I'd make an effort.' I felt as self-conscious as if I'd stepped out in my pyjamas.

'Remember when you used to wear your dad's stripy shirt under a pair of dungarees with one strap falling down?' Tilly gave a wicked grin.

'Ah yes, my "artist" look.'

'I really thought you'd go somewhere with your art. You were good.'

Not another one. 'I still draw for fun sometimes.' I thought of my sketch pads in my rucksack, and then of Danny Fleetwood. 'Guess who I bumped into at my Nan's?'

'Danny Fleetwood, I expect,' said Tilly, fanning herself with her hand. 'He's even hotter than he was back then.'

A blush crept over my whole body. 'Is he?' I'd never told them about Danny asking me to the leavers' party. Maybe I'd had an inkling he wouldn't turn up. Plus, our mantra that year had been 'sisters before misters' – we weren't interested in the 'loser' boys at school. If they'd wondered why I kept glancing at the door that night, they'd never said.

'He's definitely hot.' Meg spoke with authority. 'I don't remember him from school, but when I saw him painting the sign for the café I thought he looked a bit like that actor in *Outlander*. Jamie something?' Tilly looked blank while I gulped my tea, which had gone cold, for something to do with my mouth.

'Are you seeing anyone at the moment?' Meg asked. 'He's single, you know. Danny, I mean.'

Once again, Adam filled my head. 'I met someone recently,' I said, which was true. 'It's very early days, though, and he's… working a lot at the moment so…' I let the words hang, wishing I'd been honest then, realising Meg was about to dig for details, quickly added, 'Listen, we should all stay in touch.'

'That would be brilliant.' With touching eagerness, Meg got her phone out so we could exchange numbers, and Tilly did the same. 'I don't even know how we drifted apart; it feels like I only saw you both yesterday.'

'Legal Mystics forevah,' said Tilly, and we performed the fist-bumping movement we'd perfected long before it was a thing. 'Maybe we should re-form.'

'Never Ever,' said Meg, and when we collapsed into giggles I realised it was the first time I'd laughed properly in months.

'It's Water under the Bridge,' I managed.

'I'll stick with drinking Black Coffee,' Tilly gasped, and when we'd run out of All Saints titles to pun, she said, 'So, when are you going back to London?'

My face froze. 'Actually, I might be staying around for a while, depending how things pan out.'

'You are going back eventually, though?' Meg daintily dabbed the corners of her eyes with a napkin. 'It sounds like your skills would be wasted around here, and there'll be no chance of you meeting Kanye West again.'

'Talking about work?' It was Mum, with a fresh pot of tea in her hand and a proud smile on her lips. 'She can't stop you know, even while she's on holiday.'

'Oh?' Tilly glanced from me to Mum, as if intuiting something in my expression.

Mum put down the teapot and picked up our crumb-scattered plates. 'She's organising some events for the café for her *portfolio*, aren't you, Cassie?' She said 'portfolio' with excessive relish.

'Ooh, like what?' Meg rested her chin in her hand and looked at me with admiration. 'We could do with some entertainment around here.'

'Exactly,' I said. 'That's what I thought.'

'W-e-e-e-ll, we do have the Smugglers,' Mum seemed moved to point out. 'They have a quiz night, but Cassie thinks it's old-fashioned.'

'I never said that,' I protested, hating that Meg and Tilly might think I was being pushy.

'That pub is definitely stuck in the past,' said Tilly. 'I went for a drink there with my dad and they've still got the same carpet they had before we went to Canada.' Her expression was comical. 'I didn't realise pubs still had carpets.'

'I like it, it's retro.' Meg seemed to be enjoying the exchange in a radiant, shiny-eyed way that made me think that perhaps she and Sam didn't have many friends outside their relationship. 'And they still do karaoke.'

'I've got plenty of ideas,' I said, my earlier enthusiasm flooding back. 'The first is an exotic tea-and-coffee tasting session. Shall we say next Tuesday evening, seven until ten, Mum?' I might as well get the ball rolling. 'That'll give us time to spread the word.'

'I'm not sure…' she began. 'Ten's a bit late.'

I managed not to roll my eyes. 'Nine, then.'

'Sounds great.' Meg beamed. 'I'll make an extra batch of cakes.'

I smiled at her, glad I hadn't needed to ask. 'That would be brilliant.'

'I'll be there,' said Tilly. 'I've got quite the discerning palate, I'll have you know.'

'Oh, thanks, Tilly.' Already, I felt more supported than I had for a while. It was just a pity that Mum didn't look so keen.

'Don't worry,' I said, catching her round the waist for an awkward hug. 'You'll be home in plenty of time to get jiggy with Dad on the sofa.'

'Sounds a bit risky, though,' said Meg, as Mum walked away, pretending she hadn't heard. 'Do you think Maitland's customers are ready for the exotic?'

Chapter 10

Of course, I knew Meg didn't mean 'risky' in the sense that someone might die from drinking an earthy coffee from Peru, and she immediately qualified her words with, 'But I'm sure they will be once they've been to your taster session.'

Then, when Tilly added, 'I must admit I like my tea like my men – strong, hot and sweet,' a panicky feeling built in my stomach, and I quickly invented a call I had to make, implying it was future-work related.

'I've got to get to work too,' said Meg, while Tilly pulled some sturdy-soled shoes from a neat little backpack ready for her coastal walk. I'd noticed a group of people in walking gear starting to gather outside the picket fence.

'You've done a great job with this place,' I said to her, realising there were a lot of topics we still hadn't covered.

'Thanks.' She smiled up at me as she teased her sneakers off. 'I enjoyed it.'

'Hey, you know where to find us, so don't be a stranger,' Meg said as we stood, engulfing me in a sweetly perfumed hug. 'I love your purple hair, by the way.'

'It's Plumberry,' I said, into her shoulder.

'Great to see you again, Maitland, you've done Legal Mystics proud.' When Tilly gave me a funny boy-scout salute, I wished I'd told them about losing my job and why I was really back home. I hovered for a second, wondering if there was still time, then imagined their expressions hardening into disappointment and knew I couldn't do it. I could tell that Meg, at least, liked knowing someone whose life she thought was vastly different from her own – someone who'd 'mingled' with music stars. And, anyway, I reminded myself, tweaking the sleeves of my blouse, that life could be mine again – just on a smaller scale this time, and without Kanye West being involved.

Brushing on a smile, I 'ironically' air-kissed their cheeks before backing away, causing them much hilarity when I bashed into the same table the American had been sitting at earlier, and sent a teacup flying.

At least it hadn't broken, I reflected, driving home, which took longer and was more tiring than it should have been, thanks to Sir Lancelot's prehistoric steering system, which made me feel as if I'd been lifting weights for an hour.

Once indoors, I made some coffee and opened my laptop, trying to get into a working frame of mind. I had a quick look on TripAdvisor, amazed and proud to see how many positive reviews there were for the café, all praising the warm, friendly service, fantastic views of the cove, and the 'scrummiest cakes in Devon'. There was also an astonishing amount of love for Gwen.

She's like Mo from Eastenders! Absolute star!
I love Gwen. Reminds me of my late grandma!!

If her grandma had been related to the Kray Twins, maybe.

If you go to Maitland's, make sure you're served by Gwen.
Legend!

Baffling.

Remembering I'd promised to find some artwork to hang on the walls of the café, I typed in 'local artists South Devon' and spent an enjoyable half-hour browsing websites, but nothing appealed. I wasn't sure what I was looking for exactly, but I knew abstract squares in primary colours, and black-and-white close-ups of eyeballs wasn't it.

On impulse, I ran upstairs to drag my sketch pads out of my rucksack and shuffled through the pictures I'd drawn at the flat, whenever I'd had a spare moment. Some were of whatever my gaze had happened to land on – a lamp in the shape of an owl, and a box of half-eaten pizza – and some were views from my window (buses featured a lot). Most, though, were of trees in the nearby park, some with branches twisting up like witches' fingers to the sky, others heavy with blossom, or intricately laden with leaves. I'd always liked trees – something about the solidity of them, and how vital but timeless they were. Miss Finch, my art teacher, had been unimpressed by what she called my 'nature' paintings. She'd pushed me to experiment, but I'd been happiest creating recognisable scenes and people, as well as the occasional caricature.

In a rush of nostalgia, I opened the bottom drawer of my dressing table and glimpsed the paints and brushes still tucked away inside. The sight of them made my fingertips tingle and I picked up one of the brushes and stroked its soft bristles. I hadn't painted for years; I hadn't progressed beyond A level and had probably forgotten how. Sketching was easier, requiring only a set of pencils, and had proved to be a fun way to pass what little free time I'd had outside of work.

I slammed the drawer shut and went back down to my laptop. After sourcing a number for an artist called Connor Daley, who painted childlike seascapes he described as having 'a lot of depth and emotion', I gave him a call.

He barked out a tetchy 'Hello?' that made me blink. 'What do you want?'

'Oh, hello, my name's Cassie Maitland, and I'd like to ask if you'd be interested in exhibiting your work.' I was pleased by how well I'd slipped into 'professional' mode, even though talking to strangers on the phone still made my palms go clammy.

'You'd like to ask me, or you're *going* to ask me?'

I clicked on an image of his face. He looked to be in his forties, and about as friendly as he sounded. His angry blue gaze sliced through the screen, as if he'd been snapped in the middle of a terrible argument.

'I'm asking you,' I said, keeping my voice upbeat, mindful of the time Carlotta had caught me holding the phone away from my ear as a client held forth about why she needed to change her wedding venue less than a week before the big day.

'Why not just say that, then?'

I mentally counted to five. 'I'm sorry if I've disturbed you, Mr Daley, but I'm looking for local artists to display their work in my parents' café, and after looking at your website, I think that your—'

'*Café?*' he spat. 'You want me to put my work in a *café?*'

Anyone would think I'd suggested displaying his paintings in a public toilet. Weren't artists supposed to be grateful when people offered to exhibit their work?

'It's a very *nice* café,' I persisted, standing up and moving across the room, surprised by the sight of my grumpy face in the mirror above the fireplace. I was certain I'd been smiling, but my mouth was turned down at the corners and there was a crevice between my eyebrows. I gave myself a hard, instructive stare and hurried back to my laptop. 'I promise you the café's very popular, so lots of potential customers,' I said, in a sweet, syrupy voice. 'We stopped the cock-fighting ages ago.'

'What *are* you on about?'

'It was a joke,' I said. 'Meaning, we're really quite enlightened in this part of the world.'

His response was a grunting sound of disgust and I wondered whether he'd adopted the clichéd persona of a tortured artist, or was just a horrible person. 'Where is this *café?*' He might as well have said 'prison' or 'bear pit'.

'Seashell Cove near Salcombe.' It was quite a tongue-twister, but I managed not to mess it up.

'*Seashell Cove?*' He couldn't have sounded more scathing if I'd told him it was in North Korea. 'Why would I want to exhibit my work in a place no one's ever heard of?'

'Why wouldn't you?' A smouldering flame of anger wiped away my smile. 'Plenty of people have heard of it. Look on TripAdvisor, if you don't believe me. The café's called Maitland's and there was an American there this morning.' *Well done, Cassie. Very mature.*

'Well, I'm sorry, but I've got better things to do with my time, Miss *Maitland.*'

'It's Ms, actually.'

'Of course it is.'

I stuck two fingers up at the screen. 'I take it that's a no, then?'

'Look, I sell most of my work through my website, and as I'm currently working on a new collection for an exhibition in Plymouth next month, I'll be declining your little offer.' He spoke with such venom that something inside me snapped.

'Well, I'm sorry to have bothered you,' I said, coolly. 'Good luck with your collection.'

I ended the call, then said grumpily, 'Actually, Mr Daly, you sound like a total knob and your paintings are shit. A five-year-old could do better. And you've got a face like a scrotum.' I leant over to rid my screen of his glowering mugshot. 'I hope you don't sell a single crappy painting ever again.'

'I'm still here,' said a growly voice, and I dropped my phone in fright. Instead of ending the call, I'd accidentally put it on speaker.

'I know you are,' I lied. 'I'm trying to teach you a lesson. To be... nicer.'

He gave a nasty laugh. 'Good try,' he said. 'Don't ever get a job in public relations.' He rang off, leaving me scrabbling for a response.

Shit. He knew my name, my number, and the name of the café. What was to stop him putting a horrible review on TripAdvisor? Then I remembered – he had 'better things to do'.

Shaken that my first attempt had gone so badly, I drank my coffee and wondered whether it was worth calling back to apologise ('The customer is always right,' Carlotta had drummed into me from Day One), but decided not to waste my energy. It wasn't as if there was a shortage of artists to choose from.

I clicked on the website of a big-eyed, smiley woman, who painted delicate watercolours with simple titles like *Shoreline*, but she didn't answer her phone.

'Third time lucky,' I murmured, scrolling through the Devon Artists' web page and landing on a selection of vivid oil paintings by a youngish woman, with a cloud of black hair, called Vicky Burton. Her paintings mostly depicted the sky in varying states, and I particularly liked one with the sun's rays beaming down to the sea from behind a storm cloud.

'Ooh, I'd love you to display my work,' she said, with a slight lisp.

'That's brilliant.' I tried not to sound too grateful as I victory-pumped my arm. 'How soon could you get some paintings here?'

We arranged for her to be at the café the following afternoon, and after a few pleasantries – she was juggling her painting with a job as a nanny, while waiting for her 'big break' – and a brief discussion about commission, I rang off (double-checking I really had ended the call).

I added '*Source some artwork for the café*' to the list I'd started that morning, just so I could tick it off. It was still a very small list. I tapped my teeth with my pencil, then sketched a man playing the saxophone. I realised he looked like Danny Fleetwood, and added dark glasses and a wide-brimmed hat to disguise his face.

Music. I liked the idea of something light, maybe jazzy, to accompany the tea-and coffee-tasting session. We could always pipe it through from an MP3 player, but live music would add a touch of atmosphere. The trouble was, it would be short notice to secure a band or musician, providing I could find either, and I didn't fancy trying my luck online again. Maybe Rob would be interested in reviving his career for a couple of hours.

'No, dear Sandra, I most definitely would not,' he said, replying to my text with a call. 'I've told you, I'm not doing that any more.'

'But it's only for a night, not even that, just an hour,' I wheedled. '*Pleeeease*, Robbie Robot.'

But he wouldn't be swayed, even by his childhood nickname.

'You're the expert at this eventing lark,' he said. 'I'm sure you'll come up with the goods.'

'Eventing's to do with horses,' I replied sulkily. 'Where are you, anyway?'

'Having a late lunch,' he said. 'A meatball Subway, to be precise.'

'Not exactly brain food.'

'I'm brainy enough already,' he said. 'Plus, I'm having a break from healthy eating. I had to be fit for all that touring, and I've had my fill of protein bars and kale.'

'What about the alcohol?'

'I'm talking before all that kicked in.'

'You'll go back to it though, won't you? The touring, I mean, not the drinking.' I cleared my throat to get rid of the stern note that had crept into my voice. 'If Boss… if Emma loves you, she'll understand about you being away a lot, and that girls tend to throw themselves at boys in bands, and it doesn't mean that you're going to sleep with them all.'

There was a pause so long at the other end, I'd have thought Rob had hung up if I hadn't heard a car horn hooting in the background. 'I won't be going back,' he said, finally. 'Sorry, sis, but you're going to have to get used to being the shining star in the Maitland family.'

Yuck. Shiny I wasn't, and unlikely ever to be a star. 'So, you're not going to help me?' I said, to break another awkward little silence.

He huffed out a sigh. 'Look, I'll ask around, if you're sure there isn't anyone on your contacts list you could ask.'

'Not at such short notice,' I said, laughing internally at the thought of me having my own 'contacts list'. 'Thanks, Rob, I owe you one.'

He paused. 'Is everything's OK, Sand?' Tears fizzed up my nose at the unexpected tenderness in his voice. 'You can talk to me, you know.'

''Course I'm OK,' I said, glad he couldn't see the way my mouth had wobbled around the words. 'At least, I will be when you've found me a musician for Tuesday night.'

Chapter 11

'Wake up, Cassie, you've got a visitor.'

I came to with a violent start. In the green, subterranean light of my bedroom, Mum's face looked slightly alien and, for a second, I thought I must still be dreaming.

'Cassie!' She pressed my shoulder. 'It's Danny Fleetwood.'

'What?' I pinged upright, almost head-butting Mum. 'What's he doing here this early?'

'It's not actually that early.' Mum crossed to the window and yanked the curtains open, revealing a swatch of bright sky that made me blink. 'Your dad opens up on a Monday morning so I can have a lie-in, remember?'

'Oh, yeah.' He'd done it for years, while Mum opened the café on Wednesdays, so Dad could snatch a couple of hours extra sleep. Peering blearily at the digital alarm clock, I saw it was gone nine. 'You should have woken me earlier.' I flung off the duvet and leapt out of bed, wishing I hadn't when stars danced in front of my eyes.

'I thought you might need to rest, after waiting up for Rob.' A small frown marred Mum's face when she turned from the window. 'I told you he'd stay over at Nick's, hoping to see Emma.'

'I don't know why,' I said, tugging my crumpled nightshirt over my thighs. 'It's not like she lives with him.'

'No, but sometimes she pops in, apparently.'

'If she's asked for some space, Rob should accept that.' I was still annoyed that he hadn't let me know whether he'd managed to procure a music act for the café.

I'm interpreting your silence as a no my last message had read, as my eyelids drooped in front of a rerun of *Blackadder* on UK Gold. Mum and Dad had already retired to bed with mugs of hot chocolate and a novel each, creeping out of the room with exaggerated care as I tapped away at my phone, presumably thinking it was work-related – which, in a way, it was – but I could see by the lack of blue ticks that Rob hadn't read any of my WhatsApp messages.

'I think your brother's just keen to prove to Emma that he's serious about his new future,' Mum said with a reflexive smile, and the part of me that wasn't panicking about what to wear, marvelled afresh at how easily she and Dad had accepted Rob's news, when they used to imply that living in the area where we'd grown up – never mind the same house – would be akin to an admission of failure.

'Could you ask my *visitor* to pop back later?' I said, as Mum shook out my duvet, sending the sketch pad I'd looked through the day before flying to the floor.

'I got the impression he wants to see you now,' she said. 'I made him some coffee.' She picked up the sketch pad and stared at a picture of a bus crammed with passengers as if it was a naked man. 'What's this?'

'What does it look like, Mum?' I prised the pad off her, before she could flip through it, and stuffed it back in my open rucksack. 'Did he say what he wanted?'

'I thought you gave up art a long time ago.' I couldn't work out whether her tone was anxious or disapproving, or somewhere between the two.

'I like drawing,' I said, wondering whether it would be polite to have a shower and wash my hair before venturing downstairs. 'Is that OK?'

'Of course it is.' Mum's smile seemed less natural than it had moments ago. 'I didn't realise you still did it, that's all.'

I paused in the act of pulling on my dressing gown, having decided that Danny Fleetwood would have to take me as he found me.

'Don't worry, Mum,' I said, squeezing the words past an unexpected ache in my throat. 'I'm not planning to do a reverse-Rob and throw in my amazing career to take up painting again.'

'There's nothing wrong with painting,' she said, lurching forward to tie the belt of my dressing gown a bit too tightly. 'As a hobby, I mean.' Her eyes grazed mine. 'Although, you probably don't have much time for hobbies, with your lifestyle.'

Gritting my teeth, I shook my head and moved to the dressing table so that she couldn't see my face. 'Not really,' I said, just about managing to match her jolly tone. 'Could you tell Danny I'll be down in a second? I just need to comb my hair.'

'He's very good-looking, isn't he?' she said, as she backed towards the door. 'Not *London* good-looking, but for around here.'

As she left, an urge to giggle rose as I imagined saying, 'I suppose he's what you'd call Devon handsome. Fit for outside the city. Buff, for a country lad.' *Not London good-looking.* It was possibly the most ridiculous thing my mother had ever said.

I did my best with my hair, which was refusing to lie flat on one side, and swiped the sleep from my eyes with a cleansing wipe before dotting on some concealer and blending it in. After nipping to the bathroom for a wee and brushing my teeth, I decided my lips looked too pale so I chewed them until they went red, trying not to think about Danny Fleetwood downstairs in my parents' kitchen.

Deciding I'd be at a disadvantage in my nightwear, I ransacked my suitcase for my newest jeans, before remembering I'd lent them to Nina and she hadn't given them back. My other good pair needed washing, as did my baggy-kneed joggers, while the jeans I'd arrived in and the trousers I'd worn the day before were in a heap on the floor.

'Oh, for god's sake.' Danny was probably wondering what I was doing. I jabbed my feet into my slippers and went downstairs, to see Mum zipping her jacket up.

'I'm off to the café,' she said. 'I'll leave you to it.'

'Do you have to go now?' I went hot at the thought of being left on my own with Danny. 'I could give you a lift in Sir Lancelot.'

'I always walk on a Monday, if the weather's nice.' Mum opened the front door, letting in a blast of fresh air. 'Look at that sunshine.'

Typical. Where was the rain when you needed it? 'I'll see you this afternoon then,' I said, trying to delay her a bit longer. 'Someone's popping round with some paintings.'

'Look forward to it.' Mum hoisted her bag onto her shoulder and blew me a kiss. ''Bye, love.'

''Bye, Mrs Maitland,' came a voice from the kitchen.

'How many times have I told you to call me Lydia?' Mum lowered her voice. 'He's such a gentleman,' she said. 'He'll make someone a lovely husband one day.'

'I can hear you, you know.' Danny sounded amused.

'I'm not looking for a relationship right now,' I loud-whispered, bundling her outside.

'Oh, I didn't mean for you.' She paused on the doorstep and squeezed my arm. 'He's obviously not your type.'

She was probably thinking about Adam, assuming I'd eventually end up with someone similar, and while I had no intention of hooking up with Danny, it hurt that she thought I'd rule him out just because he wasn't 'London good-looking'.

I closed the door with a nagging feeling of dissatisfaction and, adjusting the belt of my dressing gown, went into the kitchen.

My insides jumped at the sight of Danny leaning against the stove, cradling Dad's 'Rise and Grind' coffee mug. I wished I'd got dressed. And that I wasn't wearing slippers with bunny ears.

His eyes kindled at the sight of me, in a way that might have been flattering if I'd been in the mood. 'Good morning, Miss Maitland.'

'Hi.' *Inventive.* 'Please don't call me Miss Maitland.'

He grinned. 'Sorry, I'll start again. Good morning, Cassie.' It sounded way too intimate. He had one of those husky voices that made even the most innocent sentence sound oddly seductive.

''Morning,' I said grudgingly, failing to stop my eyes from roving over him. He was wearing black jeans and a deep blue T-shirt that somehow made the details of him – skin tone, eye colour – leap out. His arms looked muscly, but not in that body-builder way I disliked, and his thighs… I quickly pulled my eyes back to his face to see him taking a similar inventory of me. Aware that my outfit hinted at a night spent twisting and turning in bed, I grew hotter and redder and folded my arms across my chest. 'What do you want?'

There was a beat where, if we'd been starring in a romantic film, he might have said, 'You.' But we weren't, and he said, 'I've got something you might like,' instead, which was almost as cheesy.

'Is it a puppy?' I glanced automatically at the corner of the kitchen where Rosie's basket used to be, feeling a pang for the dopey spaniel that had been part of my life growing up.

'I'm afraid not.' Danny put down his mug with a clownish grimace. 'Sorry, if I'd known…' He lifted his hands.

'I was joking.'

'So was I, although I do know someone whose bitch has just had puppies, so—'

'I don't want a dog,' I lied. I'd actually love a dog, to walk on the beach and to snuggle up in bed with. There'd been a 'no dogs or cats' rule at my flat in London and, before I met Adam, I'd been considering getting a house-rabbit for cuddles. 'I won't be staying here long enough, apart from anything else,' I said, to give the impression I could be anywhere in the world at any given moment. I shuffled across to the counter and picked up the lukewarm coffee jug. 'And my parents wouldn't want one. They swore they'd never have another pet after Rosie died. It was too heartbreaking. We didn't stop crying for about a fortnight...' Aware I was talking too much, I stopped.

'They become part of the family,' said Danny. He must have moved closer, because I suddenly smelt something zingy that made my stomach leap. I concentrated hard on taking a mug from the cupboard and pouring out some coffee. 'We had a lurcher called Ziggy, as soft as anything, he was. I still miss the old boy.'

A moment's silence stretched, during which everything felt heightened; the hum of the fridge, the sound of my breathing (too fast) and the contrasting colours of deep brown coffee against the bone-white mug.

I spun round, fingers gripping the edge of the counter behind me, and the rapid movement pulled the edges of my dressing gown apart.

'Do not disturb,' Danny said, reading the slogan on my nightshirt, and I was surprised to see he was still standing by the stove. 'I'm sorry if I did,' he added. 'Disturb you, I mean. I probably should have phoned.'

'I'm assuming it's part of your plan.' I tried to sound relaxed as I pulled my dressing gown closed. 'To "win me over". Only, you're not doing a very good job.'

'Ah.' He smirked. 'That's because you haven't seen what I've brought.'

My stomach dipped. 'You'd better go and get it then.' I affected a casual tone. 'I haven't got all day, and you must have work to do.'

'I've been working already,' he said. 'Moving Sylvia's things into storage. That's when I came across this box of stuff I thought you should have.'

Curiosity piqued, I urged, 'Well, go on then.'

He crossed one foot over the other and folded his arms. 'So, what is it you're up to today that's so important?'

'Danny, *please*.'

'OK, OK.' He held up his hands in surrender, a smile on his infuriatingly perfect lips. 'I'll go and get it.'

As he opened the back door and stepped outside, a welcome whoosh of air hit my overheated skin, but I'd no sooner slurped some coffee and cursed myself for pleading than he was back, tilting under the weight of the box he was carrying.

'Here we are,' he said, waiting while I cleared a space on the table so he could plonk it down.

'What's in it?' I pulled at the curling tape holding the top edges of the box together. As they sprang apart I peered inside to see it was crammed with pictures.

'Recognise them?'

I glanced up to see Danny smiling a private smile, clearly anticipating my reaction, and realised my heart was beating too fast as I dug a hand inside and pulled out one of the pictures.

'I did this.' I stared at a painting of Seashell Cove on a summer's day, the sea a great wash of aquamarine against the fudge-coloured sand. In fact, that's what I'd called it. *Seashell Cove on a Summer's Day*. Hardly imaginative, but it fully captured the essence. The painting positively oozed summer magic. I could almost feel my toes scrunching into the sand, and the golden sunshine bathing my neck in warmth. Not that I'd been there that day. I'd painted it from memory, in class, for an exam. I got top marks for it, too.

'Nan used to have this on her wall,' I said, looking it over with a critical eye. It really wasn't that bad. There was something almost naïve about it, as though the artist had painted impulsively, keen to get down the image (which I had), but somehow it worked.

'She had a lot of your paintings in the attic,' said Danny. 'She told me you didn't like seeing them displayed, that you were embarrassed and made her take them down.'

'I did.' I remembered Nan saying she used to go up to her attic and look at them sometimes, but assumed it was the sort of thing all grandmothers said about their grandchildren's artistic efforts. Mum still had a misshapen pottery vase that Rob had made her for Mother's Day, when in Year Four, while my primary-school attempt at a felt Father Christmas with a cotton-wool beard still made it onto the Christmas tree every year.

'I can't believe she kept them,' I said, pulling out picture after picture, all of them beautifully framed. Some were sketches: a pencil drawing of her and my grandfather, standing on either side of his car, smiling in a way I'd imagined rather than seen; and one of Mum and Dad stationed behind the counter of the café. Mum's hair was a crazy spiral of curls, Dad was holding up two coffee mugs, and there was a profusion of café paraphernalia all around them. There was also a caricature of a customer with big, horsey teeth and flaring nostrils, about to bite into a scone.

'I'd forgotten about that one,' I said faintly. The truth was, I'd forgotten about them all, but the memories came flooding back as I looked at each one. 'That was a terrible summer.' I prodded a painting of a storm-lashed village, the houses and cottages seeming to cower beneath a lowering sky.

'It rained solidly for three weeks,' said Danny. 'I still went fishing with my dad every day though. It was pretty miserable.'

I glanced up. He seemed lost in memories too, and not very happy ones at that. 'Are your parents still alive?'

'Hmm?' It took him a moment to refocus. 'Oh, yes. They're fine,' he said, but I had the feeling there was more to it than that. 'So, what do you think?'

'About these?' I returned my attention to the pictures spread out on the table, feeling a mix of emotions. Pride, that I'd been... not bad. Surprise, that Nan had framed them, even though I'd ordered her not to hang them up. Why had I been so silly? I was aware, too, of a strange sense of loss... for the total absorption I used to feel while painting; the sense that all was right with the world, as long as I had a canvas and a paintbrush in my hand. Teenage feelings; the sort that were bound to fade once real life crept in, but which probably explained the urge I still felt now and then to put pencil to paper and sketch something. 'Was she going to throw them away?'

'Of course not,' Danny said. 'She's kept her favourite, and asked me what she should do with the rest. I said you should have them.'

'Why?'

'I heard you were looking for some artwork to display in the café.' He picked up a picture of a younger, mop-haired Rob, sitting hunch-shouldered at his computer.

'And?' I said, wondering where he'd heard that.

He swept a hand over the box of paintings, as though it was obvious. 'So, here it is,' he said.

Chapter 12

'You are joking?' I grabbed the picture and jammed it back in the box. 'I can't put these up in the café. I'd be a laughing stock.'

'What?' Danny dragged out a different painting, of a tree surrounded by cherry blossom. 'You think people would laugh at this?' He danced it in front of my face. 'It's brilliant, Cassie.'

'Well… thank you.' I felt oddly flustered. No one, apart from Miss Finch and Nan, had really looked at my paintings before. 'But this is teenage stuff, not proper art. And, anyway, I've already found someone who'd like to display their work in the café.'

'Cancel them.'

'No!' It came out so loudly he took a step back. 'That would be cruel and, even if I did, there's no way any of this lot will be seeing the light of day, so please just take them back.'

He lowered the painting and looked at me for longer than was comfortable. 'You could always paint some new stuff, if you don't think this is up to scratch.'

I released a sigh. 'I don't paint any more,' I said, with exaggerated patience.

'Well, that's a shame.' Danny stuck out his bottom lip then popped it back in when he saw the look on my face. 'I'm serious,' he said, eyebrows pinching together. 'What a waste of talent.'

'For god's sake, Danny, why are you doing this?'

'Doing what?' He feigned an innocent look. 'Telling you that you're wasted doing whatever it is you do these days?'

My stomach gave a nasty lurch. 'Haven't my parents told you? I'm brilliant at coordinating events.'

'I'm sure you are, but' – he wiggled the picture again – 'this is something special.'

It was of the tree in our back garden, painted a few days after my fifteenth birthday. I'd been home alone after a bout of flu, and had set up my easel in Rob's bedroom, which overlooked the garden, and whiled away several hours painting the view.

'Just take them back,' I instructed, pointing to the door like a teacher ordering a disruptive pupil out of class. 'It's all in the past. No point hanging on to them.'

Danny looked like he had a lot more to say on the matter and I waited, mentally rehearsing a couple of ripostes that would leave no room for argument, but he merely slipped the painting back in the box. Expecting an apology, at least, for not minding his own business, he surprised me by saying, 'I'll hold onto them until you're ready.'

Irritation bubbled up. 'This isn't going to work, you know.'

Unconcerned, he picked up the box. 'What isn't?'

'Don't presume you know what's best for me, Danny, because you don't.'

'We'll see,' he said, with an eye-crinkling smile. 'See you later, Cassie.' He managed to open the door with his elbow and walk to his boxy white van, which had his name painted in smart navy lettering on the side, before I had time to construct a response.

I was left with a dull ache in my chest, which I had to soothe with four slices of buttered toast and a pot of fresh coffee. I couldn't seem to settle after that. I stuffed some washing in the machine, cleared away the breakfast things, then showered and dressed. After straightening my hair to within an inch of its life, I watched ten minutes of *Homes Under the Hammer* before checking my phone for messages. Nothing from Rob.

Scrolling through my photo gallery, I found the picture of Adam I'd kept and stared at it, feeling a niggle of unfinished business. We'd barely got beyond the getting-to-know-you stage, still trying to impress each other with witty anecdotes. (I'd had plenty, but it turned out investment banking wasn't that funny.) We hadn't even slept together. There'd been one night, after soaking up the London skyline from The Shard, when I'd sensed Adam was going to invite me back to his Canary Wharf apartment for a 'nightcap'. I'd been dying to see his apartment and had been dropping hints all evening, but he'd had to go back to work to sort out a complex deal and couldn't get away for the rest of the week.

And then I'd been fired.

I started as a text pinged through. It was from Nina:

I need to return your jeans. What's your address? Hope all's well. N xx

After working together for five years and living together for a month, that was the best she could do? I'd listened to her snoring, heard her singing power ballads in the shower (badly), slipped her painkillers at work when her period pains were bad, and, once, she'd advised me to imagine Carlotta as a screaming infant in a nappy the next time she yelled at me. Yet the tone of her text was as cool as if our paths had barely crossed.

I stabbed out an equally terse reply:

Good thanks, in process of organising local events prior to launching own business.

I added my address and paused, finger hovering over 'send'. We'd never been in the habit of messaging each other, so maybe it was just her way. I quickly typed: *How are things with PT?*, which was the name I'd given her personal trainer boyfriend, and added three kisses.

Good, came the instant reply. *Best of luck with career. Will post parcel later today X*

Right. So, we were never going to be best buddies, but at least I was getting my favourite jeans back.

Unsettled at how quickly I'd been expelled from Nina's life, and reminded once more of work, I picked up my notepad and plonked myself at the dining table, trying to adopt a businesslike frame of mind. I needed to think up some more entertainment fast, or there would only be one event at the café and I couldn't build a career on that.

What would get people talking?

Scrolling through my mental database of Five Star events, I recalled the singer who hadn't turned up to a wedding reception (she'd sworn she'd let me know she was having her tonsils removed), and the client who'd wanted a maze built for her guests, only for things to descend into chaos when no one could find their way out. Then there was the rooftop bash, arranged by a hapless fiancé who'd had no idea his wife-to-be was terrified of heights. When he snatched off her blindfold in front of 200 guests, she'd screamed so loudly that people on the street below had called the police, convinced she was being murdered. I'd got the blame for that, although I couldn't have known what the fiancée's reaction would be.

'You should have been more thorough in your research,' Carlotta had raged. 'Always double-check whether there's something the recipient might not like.'

'How could I, when her fiancé didn't know and the party was meant to be a surprise?' It wasn't often I answered back, and Carlotta's immobile forehead had quivered with fury as she'd struggled to find a reply.

She couldn't, but it didn't stop her from pulling me off a *Wizard of Oz* themed party and placing me on coffee and phone-answering duties for a fortnight.

In danger of losing focus, I quickly reminded myself of all the successes I'd worked on. The client who'd wanted her home transformed into a cocktail bar for her fortieth, with no expense spared, for which I'd managed to source a particularly spectacular lighting set; and a corporate event for 300 people in New York that had gone without a hitch; and there'd been a comedy night for charity that went down a storm…

Comedy. Everyone loved to laugh, didn't they? One of the comedians at the comedy night – Andy somebody – had made a point of saying afterwards how much he loved private gigs, because the audiences were generally a lot more forgiving, especially when they'd had a drink.

OK, so it would be a sober affair at the café, but all the better for appreciating his wit and giving him the attention he deserved. He was quite new on the scene, but had got everyone going with his traditional punchlines.

I grabbed my laptop and looked up *Andy comedian*, adding the name of the agency we'd used.

Andy Farrington. That was him, and he was available for bookings. Before I could change my mind, I called the number.

'It's a bit short notice, but he's had a cancellation, so if he could do Thursday instead of Friday, you're in luck,' the agent informed me.

'Thursday's fine.'

'Where is it, again?'

I repeated the postcode, twice.

'It's a café?' she said, sounding dubious. 'I don't think he'll do a café.'

'He might like the novelty factor.'

'He won't like the embarrassment factor.'

I'd annoyed her now. About to tell her to forget it, I suddenly remembered what Tilly and Meg had said about the Smugglers Inn. It sounded as if they were in dire need of some decent entertainment, if all they offered was karaoke and a quiz night. 'What about a pub?' I said.

'Now you're talking.'

She took down the address. 'OK, that'll be fifteen hundred pounds for two hours, plus travelling expenses.'

'Fifteen hundred?' It came out as a screech. 'He's not Peter Kay.'

'No, but he's been on *Mock the Week*.' His agent was clearly miffed. 'You get what you pay for.'

I thought fast. If Rob managed to find someone to play at the café I wouldn't have to pay much – they might even do it for free – and, providing whatever else I dreamt up wouldn't leave me out of pocket, I could just about afford it.

'Fine,' I said quickly, and made her read the address back to me, before hanging up. Seashell Cove was easy to miss if you'd never been before, and most people hadn't.

Fifteen hundred pounds. I cradled my head in my hands and let out a whimper. My savings weren't going to last long at this rate, and I really needed what little I had left to set myself up – and that included getting business cards printed, building a website (though Rob could help with that) and, more importantly, finding somewhere to live once I was back in London.

Should I work out a business plan and get myself a bank loan?

Business plan. Bank loan. Possibly the least sexy words in the English language.

Panic skittered across my chest as I wondered how long it was going to take to achieve the level of success required to live independently. I was almost thirty, for god's sake. Other people were getting married and trying for babies, or advancing their careers with promotions and pay rises, and leaping onto the property ladder. They weren't getting fired and moving back home, while pretending they were on holiday. How long would it take me to get a business going and start turning a profit? A year? Ten?

Banishing the idea of a bank loan – I'd manage somehow – panic surged to a new level as I realised I'd just organised a comedy act for the pub without the landlord's knowledge. Finding the number online, I called him right away.

'Sorry, love, no can do,' said Bill Feathers, when I'd presented him with my fait accompli. 'We like to showcase local talent, if anything. The regulars wouldn't like it.'

'Of course they would,' I said, stunned. He couldn't turn me down, not when it was booked, and I didn't have another venue.

'They wouldn't,' he argued.

'I'm telling you, they would,' I said doggedly. 'Think about it and get back to me by five o'clock.' I ended the call before he could answer back. If it was a definite no, I'd just have to call the agent and cancel, but I didn't want to think about that now.

I still liked the idea of a games event at the café, having helped to organise something similar before. People could bring their own, and if they didn't have any there was a stash of them in the cupboard under the stairs: Scrabble, Monopoly, Cribbage, an ancient box of Snakes and Ladders, held together with Sellotape, all discarded the year Rob got a Gameboy for Christmas and decided board games were 'lame'. It wouldn't cost me a penny.

That still left me with a couple of days to fill.

I drank some more coffee, and glanced out of the window to see Sid Turner's handsome ginger cat, Tommy, slinking across the garden with a purposeful air.

Cats!

In New York, Nina and I had scoped out a cat café as a possible venue for a children's party. It had been amazing, with a variety of cats roaming freely, or curled up by customers as they worked on their laptops, and there'd even been a corner with a camera for viewing kittens online. The party hadn't happened in the end, as the client objected to the small entry fee, but I'd gone back on a couple of occasions by myself (escaping the sex-mad housemates) and enjoyed the experience of drinking a latte with a purring tabby on my lap.

What if I could arrange something like that? I was certain there was nothing else like it in the area – probably in the county.

'Back of the net,' I said, wriggling in my chair, my spirits rising high as I logged online.

I could do this. I just needed to find some cats.

Chapter 13

'Mum, do you know anyone who works at the cat shelter near Bigbury?'

Her smile of welcome vanished as she came out from behind the counter and piloted me to a table by the window, indicating to Dad to take her place.

He excused himself from the customer he'd been chatting to and joined Gwen, who gave me a close-lipped smile that was more sinister than friendly.

'You know we believe you should do whatever you want to, Cassie, but is it wise to get a cat with your lifestyle. Would it be fair?' Mum's smile looked sandblasted on. 'What about when you go back to London?'

'Mum, it's fine, I'm not getting a cat,' I said, immediately wishing I could get a cat, even though it wouldn't be practical. I also wished I could banish the word 'lifestyle' from Mum's vocabulary. 'I've had a good idea; I think you'll like it.' Forcing a cheerful tone, I outlined it for her, and when I'd finished she dropped into a chair as if she'd received dreadful news.

'Cats? In the *café?*'

'It's a thing, Mum.' I sat opposite and showed her some images on my phone, making sure they were of the cutest cats, being petted by adorable children.

'But… what about health and safety? It can't be hygienic,' she fretted, not even properly taking in the pictures. She looked a bit weary and I wondered, not for the first time, why she and Dad didn't get a manager in and cut down their hours a bit. I'd suggested it once, a few years ago, and they'd looked at me as though I'd proposed setting fire to the premises.

'We can't afford a manager,' Dad had pointed out, adding swiftly, 'plus, we love being there.'

There was no doubting they enjoyed what they did, and on the rare occasions they'd taken a break – usually for just a few days – they'd simply closed the café, confident their customers would return once they were back. Family holidays had become a thing of the past once Dad bought the café – not that we'd gone far before, but there'd usually been a trip to Norfolk, or Yorkshire, and even Scotland one year – but now that business had picked up, and would do so again after my events, they really should reconsider employing a manager.

'… wouldn't want a death on my hands,' Mum was saying as I tuned back in, her hands twisting together on top of the table. 'We'd be closed down for good.'

'Mum, for goodness sake, no one's going to die,' I said. 'It'll all be done properly, I've looked into it.'

'But, why the cat shelter?'

'Because it will prompt people to adopt a cat, once they've fallen in love…' I started to explain, but her eyes were roaming the café as if already seeing something deadly unfolding. I'd never seen Mum look so anxious. It was as if, the longer I was around, her true feelings were breaking through her shell of positivity.

'Couldn't people bring in their own?' she suggested.

Encouraged that she seemed to be considering it, I said, 'The thing is, not enough people might have a cat, and even if they do, they might not want them mixing with other people's cats.'

'So… how does it work?'

'Someone from the shelter would be here to supervise, and they'd only bring cats that were friendly, so there wouldn't be any danger of… bloodshed.' Mum's eyes nearly popped out. 'I'm joking,' I said, reaching over to still her writhing hands. 'Honestly, Mum, it'll be lovely.' I told her about the cat café in New York.

'Well, if you think so,' she said, with a bit more confidence. 'Obviously you did a good job, judging by those photos.' Oh bugger. She *had* been looking, and had got the wrong end of the stick.

'I did,' I said, unwilling to dash her faith in me. 'I just thought if you knew someone there, you'd be the best one to call them.' I could see she was glancing at the table next to us, which needed clearing.

'I'm afraid I don't,' she said, snapping back into work mode as she stood up and beckoned the waitress over to the cluttered table. 'Shouldn't you call them, as you're the one arranging it?'

'Fine,' I said, feeling a slump inside. I didn't want to admit that I had already called and had got short shrift from the woman who'd answered, as she was dealing with a 'flea' crisis, and couldn't talk. It seemed unreasonable to feel hurt when I'd dealt with far stroppier clients, but on the back of my disaster with Connor Daley, I felt like I was losing my touch. 'Is Meg in today?' I looked around, thinking how nice it would be to have another chat with her – a proper one, catching up on everything she'd been doing for the last few years.

'Day off,' Mum said. 'She's at the doctor's with Sam.'

'Oh? Nothing serious, I hope?'

'Sam doesn't want to wait until after the wedding for them to start trying for a baby now that Meg's turned thirty,' she said, becoming gossipy. 'It's not happening though, so I think they're going for tests.'

'I see.' There really was a lot of catching up to do. 'Tilly?'

'She's leading a long walk today to Bigbury-on-Sea, so won't be back for hours.'

'Right.' I didn't fancy hanging around until four, when I was due to meet the artist, and wondered whether to go home and start spreading news of my events on social media. I'd already looked online and found Twitter and Facebook pages for the café, so it wouldn't be too hard. No need to spend money on printing out flyers these days.

'Will you let your customers know what I'm doing?' I said, before Mum became swallowed up in work again. 'Perhaps write something on the board outside?'

'Of course I will, love.' She turned to a woman navigating the tables with a double buggy. 'Excuse me, but my daughter's organising some exciting events at the café,' she said, in the too-bright voice of a weather presenter. 'I do hope you can attend.'

'What?' said the woman, almost running over my foot with the buggy, which contained two runny-nosed toddlers trying to belt each other with their sippy cups.

'Events, here, at the café.' Mum looked at me for approval, frowning when I drew my finger across my throat. This clearly wasn't the right moment.

'I dunno what I'm doing this afternoon, never mind tomorrow or the day after,' said the woman, with the slightly manic smile of someone who'd barely slept. 'These two keep me pretty busy.'

'There'll be cats,' Mum said, bending to grab one of the sippy cups before it was hurled across the floor, just as one of the toddlers started grizzling.

'They're allergic,' said the woman, flinging her buggy forcefully towards the counter, as if trying to transport the children into the future, where fights and tears were a thing of the past.

'They're allergic,' Mum repeated, turning to me with an urgent look I recognised. She was bracing herself to be firm. 'Cassie, I really don't think—'

'As long as people know, they can avoid coming that day,' I cut in. 'It's one day, Mum,' I added, as she opened her mouth to protest. 'You're not going to lose business in one day. In fact, you're going to gain coachloads of new customers.'

'Oh, I hope not,' she said contrarily, glancing vaguely in the direction of the car park. 'There's not enough room out there as it is.'

'Oh, Mum.' Frustrated, I stood up, unsure what to do next.

'Your nan might be the best person to call,' she said, suddenly. 'I'm sure she got Fleur from that cat place.'

Fleur! I'd completely forgotten Nan's brief attempt at housing a stately grey cat that turned out to be a ruthless killer, bringing in bloodied remains and depositing them at Nan's feet like grotesque gifts. 'Didn't she give her back though?'

'No, she gave him to a farmer she was seeing at the time. I think it worked out for the best. For the cat, I mean, not your nan's relationship.'

Declining an offer of lunch, I decided there was enough time to pay Nan a visit before Vicky Burton turned up with her paintings, so set off back to the house to pick up Sir Lancelot. I wondered whether Danny would be at Nan's. Not that I had any intention of chatting to him if he was. It was a work-related visit, nothing more. And to see how Nan was doing. I was still unsure about her using an outside toilet and hoped to persuade her that she could live a more environmentally friendly life without going the full Bear Grylls.

Nan was in her almost empty living room when I arrived, and I had to admit that, without all the boxes and bags, it was an oddly relaxing space, filled with natural light flowing in through the uncurtained window. No television blaring, no clutter – no furniture, apart from a wooden rocking chair, and a side table piled with books that looked to be about self-sufficiency.

She was standing up, reading one titled *Harnessing Solar Power*, which prompted an image of her lassoing the sun. 'Sweetheart, have you come to meditate with me?' She put down her book and gave me a sunny smile. 'We should go into the garden and earth ourselves,' she said. 'It's all about being at one with the soil.'

'I'd rather stay in here, if that's OK.' I kissed her soft cheek. 'I expect Danny's busy in the garden,' I added, not sure why I'd even brought him up.

'Oh, he's not here at the moment,' she said. 'He's been spiriting all my worldly goods away, and then he's going to pick up a pipe for my butt.'

I reeled away from her. 'Nan, I think that's going too far.' I had a horrible memory of a TV programme I'd seen, about celebrities having daily enemas as part of a brutal detox regime. 'It's *dangerous*, and not as healthy as you might think.'

The lines on her face deepened. 'What are you talking about, Cassandra? I won't be drinking the contents, though I'm sure it would be perfectly safe to.'

'*What?*'

'I'll be using it for the garden, *chérie*, don't worry.' Her face softened as she cupped my elbows in her palms. 'It's lovely of you to be concerned, but it's entirely natural,' she said. 'People have collected rainwater for years.'

It took a second for the penny to drop. Hadn't Danny mentioned something about it, earlier? 'A water butt,' I said weakly.

'I've been meaning to sort something out for a while, but it's one of those jobs a man can be useful for, and I didn't want to bother your father.'

I nodded, wondering how on earth my mind had taken me in such an unsavoury direction. 'How much are you paying for Danny's help?' I said, to cover my embarrassment.

'Not as much as you might think.' She gave my elbows a little squeeze. 'Don't worry, I'm not squandering your inheritance.'

Horrified that she'd misunderstood, I said, 'I'm not worried about that, Nan. You know I don't want your money.'

'I was teasing.' A frown replaced her smile. 'You really do need to relax, *ma puce*. Close your eyes.'

Her endearment – *little flea* – reminded me I'd come to talk cats, but she'd already shut her eyes, and was making a humming sound that seemed to travel to her hands and vibrate through me. It wasn't unpleasant. I studied her lids, but they were almost translucent, giving the impression she could see right through them, so I allowed my eyes to drift shut.

'Concentrate on your breathing,' she directed. 'I-i-i-i-n and out, i-i-i-i-n and out.' She demonstrated with swooshing noises, and I found myself copying her, feeling the rise and fall of my chest.

'From your tummy.' I felt her hand, firm against my ribcage. 'Inflate from below your belly button.'

I tried again and felt an immediate difference. My shoulders dropped down from wherever they'd been lurking, and a tiny space opened up inside my head. A calm space, empty of thoughts and feelings, filled with a soft, white light. A space I'd liked to have stayed in a little longer, but a cat sauntered through it and gave me a taunting look.

'Nan, do you remember where you got Fleur?' I cracked one eye open to see her looking at me intensely. 'Nan?'

'You should keep breathing,' she said, letting go of my elbows.

I felt oddly unstable for a second, as though I might tip over. 'I know how to breathe, Nan, but thanks.' I pushed my hair behind my ears. 'I'm afraid I've got things to do.'

'You shouldn't be afraid of the things you do.' She'd gone all serious, and I remembered how it had amused Rob and me when she'd go into what we called her Dear Deirdre mode, after the agony aunt whose column we used to read in the newspapers that customers left behind at the café. The letters had salacious headlines, like *Sexy Cabin Girl Showed me the Ropes on Ferry*, but Deirdre's answers were always earnest and sensible.

'It's just a saying, Nan,' I said, even as it struck me that maybe I *was* a little bit afraid. But only of getting things wrong, when I needed them to go right. 'I was wondering whether you had a contact at the cat rescue place near Bigbury.' It sounded silly – as if I was planning to break in and set them all free.

'Oh, I'm barred from there,' Nan said, gliding across to the window. Her posture had definitely improved – perhaps because she wasn't weighed down by jewellery, expensive knitwear and hairspray. 'I gave them a piece of my mind, I'm afraid, for not warning me that Fleur was unstable.'

A giggle lodged in my throat. 'I think she was doing what cats do,' I said. 'It's not like they can psychologically profile them all.'

'Hmmm.' She turned, her eyebrows riding high. 'Why do you ask?'

'I'm organising an event for the café, involving cats,' I said. 'I thought it might help my case if they knew you'd previously adopted one, but clearly not.'

'Danny helps out there sometimes,' she said unexpectedly. 'You could always ask him to have a word, when he gets back.'

Bloody hell. Was there any pie Danny Fleetwood didn't have a finger in? 'And of course he has the van, if you needed anything transporting.' She seemed to like that word.

'It's fine, I need to sort it out today, really.'

Nan looked at me a moment longer, as if trying to work me out. 'I was going to pick some radishes to make soup for my dinner, would you like to help?' she said at last. 'It's very... how do you say it?' She tilted her head, seeking a suitable French phrase, instead of just saying the English one she knew perfectly well.

'Grounding?' I suggested. 'As in, fingers in the ground, connected to nature, the soil, et cetera.'

'No, no.' She thought some more, then snapped her fingers. '*De la terre,* that's it.' Her eyes gleamed with satisfaction. 'It means, of the earth.'

'That's what I just said.'

She tutted. 'You were always mischievous, even as a child,' she said fondly. 'Don't lose that, Cassandra. Being a successful businesswoman is all well and good, but you must have fun as well, like I have had since your grandfather died.'

Fun. The word gave me a jolt. It was what Danny had been implying with his 'all work and no play' comment, but now I thought about it, when *had* I last had fun? Talking to Meg and Tilly, yesterday. Before that? Being out with Adam had been fun. OK, it had been a bit fraught with tension, too, knowing I could get called in to work at any moment, and trying to be bright and witty all the time, but we had laughed a lot. And in New York, I'd enjoyed walking through Central Park, kicking through leaves like a character in a movie, before Nina had called to tell me I was late to a client meeting.

'Cassandra, do you enjoy your job?'

I hadn't realised that Nan was still observing me from the window. She looked like a mystical figure in her robe, with her long silver plait dangling over one shoulder, and the light from the window haloing her head.

'Of course I do!' It sounded shriller than I'd intended. 'I'm in a transition period at the moment, that's all,' I said, levelling my tone. 'I'm hoping to start something on my own.'

'And you need cats for this?'

Relieved she'd taken me at my word, I smiled and said, 'Maybe.'

'Just call and tell them what you want,' she said. 'They can only say no.'

It sounded simple put like that, but if they said no, I'd be back to square one. 'You're right,' I said. 'I'll do it now.'

Nan gave a little bow, playing up the wise-woman role. 'I'll be in the garden if you need me,' she said.

When she'd gone outside, I took a breath and called the shelter again, praying I'd get hold of someone more approachable.

'Sounds like a fab idea,' said a woman called Liz who answered the phone this time. After I'd explained what I wanted, using more words than necessary, including telling her all about the cat café in New York, she said, 'Let's do it.'

Having gone through the details and arrangements, we settled on the time and date and, afterwards, I stood for a moment in the quiet room, amazed it had been that simple.

I glanced through the window, wondering when Danny might be back, and jumped when my phone rang in my hand, the ringtone too loud in the silence.

'Hi, Mum.'

'Cassie, there's someone here to see you.' She sounded unusually rattled. 'Her name's Vicky.'

Oh god, I'd completely forgotten the time. 'Tell her I'm on my way,' I said, glad I'd brought the car instead of walking. 'Take a look at her paintings, Mum, they're great.'

'I already have.' Her voice was stiff with disapproval. 'I'm a bit surprised, to be honest, Cassie. I thought you knew about art.'

My heart dropped. 'Don't you like them?'

'They're nicely done, I suppose,' Mum said. 'But they're hardly appropriate for a family establishment.'

I thought of the tasteful sunsets and sunrises on Vicky's website – the sunburst storm cloud. 'In what way?' There was a pause. 'Mum?'

When she finally spoke, I wished she hadn't. 'The people in them don't have any clothes on,' she said.

Chapter 14

I half expected to find that Vicky had been banished by the time I rushed through the café, grimly avoiding Mum's eye, but she was sitting at a table out on the terrace, a beatific smile on her face as she studied the view.

'Gorgeous, isn't it?' she said without turning, as if divining my approach. Or maybe she'd heard my heavy breathing. I felt as if I'd run all the way from Nan's.

'Sorry I'm late,' I said, seeing Dad miming a tipping mug from the doorway and shaking my head. I wasn't in the mood for refreshments. 'I gather my parents have already viewed your work.' I moved in front of her, rolling down the sleeves of my top. A breeze had sprung up, sending tufty clouds chasing across the sun, but Vicky didn't seem bothered. She was wearing the sort of lacy dress that would have made me look like an overgrown baby, her explosion of black hair billowing around her cheeks. 'Your work,' I repeated, as she shut her eyes and tilted her head back, deeply inhaling the air. I wasn't in the mood for artistic quirks – or even someone appreciating their surroundings. 'May I have a look, please?'

She peeled open her eyes and put down her half-empty cup. 'Of course,' she said, reaching for a black leather portfolio at her side. 'I'm so pleased you asked me to come.' She broke into a smile, revealing rabbity teeth. 'The café's adorable, and your parents are lovely. They're very proud of you.'

'So I've heard.' Mum and Dad obviously hadn't commented on her nudey paintings.

'I'm not sure what they made of my work, though.' Vicky unzipped the portfolio and released a picture of a woman standing in the middle of a sheep-strewn field.

'She's naked,' I said, when I'd been silent too long.

Vicky darted me a confused look. Her eyes were too close together, giving the overall impression of a pretty rodent. 'It's to represent her oneness with nature.' *Of course it was.* 'And this one is showing how, even among people, we're naked, at least on the inside.' She took out a picture of the same woman, this time at a party, surrounded by guests in full evening dress, her nipples the colour of raspberries.

'Couldn't you pop a dress on her?' I said, aiming for a jokey tone to hide my frustration. 'She'd look lovely in green, with all that flowing red hair.'

Vicky's head jerked, as if I'd slapped her. 'But that would be missing the point,' she said, placing a hand over the woman's breasts to stop the painting from blowing away.

Pushing my hair off my face, I dragged my eyes from the next picture out of the portfolio – a naked man doing a cartwheel – *presumably to demonstrate what a complete muppet he was.*

'You were supposed to be bringing the paintings I saw on your website.' I fixed her with what I hoped was a relaxed smile. 'The sunsets and seascapes?'

'Oh, I know, but I thought they were a bit... *safe*,' she said, with a dismissive waft of her hand. 'I'm in a completely different phase now.'

'But, you can see these aren't suitable for the café?'

From the gormless look on her face, she couldn't.

'There'll be children here,' I said bluntly. 'And nobody wants boobs and bums in their faces while they're drinking their tea. They want sunsets and seascapes and...' I pushed away the picture on the table. 'Not this.'

Her face was uncomprehending. 'We should be embracing nudity.'

'I wouldn't embrace that.' I pointed to the cartwheeling man. 'I wouldn't want him on my wall, either.'

'Being naked is a natural state,' she said with a petulant pout. 'It's how we were born.'

My patience ran out. 'Wearing clothes is natural, especially outdoors. If I stood in a field, flashing my bits, or turned up at a party with my boobs out, I'd get arrested.'

Vicky began to snatch up her things. 'People are so close-minded,' she said, quite bitchily. 'They're the best work I've ever done, yet nobody wants them.'

'Maybe you should stick with your seascapes,' I suggested.

'I wouldn't be being true to myself if I did that.' She snapped her portfolio shut. 'That's more important to me than money.'

She sounded like Danny, and I wondered what the fuss was about 'being true to yourself'. Doing what you wanted was all well and good, but what about financial security? You could learn to love what you did, if the rewards meant you didn't have to worry about paying the bills.

'Most people just don't understand art, that's the trouble.' Vicky got to her feet. She was tiny, even in heels. 'I'm sorry for wasting your time.'

'I do understand about art,' I was moved to say. 'I used to paint myself.' That sounded wrong. 'I mean, I used to paint. A long time ago.'

'That's exactly my point.' She plucked a cropped denim jacket off the back of her chair and slung it around her shoulders. 'Everyone who's ever picked up a paintbrush thinks they know about art.'

'I know what I like!' I sang through a smile, even though my teeth were clamped together. Dad was hovering in the doorway again, clearly keen to know what was going on.

'I wish I hadn't wasted petrol driving over here, now.' Vicky flounced away far more elegantly than I'd have managed in heels, leaving me with a confusing mishmash of feelings swilling around in my gut.

As the first drops of rain began to fall, I hurried inside. 'It's not happening,' I said to Dad. 'Her work wasn't suitable.'

'No,' he said, a look of relief sweeping over his face. 'They were a bit rude.'

'They weren't the paintings I looked at on her website.'

'Maybe you should have looked at them in person.' There wasn't an ounce of criticism in his voice, but all the same I was slammed with a sense of failure. It was the kind of thing Carlotta would have said, with slitted eyes and a steely edge to her voice.

'I'll find something else,' I promised.

'You don't have to.' He sounded concerned – probably imagining the pristine walls littered with pictures of corpses, or mating animals, or something else inappropriate.

'I want to,' I said, rolling my sleeves up again. It was warm inside, and I was tempted to slump at a table with a cup of something hot, and the biggest slice of cake I could get my hands on. Sour cherry and pistachio was the special of the day, and Mum was carving out a sizeable chunk for a man with a paunch pushing over the waist of his jeans. 'I just think the café would look even better with artwork on the walls.'

It suddenly seemed imperative that I do this one thing – the first thing I'd said I would do. Otherwise, I'd have failed at something even Rob could have arranged, and he didn't know his Monet from his Banksy.

'Okey-dokey, then.' Dad was giving me a similar look to the one Nan had given me earlier – they were so alike when they frowned – and I suddenly couldn't bear it. I felt like a pinned butterfly, only not delicate and pretty.

'Tell Mum I'll cook dinner tonight,' I said, and left before he could object.

♥

Mooching round the shops in the village, I tried to rescue my positive mood by thinking of some of the Instagram quotes that Nina was such a fan of, often reading them out to me like a mother encouraging a toddler. *Stay positive, work hard, and make it happen*, had been a favourite, along with: *The best preparation for good work tomorrow is to do good work today*, and: *Easier to do a job right, than explain why you didn't.*

Maybe if I designed a menu for the taster session tomorrow night, I'd feel more in control. There was a cute little arts and crafts shop tucked between the butcher's and the Old Bakery, where Meg still worked most mornings. It was shut now, the display shelves in the window empty of the loaves, cakes, and pies they used to sell all day, when the aroma of baking would draw people like a magnet, and Mum would send Rob and me to buy a batch of scones for the café if she hadn't had time to make any.

In the craft shop, I became sidetracked by a selection of sketch pads in varying sizes, and ended up buying two – one for watercolour painting – and a set of waterproof, smudge-proof coloured pencils that cost more than I could afford, but which I couldn't resist.

My phone rang as I came out of the shop. It was Bill Feathers, from the Smugglers Inn. 'OK, love, you're on,' he said, without preamble.

'He'd better be good, though, this comedian of yours. Our reputation's on the line.'

'You won't regret it, Bill, thanks,' I said, wondering what reputation he was talking about. The one for having the stickiest carpets in Devon? Even so, I was smiling when I ended the call. Everything was coming together.

It was only when I got home that I realised I'd forgotten to buy something for dinner, but a rummage through the fridge and cupboards provided the ingredients to make a big dish of macaroni cheese – the one dish I'd perfected, living in London, because it was quick, easy and cheap.

Once assembled, I put it aside to pop in the oven later, and shot upstairs into the back room my parents used as a study, where a newish computer with a printer and scanner attached were housed. Normally, at work, I'd have outsourced the printing of invitations or menus to someone who knew what they were doing, but as that wasn't an option I opened a document and fiddled about for a while with a graphics programme, wishing Rob was around to help. Nothing I came up with looked right. Maybe it would be easier to do something by hand.

Enthused, I ran downstairs and took out my new coloured pencils, then located the delivery note for the teas and coffees and settled myself at the kitchen table. An hour later, I'd carefully scripted all the different blends of tea and coffee and surrounded them with delicately outlined cups and saucers, spoons and coffee beans, and plump little muffins bursting with fruit.

Back upstairs, I scanned in the page and printed out several copies on standard A4 paper, because there wasn't anything nicer, and even though they came out black and white, they still looked good.

On impulse, I retrieved my paints from my bedroom drawer, mixed them with water, then painted Meg's blueberry-and-buttercream cake from memory, resplendent beneath a glass dome, exaggerating the cake's dimensions and the purple shade of the fruit, until my mouth was watering. It wasn't until I heard the key in the door that I realised Mum and Dad were back, and I'd forgotten all about dinner.

'What's all this?' said Dad, as I leapt up and switched on the oven. My fingers were splotched with paint and I wiped them on my top, feeling as if I'd been caught doing something illegal.

'Just messing about,' I said, as Mum came through, shedding her bulging bag and fleecy jacket. 'I forgot the time.'

'Not to worry,' she said, efficiently slipping the macaroni into the oven before setting the timer. 'It was lovely of you to make this, Cassie.'

'No trouble.' I shoved my hands in my pockets. 'I don't expect you to wait on me hand and foot.'

'And you've done some washing.' Smiling, she opened the door and started tugging out damp clothes.

'I should have hung them on the line,' I said, wondering what was happening to the iron-clad focus I'd always had when working. 'I got a bit distracted.'

'It's OK,' Mum said, pushing the items into the tumble dryer. 'The weather's turned, anyway.'

I looked at the window and saw that it was still raining.

'This is good.' I turned to see Dad squinting at my painting. He was supposed to wear reading glasses, but said they made him feel old. 'You always were good at drawing.'

I plucked it out of his hands and laid it on the worktop to dry properly. 'What about these?' I said, showing him the taster menu I'd designed.

'You did this?' I nodded, thinking *who else?* 'It's lovely, isn't it, Lydia?'

'Yes,' she said doubtfully, and exchanged a look with Dad that I couldn't interpret.

'What?' I said, alert to criticism.

'Nothing.' Dad was wearing the shifty look he used to get when Rob and I begged him to tell us what we were getting for Christmas.

'It's obviously something.'

'It's just that we were wondering whether you should be working so hard, when you're meant to be having a holiday,' he said, shooting a look of apology at Mum.

She was shaking her head so much her curls bounced. 'We can see how much you love your work, and obviously we want you to do whatever you want, but we're worried you might be addicted. To work, I mean.' Redness burst over her cheeks. 'We're *so* proud of you, love, but we don't want you to burn out, and what about your eggs?'

'Sorry?' Gobsmacked by her eruption, I glanced at the novelty egg holder in the shape of a helter-skelter by the fridge. 'What do you mean?'

'Do you think you should freeze them, for later?'

Confused, I said, 'I didn't know you could freeze eggs.'

'I read that a famous actress put hers on ice years ago to focus on her career—'

'Lydia.' Dad sounded like a man trying to stop a runaway horse, but Mum had got the bit firmly between her teeth.

'Even if they were defrosted now, she's probably too old to become a mother, and I wouldn't want that for you.' She clapped a hand across her mouth as if she'd just been sick.

'You're talking about *my* eggs?' I pointed to my lower abdomen, in case there was any doubt.

She nodded. 'I'm sorry,' she whispered through her fingers.

My eyes swivelled from her to Dad. They looked crushed, as if they'd broken a vow of silence and knew there was no going back.

'I didn't realise it was something that bothered you,' I said, astonished that they'd expressed an opinion about my future that didn't involve the word 'proud'.

'Oh, it doesn't, not really,' said Dad, but I could see from the looks he was flinging at Mum it was something they'd discussed, probably more than once. 'We're not like those parents who are desperate for grandchildren, or think you should be in a relationship or anything.' Dad made a *pfft* sound, presumably dismissing the very thought. 'We just want you to be happy, and not to have a breakdown.'

'That's all it is,' Mum said, flapping her hand as though to shoo away her previous words. 'Take no notice of us. We want what's best for you, always have. You don't have to do anything to please us.'

Looking at their hunted expressions, I tried to work out what I felt. Anger, that they'd discussed me behind my back? Outrage, that my eggs (so hard not to picture them with freckled shells) had been the topic of conversation? Humiliation, that – at twenty-nine – they were worried my childbearing years were already behind me? Strangely, I felt none of those things. Instead, I was disproportionately pleased that they cared enough to worry and, for once, to let me know – even if it was reluctantly – and that they'd felt it necessary to retract their words right away.

'You two,' I said, placing my arm around Dad's waist and drawing Mum in for a cuddle. 'You're a pair of numpties, but I love you.'

Chapter 15

'They smell so good,' I said to Meg, peering into the tin. 'What's in them?'

'Ginger and lemon.' She playfully smacked my hand away as I reached for one of the delicious-looking muffins. 'These are for customers,' she said. 'I've held a few back if you'd like one.'

'Maybe later.'

I peered through the door into the café. My stomach was a cauldron of nerves, and I'd developed a new itchy patch above my right wrist that I was trying not to scratch. It had always happened right before an event, but I'd thought this evening would be easier. It wasn't as if I'd invited 400 guests, or had Carlotta hissing last-minute orders into my earpiece, and no one's night was going to be ruined if the lighting wasn't perfect, but I needed to pull it off.

Your future is directed by what you do today. Another of Nina's quotes. I couldn't seem to get them out of my head. *Don't wish for it, work for it.* At least she'd been true to her word and returned my jeans. They'd arrived that morning while I was updating the café's Facebook page:

Come and try our new range of teas and coffees this evening, 7–9, and let us know what you think. There'll be music, and cake, so tell your friends and don't miss this one-off event!

I copied it onto Instagram with multiple tea- and coffee- and Maitland's related hashtags.

I'd been careful not to specify what kind of music, as Rob had informed me over breakfast that he was still 'firming up' an act called Rodney's Dad.

'What do you mean, "firming up"?'

'He usually visits his granddad on Tuesdays. He's in a care home. His granddad, not Fletcher.'

'Fletcher?'

'Nick's mate, the one I told you about.'

'I thought you just said he was called Rodney?'

Rob had looked at me as though I was being deliberately obtuse. 'Rodney's Dad's his stage name, Sandra.'

'Well, it's a stupid name.'

'No, it's not, it's meaningful.'

His class didn't start until ten, and I thought how unfair it was that he looked so fresh when he hadn't come home until gone midnight, waking the rest of us by clicking on lights and singing a chorus of 'All Things Bright and Beautiful'. Not drunk, he'd informed us, when we'd staggered onto the landing to see what was happening. Just happy that Emma had agreed to consider giving their relationship another go, once he'd finished his course and started his new job. He'd had an aura about him that had made me want to simultaneously throttle and hug him.

'The name's for his granddad,' he'd said at breakfast, when I'd continued to look blank.

'How do you work that out?'

'His dad's called Rodney, which means Rodney's dad is Fletcher's granddad.' Rob had picked up one of my new coloured pencils and torn a page from my sketch pad to scribble a crude family tree, complete with arrows and smiley faces. 'Do you understand now?'

I'd leaned over and dislodged his glasses, which he hated. 'Why not just use his granddad's name?'

'Because no one would take him seriously if he called himself Nobby.'

We'd cracked up then, and for a moment the upcoming event had faded into the background, and I'd wished we could stay in the kitchen messing about.

Now, smoothing my hands down the snug-fitting jeans I'd been reunited with – maybe they'd become my lucky jeans – I wondered whether Rodney's Dad was going to make it. Time was getting on, and I assumed he'd need to prepare.

As if on cue, my phone buzzed with a message.

Fletch on his way, sis X

Brilliant! *I owe you* I replied, feeling my shoulder blades loosen slightly. *You coming?*

Wouldn't miss it for the world!!

I didn't like the sound of that, but there wasn't time to ponder it.

'Anything else I need to do?' Mum's smiling face appeared. After closing the café at six as usual, I'd persuaded her to change out of her work clothes, in favour of a flared, black skirt and scoop-necked top, which I'd brought to the café with a pair of kitten heels and some tights, but it was obvious she didn't feel comfortable. She kept tugging her skirt down as though it was showing her thighs, instead of her neatly shaped calves, and she was convinced her top was hugging her 'spare tyre'.

'You look lovely, Lydia,' Meg had said, when Mum came out of the Ladies, looking self-conscious as she fiddled with her waistband and pretended to stumble in her shoes. 'I don't think I've ever seen you wear make-up at work.'

Mum's pink lipstick had worn off already, and the hairspray I'd brought hadn't had the desired effect of fixing her curls in place. Instead, they'd gone limp, so she looked as if she'd been caught in the drizzle still falling outside.

'You've labelled the teapots and checked you've got enough strainers?' I said. 'We don't want the cups full of leaves.'

Mum nodded. 'Yes, and I made myself some strawberry crush, and it was delicious.'

'That's good,' I said, pleased she was on board, but sorry she seemed ill at ease in spite of her rigid smile. *Great things never came from comfort zones.* 'You'll be able to recommend it,' I said. 'Is Dad OK with the coffees?'

I peered past her to see him polishing the coffee machine with the same sort of zeal that Sid Turner buffed his car. He'd changed, too, into grey suit trousers and a lilac shirt with the top button undone. He'd sworn off wearing ties after leaving his banking job, except at weddings and funerals.

'He's fine,' Mum said, pointing to a row of white cups lined up on the counter, which I'd instructed him to fill with the different flavours of coffee beans. 'They're all labelled too.' She scrunched her face into an expression of excitement that didn't quite convince. 'I must say, the Peruvian coffee sounds… exciting.'

'And you've both had a look at the packets, so if anyone asks you can say where the teas and coffees are from and answer any questions?'

'We did our best, love, but it's been quite busy today.'

'Well, I've done some reading up, too, so I can help,' I said. The planner wasn't supposed to get involved in the event, just blend into the background and oversee its smooth running, but I really needed to prove myself – to show my parents I could make the café even more successful – and hopefully impress any potential future clients.

I rubbed the skin on my wrist as I tried to remember whether I'd forgotten anything.

'What's that?' Mum took hold of my hand and looked at the rash.

'I must be allergic to your washing powder,' I said, pulling the cuff of my blouse over the offending patch. 'Don't worry, Mum, it's fine.'

'There's some antihistamine cream in the first-aid box, I'll go and get it,' she said, seeming relieved to have an excuse to leave the café. She started to take tiny steps towards the office, as though genuinely worried about falling off her heels.

'You're good at this, aren't you?' Meg said, joining me in the doorway. I was grateful she'd offered to stay and help, especially as she'd been on her feet all day and was probably keen to get home. 'It's funny, really, when you didn't used to like organised dos.'

I turned to her in surprise, hit once more by a wave of pleasure at seeing her again. 'Didn't I?'

She dimpled into a smile and nudged me with her shoulder. 'You refused to come to my sixteenth birthday because it was fancy dress, remember? And when your mum wanted to arrange something for yours, you said you'd rather hang out with Tilly and me. We went to see *The Others* at the cinema in Dartmouth, and Tilly didn't realise it was spooky and kept her eyes shut.'

'Oh god, yeah, I'd forgotten about that,' I said, momentarily distracted from the sight of Dad rubbing the window with his tea towel. 'But we're grown up now, and bound to be different to how we were back then.'

'Oh, I don't know.' Meg slipped her arm through mine in an easy gesture. She smelt faintly of vanilla essence with a hint of something fruity, and I leant against her and discreetly breathed it in. 'Obviously you are, but I don't think Tilly or I have really changed that much.'

'I'm glad you haven't,' I said, feeling peeved in a way I didn't understand. 'Is Tilly still coming this evening?'

'As far as I know. She's dying to see you again.'

Warmed by the genuine feeling in her voice, I said, 'Shall we get your muffins out?'

Sniggering childishly, we arranged them on cake stands, alongside the Bakewell tart, its icing as shiny as a tile, and a farmhouse-style fruit loaf scented with cinnamon. After checking that every table had one of my tasting menus on it, I began to rearrange them, moving them closer together to create a more intimate space.

'Cassie, don't do that,' scolded Dad, alerted by the sound of wood scraping across the floorboards. His smile looked more like a grimace. 'We had it just how we liked it.'

'But this is cosier,' I said.

'It'll be cramped when everyone's sitting down.'

'I'm creating a harmonious zone.'

Dad subsided with a shrug. 'OK, love, you're the boss,' he said, turning back to look outside, where the lowering sky was making it look later than it was.

I took a last look around the café, my gaze snagging on the bare walls. Some lucky artist could have made a killing tonight, but it was too late now. Vicky Burton's paintings would probably have broken some indecency laws, and I couldn't risk my reputation – never mind the café's.

Mum bustled through with a tube of cream and I let her rub it on my rash, thinking perhaps I did have an allergy and the ointment would magic it away. 'You definitely told people about tonight?' I said, glancing at the door. The time was ticking down to seven o'clock and I'd expected to see people queueing outside, but apart from an elderly man with a stiff-legged dog there was no one around.

'Of course I did.' She slipped the tube of cream in her pocket and moved round to the sink to wash her hands. 'I just think…'

'What?'

'It's a bit of a funny time, that's all. People will be having dinner and settling down for the evening.'

I stared at her back. 'I suggested holding it later, but you wanted to be home by ten.'

'So, it's my fault if no one turns up?' Mum's voice had gone a bit high-pitched and Meg shot a look at me that said, 'What's going on?'

'Of course it's not your fault, I'm just saying…' I said, then almost left my skin when Dad yelled, 'Someone's here!' like a castaway spotting a rescue boat on the ocean.

'Thank Christ for that.' I smoothed a hand over my ponytail before picking up my checklist. 'Leave the door open, Dad,' I instructed, straightening my shoulders to give the impression I was in charge, and he pushed it wide and stepped outside to greet the first customer.

'Welcome to our taster night,' he said in a jolly voice, a tea towel folded over his arm like a waiter. Mum sprang forward and placed her hands on the counter, an over-the-top smile on her face, and something inside me shrivelled at the sight of my parents trying to play roles that normally came so naturally to them.

They'll settle into it, I told myself. It was only because they were outside their normal routine.

'No need for a welcome committee, it's only me,' said Rob, slapping Dad on the back as he strode in.

Mum's high-wattage smile dimmed to a normal level. 'Is Emma coming?' she asked, as though they were best friends now.

Rob shook his head. 'Just this dude.' He swept his arm in an arc, as the friend I assumed was Fletcher came loping in, a guitar slung across his lanky body. Everything about him seemed droopy, from his middle-parted hair and moustache, to his sloping shoulders and the flappy beige trousers that looked like they might have once belonged to his granddad.

'Helloooo,' he said, swinging round in a circle, arms outstretched, as if greeting a horde of people. Confusion crossed his face. 'Where is everyone?'

'On their way,' I said, hoping it was true. 'He's the musician,' I explained on seeing Mum and Dad's muddled faces, and remembering that I hadn't mentioned Fletcher in case he didn't turn up. 'I thought some live music would be nice for ambience.'

'If you'd said, I could have asked my friend Jim to bring his saxophone in,' Dad said. 'He'd have done it as a favour.'

'Oh.' (*Failure to communicate with your client is a sure-fire way to disaster.*) 'Well, I think Fletcher's doing it as a favour…' my words trailed off as I saw him shaking his shaggy head, as mournful as a bloodhound.

'S'not possible, sorry, no way,' he said. 'I've got fees to pay. Grand-dad's care home don't come cheap, mate.'

He grabbed his guitar and bashed out some tuneless chords that brought Mum's hands crashing to her ears. 'Talent like this don't come cheap either.' He dropped onto the nearest chair, like a puppet whose strings had been cut, and, as he began to giggle helplessly, I realised that Rodney's Dad was high as a kite.

Chapter 16

'What the hell were you thinking?' I hissed at Rob, once we'd wrangled a tittering Fletcher into the office and left him stroking his guitar and making little crooning noises.

'Honestly, he wasn't that bad in the car on the way over, or I'd never have got in with him.' Rob tried to keep a straight face, but was obviously finding the whole thing hilarious. 'He's been at his granddad's medication again.'

I snorted with disbelief. 'Not long ago, you had the world at your feet, and now you're hanging around with idiots like *him*.'

'Hey,' he said, losing the grin. 'You asked me to find someone at short notice, and Nick recommended him. I didn't *know* about his little habit, and I don't think Nick does either.'

'Well, thanks for nothing.' I felt a hot flare of resentment. 'Now the evening's spoilt.'

'Look, I'm sorry,' he said, then held up his hands as if I was advancing with a sword. 'Don't look at me like that, I'm not doing it, Sandra. I've told you, I'm finished with music.'

'Just this once, as a favour to me.'

He shook his head, his glasses sliding down his nose. 'Why won't you take me seriously?'

'What's the problem?' I felt an ache of tiredness in my back. 'It's just a few songs while people drink tea, not a three-hour set at the O2.'

'That's not the point, sis. You're asking me to do something I've expressly told you I'm not happy doing any more.'

'Oh, for goodness sake.' I was suddenly close to crying. 'You just wait until you're in front of a bunch of spotty students, you'll soon be wishing you were back on the road.'

'How do you know that?' Rob's colour deepened as he fidgeted his glasses back into place. 'You don't know what I want. When did you last even talk to me properly?'

'What?' Shock stilled the urge to weep. Rob and I had always bickered whenever we were in the same room, but there'd never been anything malicious in it. Now, he looked as though he'd like to shove me over. 'I'm always WhatsApping you,' I said. 'And we FaceTime.'

'Yeah, thank god for technology.' His tone rocked me to my core. Rob didn't do bitterness – at least not with me. 'I'd probably never have heard from you otherwise.'

'But… we've been busy with our lives.' A fluttering feeling started up in my chest. I couldn't be having this conversation, not now. 'I thought you were out there having a brilliant time, not sitting around waiting for your sister to call.'

'I wasn't "sitting around".' His arms dropped to his sides. 'I missed you, that's all.' His eyes were big and shiny behind his glasses, reminding me of when he'd cried after a routine eye test, aged seven, had revealed his long-sightedness, and he'd worried his friends would laugh at him in his glasses. 'Look, forget it,' he said, appearing to cave in. 'I'll borrow Fletch's guitar and do a couple of numbers, if that's what you want, though I'm not as good on the guitar as I am on the keyboard.'

'No, wait.' Flooded with guilt that he was willing to capitulate to please me, I held out my hand. 'It's OK,' I said. 'They don't need music to drink tea by. I'm just being silly.'

'No, you want things to go well, and I'm being a bit of a twat.'

'No, you're sticking to your guns,' I insisted, relieved he seemed like his usual self again. I tugged the sleeve of his baggy shirt. 'Thanks for offering though.'

'Cassie, if a customer wants to sample *all* the teas, how does that actually work?'

I turned to see Mum's head poking round the door.

'Have people turned up?'

'Yes,' she said, eyebrows high. 'We're nearly full. I was thinking of asking Gwen to come in.'

'No need,' I said, too quickly. 'We'll come and help.' I looked at Rob, willing him to be OK.

He gave a rueful smile. 'I can wash spoons or something, I suppose.'

'Or take some photos to put on the website,' I said, thinking too late that I should have invited someone from the local paper to cover the event. The words *EPIC FAIL* flashed through my head in lights. I couldn't believe I'd taken my eye off the ball, when I'd usually been so meticulous in the past, checking and double-checking every detail. 'Let's go.'

Although the café wasn't quite as busy as I'd seen it during the day, I was pleased to see people were still trickling in, looking a bit furtive, as if turning up to an illegal cage fight.

Meg, behind the counter, looked fresh and pretty in her blue-and-white floral tea dress and gave me a thumbs up, which I returned – even if it was a little shaky. Pushing aside my altercation with Rob, I watched a well-dressed couple squeezing themselves in at a table – Dad had been right, the tables *were* too close together – and settled down to study the menu. The woman called Dad over, and after they'd spoken he pointed me out, then beckoned me over with a curl of his finger.

Oh god. I tried to remember what I'd read about the origins of the different drinks, mumbling under my breath as I approached the table. 'The Fadenza coffee is from a small region of Brazil and has been processed using the honey method, offering complex flavours of...' Of what? Butternut squash? And was it Brazil, or Peru? And what the hell were peaberries?

'They were asking who designed the menu,' Dad said, helping me round a tight cluster of chairs. 'I told them it was my clever daughter.'

'Oh.' Thrown, I looked at the woman, who was probably around forty, with a glamorous sweep of auburn hair and so many freckles they'd melted into splodges.

'I'm throwing a golden wedding anniversary for my parents later this year,' she said, smiling pleasantly.

My heart started racing. I'd hoped people might ask who'd organised the evening without me having to network too much, but hadn't expected it to happen right away. 'You'd like me to plan it for you?' A blend of excitement and dread rose in my gullet as I flipped my checklist over and unclipped my pen. 'Did you have a theme in mind?'

Her brow wrinkled and she exchanged a look with her partner, as if checking she'd been speaking plain English. 'That's all in hand,' she said, returning her gaze to me. 'I was wondering whether you'd be interested in designing the invitations.'

'Invitations.' I scribbled on my pad, to buy myself a moment. Literally, scribbled, as I tried to make sense of her request. 'Of course,' I said perkily, slamming the pad to my chest so she couldn't see my squiggles. 'I'd love to.'

'Great!' She was all smiles again. 'Do you have a business card?'

'I, er, not on me at the moment.' I patted my backside, as if I normally carried hundreds of them in my pocket. 'I'm actually in the process of getting some new ones printed.' At least that much was true. Almost. 'Why don't you give me your number, and I'll call you to discuss details?' *What was I doing?*

'Sure.' She reeled it off, along with her name, and I dutifully wrote it all down. 'Brilliant,' she said, beaming at her partner, who beamed right back, and as Dad was beaming too it seemed only fitting that I joined in, even though I was thinking, *What the HELL?* Designing golden wedding invitations wasn't even on my list of things to do, but it was a job of sorts, and I wasn't exactly in a position to turn down work.

'Won't you be back in London by then?' Dad had stopped beaming and was looking puzzled, but luckily the woman spoke at the same time and I didn't have to reply.

'Could I taste the lemongrass and dill tea? And my husband wants to try the Peruvian coffee.' She gave him a wicked grin. 'He likes a challenge.'

'Of course.' I snapped back to the current event. 'The tea is... well, the flavours speak for themselves, and the coffee is...' *What is it, Cassie?* 'It's earthy,' I improvised, 'with quite a kick.' I mimed a little kicking motion, narrowly missing her slender shin. 'Dad, could you bring the tasters over?' I grabbed his arm for support as I edged round the table on tiptoe, trying not to stand on bags and shoes as a group of women crowded round, pulling their chairs closer together to look at the menu.

'This is cute,' I heard one of them say. 'Wish I was artistic.'

'You're good at painting the town red,' said another, and they burst out laughing, even though it wasn't very funny.

'Mum, do you still have a radio out the back, or a music player somewhere?'

'What?' She looked up from straining tea into a cardboard takeaway cup, and some of it dripped down the side. It was bright red, like fresh blood, but the customer seemed entranced, inhaling the steam as though trying to clear his sinuses.

'Radio?'

She shook her head and I suppressed a sigh as I went to join her and Meg, who was slicing her Bakewell tart into even slices. Maybe it was better without music, I thought, seeing everyone was entering into the spirit of things, discussing and comparing flavours and appearing to be enjoying the novelty of it all.

Music might have been a distraction, now I thought about it.

Think through every aspect of the event, and make sure you've judged it correctly. Carlotta's voice this time. No wonder she'd been bad-tempered, thinking about it. All that thinking and judging.

'Do I have to spit it out, like wine?' someone was asking, and I hastily shook my head when Mum turned querying eyes my way.

'That coffee's rank,' said a man with a face like a bulldog, screwing up his nose in disgust. 'I think I'll stick with my usual espresso, please.'

'Oh, we're not serving our usual drinks this evening,' Dad said, looking a bit hot and bothered. 'Only the new stuff.'

The man opted to taste one of Meg's muffins instead, not bothering to sit down before biting into it, spilling crumbs down his shirt.

'How much are you charging for those?' I asked her.

She put down the knife she'd been using. 'I thought everything was free.'

'*What?*' I looked around at the rapidly filling café, with a cold, tight feeling in my stomach. The idea had been for customers to taste the drinks and then order a cup of their favourite and pay in the usual way – *Had I put prices on the menu?* – but now I noticed people were tasting all the flavours on offer before helping themselves to cake, and not parting with any cash.

'Were they supposed to pay?' Meg looked a bit panicked, and I tried to remember whether I'd spelt things out – another golden rule of event planning – and they'd just forgotten, or the words had stayed in my head.

It's fine, don't worry,' I said, twirling my ponytail round my finger as I paced behind the counter, getting in everyone's way. It didn't seem right that Mum and Dad were now losing money, but it felt too late to start asking people to cough up. I'd have to cover the cost of the evening out of my own rapidly depleting pocket.

'Mum, are you getting everyone to make a note of their favourite drink so you can stock it in future?' I said, as she reached past me for another cup.

She froze, as though she'd spotted a rat. 'Was I meant to?'

Oh, help. 'That was the general idea.' I'd run her through it when I'd arrived with her change of clothes, even writing down the flavours so that she and Dad could put ticks against each one. I glanced at the pad, which was still sitting by the hot-water dispenser, and mashed my palm against my forehead. 'How will you know which ones to order, if you don't know what's popular?'

'Ah.' She looked at the packet of tea in her other hand. 'I thought it was just a novelty thing, not that we were going to be *buying* any.'

'You won't be buying *all* of them,' I said, going dizzy as Rob spun me round on his way to help Dad, whose face had gone all shiny from the steam. 'Just the ones that people like the most.'

'Apparently, this one tastes like dishwater.' She waggled the packet with the expression of a Labrador hoping to please its mistress.

'Oh, *Mum.*'

'Don't get cross with your mother,' Dad scolded, chucking an empty coffee-bean packet in the direction of the bin.

'Don't throw that away, it has the provenance on the back.'

'I don't think anyone's interested in the coffee's upbringing, they just want to drink it,' he said, pausing to watch a man pulling a face as he drank. 'Or not.' He winked at a wild-eyed pensioner who was asking for another taste of 'the one like nectar'. 'She's already had four of those,' he said round the side of his hand. 'She's completely wired.'

'Dad! Just one taste, like I said, or there won't be any left for anyone else to try.' Despair flowed through me, and not even the sight of Tilly's friendly face, as she approached the counter, could dispel the feeling that I'd made a terrible mistake.

'How's it going?' she called, above the rising babble.

'Great!' I replied with a wave, envying the easy way she greeted people, and how they responded, seeming to light up in her presence. 'Try some cinnamon and ginger tea.'

Mum poured her half a cup – far too much for a taste – and Tilly swilled it around her mouth and nodded her approval. 'I like that,' she said, when she'd swallowed. 'Make sure you get some in.'

'Really?' Mum made a face. 'It's quite expensive.'

'Mum! You're not supposed to say things like that.'

'It's only Tilly,' she said. 'And, anyway, it *is* too expensive.'

Resisting the urge to stamp my foot and scream, I somehow arranged my face in an understanding smile, in case someone was thinking they'd like to host a similar event – but better – and wanted to know who'd arranged this one.

'It would be better if it was cocktails,' said one of the women whose foot I'd almost trodden on earlier. 'And if there was music,' added her friend, who'd clearly tasted too many of the stronger coffees, judging by her jittery arm movements.

'They've really missed a trick, haven't they?' Now one of the other females was joining in, glancing at her watch with a dissatisfied look. 'Can't even sit outside, 'cos it's pissing down.'

'We should go to the Smugglers Inn later on, they've got karaoke tonight.'

I caught Tilly's sympathetic look, and gave a 'what can you do?' shrug, careful to keep smiling even though my head was starting to thump. What I wanted to do was go home. What I needed to do was start networking, but I couldn't seem to summon the energy.

'Cassie, how do you pronounce this?' Dad was waving a packet of Himalayan coffee beans at me. 'Claude reckons it's Hula,' he said, winking at a big-bellied man with a huge white beard, who looked like he should be unloading Christmas gifts from a sack.

I peered at the letters. *Huila.* 'Erm, I can't help you there, I'm afraid,' I said, wishing he'd asked me something I could answer.

'Cassie, did you order anything decaffeinated?' Mum tapped my arm. 'Stop that,' she said, and I realised I was raking my itchy wrist with my fingernails.

'Sorry, no, I thought I had,' I said, 'but if there's nothing there then… No, sorry.'

The room was spinning. It was hot and my clothes felt too tight. I headed for the terrace, not caring that it was raining, just desperate to get outside, but was stopped in my tracks by the sound of a Spanish guitar being played with expert precision.

Around me, the chatter died away, and I turned with everyone else to look for the source of the music. It was Rodney's Dad, sitting on one of the tables, head lowered over his instrument, the fingers of one hand plucking the strings while the other hand danced gracefully over the frets. His face was curtained by hair, but it was obvious the effects of whatever he'd taken earlier had worn off.

Astonished out of my panic, I looked at Rob, and saw that he looked as stunned as everyone else. We exchanged relieved smiles, and as the music danced around the café, pulling everyone towards the source like a magnet, some of my tension evaporated.

Every event needs a 'wow' moment that people will remember.

I looked at the rapt expressions on the faces around me, and knew that this was it. Smiling, I backed to the counter, careering sideways when I came up against something solid.

A strong pair of arms shot out to catch me just before I hit the floor. 'Falling for me already?' said Danny Fleetwood.

Chapter 17

I hurried down the ribbon of path to the beach, wrenching my ponytail free of its band so that my hair lashed round my face in the rain-soaked wind.

'Hang on, where are you going?' called Danny behind me, but I didn't stop until I was panting on the sand, with nothing but the darkening sky above and the steely glitter of the sea stretched out in front of me.

'I'm fine,' I said, as Danny caught up, not sure how to explain that the feel of his hands on my arms as he'd steadied me, combined with the music and heat of the café had sent my emotions into a tailspin. Frantic to escape, I'd mumbled that I had a headache before fleeing.

'I don't normally have such a dramatic effect on women,' he said, facing the sea alongside me, not even slightly out of breath. 'They normally run *into* my arms, not sprint in the opposite direction.'

'You're pretty full of yourself, aren't you?' Hugging my arms around my waist, I turned to look at his annoyingly perfect profile, wondering exactly how many girlfriends he'd had. 'Why are you wasting your time trying to "win me over" when you can obviously have your pick?'

'Hey, lighten up.' Bending his knees so our shoulders were level, he gave me a gentle nudge. 'I was only joking, Cassie.'

The collar of his woollen jacket smelt damp and his stubble glistened with raindrops. The rain was falling steadily, flattening our hair to our scalps, but where it didn't detract from his good looks, the drowned-rat look didn't flatter my egg-shaped head.

'Sure you're OK?'

Keen to escape his scrutiny, I fixed my gaze ahead as if hypnotised by the waves. 'Why wouldn't I be?'

'You seemed a bit tense back there.'

'Of course I was,' I said, wondering how long he'd been watching me. 'Events are always nerve-wracking.'

'Even a small one like that?' He turned, and I glanced over my shoulder at the brightly lit café, where silhouettes of people were bobbing about. Faint guitar music drifted down, faster than before, and I imagined everyone dancing and wished I'd not let my nerves get the better of me. I'd caught a glimpse of Meg's startled face as I shot past and heard Tilly call my name, but hadn't looked back.

'There's more pressure when it's family,' I said.

'You want to be careful of that.'

'Sorry?'

'Pressure. It can do bad things to a person.'

What did he know about pressure with his casual approach to work? 'Pressure produces diamonds,' I said, citing Carlotta, who'd been as fond of a pointless sound bite as Nina was of inspirational quotes.

'It can also burst a pipe.' Danny flipped up an eyebrow, and looked as if he was waiting for me to appreciate this startling insight.

Hoping for a quick exit from the conversation, I said, 'Thanks for doing the sign for tonight's event.' I hadn't noticed it until I'd arrived at the café. A sandwich board, with the words *Taster Session tonight, courtesy of Cassie Maitland. Come and wet your whistle between 7 and 9 p.m.* written in swirly script.

'My pleasure. I'll do one for your cat day too, if you like.'

'How did you know about that?' I realised as soon as I said it that Nan must have told him.

'Sylvia mentioned it,' he confirmed. 'I volunteer at the shelter sometimes, so I called and put in a good word for you.'

'Which good word, when you don't even know me?' I couldn't help making the dig again, thinking how little he really did know.

His eyes sprang wide with surprise. 'I said you'd had lots of experience at arranging these sorts of events, and that the cats would be in safe hands.'

For some reason, while he was speaking, I was imagining us in a soapy embrace in the shower. Chasing the image away I said, 'I wouldn't say *lots* of experience.'

'You don't have to pretend to be modest.' I felt the weight of his gaze again. 'Your parents are obviously proud of you for a reason.'

They wouldn't be if they knew I'd been fired. 'All parents are proud of their children's achievements.'

'Not true,' he said. 'I know plenty who aren't, and for good reason.'

'Speaking from experience?'

He was silent for a moment, and I wondered if I'd gone too far. I didn't want to encourage him, but I was coming across like a bitch.

'My parents are proud,' he said lightly. 'But they're not the type to shout about it.'

'Like mine, you mean?'

'I wasn't saying that. God you're touchy.' He gave a little laugh. 'I'm really going to have my work cut out, persuading you I'm worth getting to know.'

I gave a snort. 'You're full of it, Danny Fleetwood.'

'If you mean good intentions, then yes, I am. Hopefully, I can convince you of that over a meal tomorrow night.'

'No, thanks, and anyway, I can't.' I rubbed my upper arms. My thin, wet blouse was no match for the bracing wind wrinkling the sea into creamy-white peaks. 'I've arranged a games evening at the café.'

'Sounds fun.' His lips curved into a smile. *Why did I keep looking at his lips?* 'I'm lethal at Scrabble.'

The thought of him coming to the games night made my wrist itch again. 'Won't you be working at the restaurant?'

'Night off,' he said. 'I could bring my mum.'

'Great.'

Apparently choosing to ignore my sarcastic tone, he said, 'What about Thursday? I'll cook you the best meal you've ever had.'

My heart did a great big bounce. 'I've already told you, you're wasting your time with me.'

'But you will at least come for a meal?'

I sighed. 'I've arranged a comedy night on Thursday, at the Smugglers Inn. Andy Farrington. It's on the website.'

'Ah, yes, the comedy night.'

I didn't bother asking how he knew. He clearly knew everything. 'He's good,' I said. 'He did a big charity gig I was at last year in London.'

'Oh, I know who Andy Farrington is.'

Confused by Danny's mischievous tone, I said, 'Well... good for you.'

'I guess it'll have to be Friday, then. The meal, I mean.'

'Fine, whatever.' I puffed the words out on a sigh as I stamped my feet on the sand. My teeth had started to chatter and, before I could object, Danny had removed his jacket and swung it around my shoulders. The lining was warm, and held the scent of him, and – in spite of myself – I snuggled into it.

'Let's get you back inside before you catch cold,' he said, turning and leading the way back to the path. 'Unless you'd like me to walk you home?' It was almost as if he'd sensed my reluctance to go back into the café.

'Thanks, but I've got the car,' I said. 'Plus, I should really stay for a bit and help my parents clear up.'

'I'm sure they'll manage without you.'

'This wasn't their idea,' I said, watching his outline in front of me, pushing along with easy strides while I puffed behind in my slippery-soled black loafers. 'They'll be wanting to get off home.'

He stopped suddenly, halfway up the path. 'Aren't they on board with your plan to "boost their business"?'

Why had he emphasised the words? Had Mum and Dad said something? 'I'm doing it for their benefit.'

'I didn't say you weren't.' He turned to face me, but I couldn't read his expression in the failing light. 'But I got the impression they thought you were here on holiday.'

For god's sake. Why did they have to talk about me to *everyone*?

'But they want to help,' he said.

'Oh, they want to *help*, do they?' I had no idea why my voice had risen an incredulous semitone. 'I'm the one doing *them* a favour, not the other way round.'

The wind had dropped and the silence that fell was a solid wedge between us. Behind him, I noticed that Meg and Tilly had come out onto the terrace and were looking over, their faces a pale blank gleam.

'I guess you're helping each other,' Danny said finally, and I switched my gaze back to his shadowy frame. 'That's what families do, isn't it?'

'Families are a pain in the behind.'

'Don't take your family for granted, Cassie, they're part of your history, of who you are.'

Ashamed of my snappy tone, I said, 'I suppose so. It's just… ' I looked at my shoes, which were covered in sand.

'Just what?'

'It's hard work, that's all… ' *Pretending I haven't potentially messed up my future.* 'If I'm going to be my own boss, I need to put myself out there. I can't afford to lounge around doing nothing while I'm here, especially as Mum and Dad think I'm going back to London soon.'

'Aren't you?'

'Well, yes, but…' Unwilling to admit that I currently had no home there, I said vaguely, 'I was thinking of New York, too. I lived there for a while and know a few people.' *None who'd be willing to offer me a free home.*

'I quite fancy visiting New York.' He grinned, and although I had the feeling it wasn't what he'd intended to say, I was relieved when he didn't pursue it. For a horrible moment, I'd felt a dragging desire to tell the truth about everything and, as he continued on his way, I lagged behind so there were no more opportunities for conversation.

♥

Everyone seemed subdued the following morning. I'd risen early, determined to have breakfast with my family before they left the house, but attempts to analyse the evening's event were met with a lacklustre response.

'It went very well, love,' was Mum's best offer.

Dad's was worse. 'I ache all over this morning,' he said, moving stiffly with his hand pressed in the small of his back. 'Those extra couple of hours made a real difference.'

Maybe their lack of enthusiasm was because, in the end, I hadn't been able to face following Danny back into the café – even to return his jacket. I'd invented a migraine for Meg and Tilly's benefit, my bedraggled appearance adding credence to the lie. Although it hadn't been a total lie, as my head really had been pounding. They'd been touchingly sympathetic, with Meg promising to tell my parents I'd had to go home, and when Mum had stuck her head round my bedroom door just after ten, I'd pretended to be asleep.

'Rodney's Dad demanded two hundred quid,' Rob said, once Mum and Dad had left for work, their goodbyes to me accompanied by worried smiles and admonishments to 'take it easy' because I was 'obviously very tired'.

'*Two hundred quid?*' I almost dropped my coffee mug. 'You didn't pay him?'

Rob shook his head.

'Mum did, though.'

'WHAT?' I clattered my mug onto the table. 'The little shit,' I stormed, pushing my fingers through my bed-tangled hair. 'Considering the state he was in when he arrived, he's got a bloody nerve. I mean, he came good in the end, and he'll probably get more bookings on the back of that performance, but he should be thanking us for giving him a second chance, not demanding cash. In fact, I've a good mind to call him—'

'Dial it down, sis,' Rob said calmly, placing his cereal bowl in the sink. He still ate Cheerios for breakfast, like he had when he was ten. 'I told him I'd tell his granddad about his little habit if he didn't give back at least a hundred and fifty.'

'And did he?' I seemed to be angry out of all proportion, my heart banging too hard in my chest. I imagined leaping on Fletcher and pummelling him to the ground, then bashing him over the head with his guitar.

'Yes, he did.' Rob took off his glasses and cleaned them on the hem of his shirt. 'I said he could keep forty, to pay for his petrol.'

I glared at him. 'Why didn't you lead with that, instead of letting me get all worked up?'

'Didn't take much, did it?' he said, replacing his glasses and leaning back against the worktop. 'Maybe you *should* be taking a holiday, instead of working while you're here.' His reprimanding tone gave me a crippling sense of inadequacy. Far from being impressed by my endeavours, everyone seemed to be worried about me. Hardly the effect I'd been hoping for.

I picked up my mug and took a careful sip of coffee to prove that I was fine. 'It went well though, didn't it?' I said. 'Eventually, I mean?'

'It could have been worse,' Rob acknowledged. 'I don't think it's really Mum and Dad's kind of thing, though. Expensive brands of tea and coffee, I mean. They liked the guitar playing.'

Bloody hell. That was the bit I'd had nothing to do with, other than to pester Rob with sibling blackmail, and Rodney's Dad could have died from whatever he'd taken, now I thought about it. 'What if customers start requesting the tastier brands?' I said, attempting to keep my cool.

Rob picked up a slice of cold toast and took a bite. 'Mum and Dad will have to order them in, they won't have any choice,' he said, through a mouthful.

'You make it sound like a chore.'

'Well, it's not like they asked for any changes, is it?' he said reasonably.

'We're talking about stocking new flavours, not bulldozing the café and building a brothel.'

Rob looked like he was picturing it for a moment. 'Yeah, but they're pretty set in their ways,' he said. 'Remember, you and me were the ones who were supposed to escape the drudgery and set the world alight with our brilliance.'

'They did used to go on about it, didn't they?' I said. 'Especially Mum.'

He shrugged. 'Parents want their kids' lives to be different from theirs. If theirs has been unhappy, I mean.'

I put my mug down again. 'Mum and Dad *are* happy.'

'They are *now*, but they weren't when they were younger, with Mum's mum being sick all the time, and Dad having to pick up the pieces with Nan whenever Gramps had another one of his flings, and getting caught in the middle of it all.'

I stared at him, wondering whether he really *had* been in therapy. There'd been a time he hadn't even known our parents' first names were Edmund and Lydia – he'd just thought of them as Mum and Dad.

'I know that's why they pushed for us to get away, and that they were terrified of placing demands on us, but that didn't mean we were going to end up happier, did it?'

'No, but at least I gave it a good shot,' Rob said, and I realised he thought I was referring only to his happiness, not my own. And why wouldn't he, when I kept banging on about how brilliant my life was?

I suddenly remembered him calling in to see me, just after I'd finished working on a fashion gala attended by pop stars, models and magazine editors, and I was on a high, despite hardly any sleep. He'd been heading to Amsterdam with X-Y-Zed and, thinking back, he'd mentioned that Emma wasn't happy about him going away, and I'd said something catty about her having to suck it up.

Guilt jabbed beneath my ribs as I wondered about the conversations we hadn't had over the last few years. What would we have talked about? Would he have admitted he was struggling?

Would I?

'Listen, Rob, I'm sorry I wasn't in touch with you more while you were away. I had no idea you weren't enjoying your life.'

He swallowed more toast and went a bit pink around the ears. 'No worries,' he said. 'I could have called you, I suppose, but I knew you were busy all the time, and, anyway, it's not easy to… you know.' He scratched his nose. 'Admit you're not doing well. Emotionally, I mean.'

'No,' I agreed. Hopeless tears welled and I blinked and stared hard at the table.

'Hey, it's OK. I'm good now, I promise.' The fact that he was at pains to make me feel better, only made me feel worse. 'Better than I've ever been, in fact.'

Something about the tenor of his voice brought my head up. His face was a watery blur, and I blinked to clear my vision. 'How so?'

His eyes were as shiny as marbles. 'I haven't said anything yet because Emma doesn't want anyone to know until she's past twelve weeks, and she still wants to be sure I'm going to stay around—'

'Oh good god.'

'She's pregnant, Sandra.' His grin was wide enough to split his face. 'I'm going to be a dad.'

Chapter 18

'You're going to be an auntie,' Rob continued, as I stared in stupefied silence. 'Mum and Dad are going to be grandparents, Nan's going to be a—'

'Great-grandmother, I get it.' A show reel of images flashed through my head: Mum knitting baby clothes, though she'd never knitted in her life, for a scrunch-faced baby with Rob's hair; me reading bedtime stories to a dimple-cheeked toddler; Rob pushing a baby stroller around Seashell Cove, Bossy Emma clinging to his arm, issuing instructions.

I'd have to pretend to like her.

I'd have to learn how to change a nappy for babysitting duties.

I'd need somewhere to live so my niece or nephew could come and stay.

I needed a proper job to pay for somewhere to live—

'Sandra?'

My escalating thoughts screeched to a halt. 'How did that even happen?' I said, in a daze.

'Well,' Rob adopted a wise-man expression, 'when a lady and gentleman are attracted to each other…'

I tutted. 'I mean, you've only been back five minutes, how have you managed to conceive a child?'

He pulled the crust off the last piece of toast and rolled it between finger and thumb. 'Ah, well, we might have met up when I was, you know, having a bit of a meltdown. She came out to Berlin to see me a couple of months ago and… well, one thing led to another.' He glanced at my face. 'We were boyfriend and girlfriend, she didn't take advantage of me, or anything.'

'So, how come you're "on a break" if she's pregnant?' I said.

'Because, I've promised her in the past that I was going to give up the band, but never did it.'

'So you *are* doing it to make her happy.'

'No, Sandra, I'm not. I left because *I* wasn't happy.' He jabbed his chest. 'And I want to be with Emma. But I'd said it before and didn't stick to it, so I need to show her I'm serious this time.'

'Well, obviously you're going to stick around if she's having your baby.'

'That's not the only reason.' He looked mildly offended that I might think otherwise. 'The baby's just the icing on the cake.'

'But, you're not even thirty.' I was struggling to take it in. 'People don't become parents until they're in their forties, these days.'

'Fine, if that's what they want, but this is what *I* want.'

'What about Mum and Dad?' I studied his face for a hint of doubt, or indecision, or even a trace of panic – had Bossy Emma trapped him by getting pregnant on purpose? – but I could only see the same look he'd had the year he got his own computer for Christmas. 'I doubt becoming grandparents is on their list of things to look forward to this year.'

'Maybe not, but it's happening, and they'll be happy for me.'

I tried to swallow, but it felt like I had a pellet stuck in my throat. My little brother was going to be a *dad*. He'd be getting married next, and would be working as an IT tutor by the time the baby was born, with a proper income and everything. He'd be living with Bossy Emma, probably cooking her dinner every evening, while she pumped breast-milk for him to feed the baby in the night. My brother was a grown-up who knew what he wanted and had been brave enough to say so.

'I guess congratulations are in order.' I said it with such loud, bright energy he jumped. 'Sure you don't want to tell the parents, yet?'

'No, and you'd better not either.' He threw the mangled toast crust back on the plate. 'I shouldn't have said anything really, but you looked like you needed cheering up.'

'And you thought providing me with proof of how fertile you are would do the trick?' I lobbed the crust back at him. 'Thanks a billion, bro.'

He ducked and picked up his rucksack, a grin all over his face. 'I wanted you to know, anyway,' he said. 'We always told each other stuff like that when we were kids.'

'I don't remember ever telling you I was with child.'

He pretended to gag. 'That's revolting.'

'You're going to be late for class… *Dad*.'

'Please, don't call me that in front of anyone.'

'I won't,' I promised, letting his secret settle in. 'Now, go. You've a sensible, pension-clad, nappy-changing, slipper-wearing future to work towards.'

He gave me the finger and left, and I stood for a full two minutes, staring at the door, the words 'Rob's having a baby' revolving around my head.

On balance, I decided I was glad he'd told me. It showed he'd forgiven me for neglecting to stay in touch, and hinted at an improved relationship between us in future. Providing I didn't let anything slip in front of Mum and Dad, which shouldn't be too difficult. After all, I was good at hiding things from them.

Unsure what to do with myself once I'd got dressed, and had smothered my itchy wrist rash in some more antiseptic cream, I logged on to the café's Facebook page to see if there'd been any feedback from the night before.

Nothing. No comments on the classy new website either, and only a few likes on Twitter, but someone had posted a photo of Rodney's Dad on Instagram with the hashtags *guitarmagic* and *whoisthisguy.* Shame no one had mentioned the tea- and coffee-tasting, but what had I expected? *Amazing event organised by Cassie Maitland #best-nightever?* I should have taken some photos myself and posted them up, but I wasn't very good with a camera. I'd once chopped the heads off some guests at a footballer's wedding reception in a publicity shot for the website.

I updated Facebook and Twitter with: *Games Night – bring your board game to Maitland's Café at 7 p.m. for another fun-filled event.* I added a couple of celebration emojis, took them out, added: *Come early or all the Monopoly seats will be taken*, then deleted it because it didn't make sense, and wondered why I was finding it so difficult to do the things I'd had no trouble with at Five Star.

Hopefully, Mum and Dad would spread the word, and the older customers at least – nostalgic for days when tablets were things you took for a headache and people weren't glued to their phones – would turn up in their droves. In the meantime, I should go down there and subtly network, without alerting Mum and Dad, who still believed I should be 'relaxing'.

On a whim, I gathered my sketch pad and coloured pencils, and shoved them into my bag, then pushed my feet in a pair of low-heeled ankle boots, which looked good with my freshly washed jeans and a pink cashmere jumper. With my hair styled in a bun, and subtle make-up to hide the troughs beneath my eyes (despite being worn out, I hadn't slept well), I looked like the sort of person that people might want to arrange a party or corporate event with – if people in this part of the country bothered with corporate events.

Outside, the weather had brightened and, although there was still a cool breeze, the sun was sliding between chalky-white clouds and the sky in between was blue. I decided to walk to the café, taking the shortcut. I fidgeted with my bun, which the wind seemed determined to loosen, and halted when I caught sight of Danny's van in a corner of the car park. Perhaps he'd come to pick up his jacket, which I'd left hanging over the arm of the chair in my bedroom. There was no other reason for him to be there when he lived in Kingsbridge, and was presumably still doing odd jobs for Nan.

I wished my heart would stop leaping whenever he was around, or even if I thought about him. Which I definitely hadn't been doing – at least, not since I'd clambered out of bed that morning. And even before that, tossing about in the darkness, the only reason he'd been at the forefront of my mind was because I'd kept returning to our conversation on the beach, and wondering whether he'd discussed me with my parents. I should have asked them outright, but it sounded so childish and needy.

Has Danny Fleetwood said anything to you since I came home, and if so what, and what did you say back? Pathetic. And, OK, I might have thought about his eyes a bit, as I drifted into a doze around dawn, but only because they were such a nice colour and always looked smiley.

Now I was thinking about his eyes again, and those little smile lines at the corners, and the way he'd looked at me when he stopped me from crashing to the floor in the café – as though he'd caught a Ming vase in the nick of time.

Adjusting my bag, which seemed to have grown heavier while I was walking, I decided to wait until he'd gone. I turned to look at the wide blue horizon of sea and sky that seemed to blend into one, moving aside as a gaggle of colourful women approached, laughing, arms swinging, and when they'd passed with cheery 'good mornings' I sat on the grass and took out my sketch pad. A couple of yachts had appeared on the water, zigzagging between frothy waves, sails blossoming in the breeze, and taking out my coloured pencils I drew quickly, absorbed in the simple motion of moving my hand over the paper, bringing to life the scene in front of me, layering on colours, carried away on a rush of enthusiasm.

I added some final flourishes, startled when something tickled my face. I brushed it away, realising it was my own hair. My bun had collapsed, but I couldn't be bothered to sort it out. Instead, I studied my drawing, enjoying how the yachts seemed to be racing each other, and how every aspect of the scene had personality: the boats looked cheeky as the bucking blue sea urged them on, the clouds smiling down benignly from a cornflower sky. It was a slightly exaggerated view, which, Miss Finch had once pointed out, seemed to be my speciality, if it could be called that: to slightly distort and enhance, but still retain a likeness.

Pleased with the result, I sat a few moments longer, enjoying the air on my face and the fact that my head felt lighter. Shielding my eyes as the sun slid out once more, I glanced back at the café and saw that Danny's van had gone.

Unsure whether my initial reaction was relief or disappointment, and unwilling to examine it further, I thrust my things into my bag and stood up, aware of a creeping wetness through my jeans. Craning my neck, I saw a damp patch across my bottom, which was also covered in grass stains. Debating whether to go home and get changed, I spotted a glint of bright hair in the car park and realised it was Meg.

'Hey!' I scooped up my bag and hurried down the path, but by the time I reached the café she'd driven off in a little white Clio and was too far away to see me waving madly. Resolving to arrange a proper get-together soon, I stepped inside the café, instantly soothed by the ambient sounds of clattering plates and the whir of the coffee machine. The aroma of roasting beans, and the sight of Meg's cake of the day – lemon and coconut – propelled me straight to the counter, where Gwen was cleaning the area around the coffee machine as though preparing it for surgery.

'Have you seen my parents?' I said, surprised neither of them was serving.

'Out the back,' Gwen replied, without looking round. 'Be wiv you in a mo,' she added, presumably to the man standing next to me waving his bill.

'Whenever you're ready,' he said, cheerfully.

I was pleased to see the leftover boxes of tea and coffee from the night before lined up on display behind the counter.

'Has anyone ordered any?' I said, gesturing at them when Gwen paused her scrubbing to give me a suspicious glare.

'Nope.' She didn't even look to where I was pointing.

'You might have to ask people if they'd like to try them.'

Her face took on the look of a belligerent bulldog. 'Why would I do that?'

'Er, because they might not know about them otherwise?' I was starting to feel a bit belligerent myself.

'Got eyes in their 'eads, 'aven't they?'

Which charm school did you go to? I said, in my head. 'Is Meg coming back?'

'Nah, not today. Did extra hours last night, didn't she?' Another fierce glare. Maybe she was put out at not being asked to work. 'I 'eard the café took an 'it.'

'Sorry?' An image of a lit rag being chucked through the door sprang to mind.

'Lost revenue.' More glaring, accusatory this time.

I puffed out my cheeks and counted to five before releasing my breath. 'Could I please have a milky coffee and a slice of lemon-and-coconut cake?'

'TAMSIN!' Gwen bellowed, and the young waitress materialised, looking petrified.

'I'll bring it over,' she said, when she'd taken my order and tapped it into the till with a shaky finger. 'Where will you be sitting?'

I turned to look for an empty table, preferably by the window. I needed to engage in some covert networking about this evening's event, highlighting that refreshments would have to be paid for. My gaze snagged on the wall opposite the counter and my mouth dropped open.

How had I not noticed the artwork as soon as I'd walked in?

An eclectic mix of paintings and drawings in a variety of frames had been arranged in clusters along the length of the wall, and although not much thought had been put into their arrangement, they seemed to be attracting the attention of the people seated nearby – particularly a couple of caricatures I recognised.

In fact, there was nothing I didn't recognise, from the tree on its carpet of pink cherry blossom, to the stormy village scene, to the picture of woman with giant, horsey teeth and flaring nostrils, about to bite into a scone.

I recognised them, because I was the artist.

Chapter 19

'Who put those there?' I turned back to the counter, heart thumping as though I'd been chased.

Gwen had finished her cleaning and was peering at the customer's bill as though it was written in Sanskrit. 'Put what, where?' she said.

'The artwork?'

Her eyes twitched to the wall. 'Oh, those,' she said, as if she hadn't noticed the wall had been covered with pictures. 'That bloke wot painted the sign for the caff put 'em up,' she said. 'The fit one.'

I'd known she was going to say it before I asked – not the bit about Danny being fit, accompanied by an unpleasant leer – because who else could it have been?

'Dunno who the artist is, but she's got a way with a pencil, I'll give her that,' Gwen added, her sly look telling me she knew very well that the artist was me. 'I like the cartoon ones best.'

Having assumed she'd be at best indifferent, at worst scathing, my cheeks began to heat up – even though I was fuming with Danny for hanging the pictures without telling me, or even asking permission. 'Thanks,' I said, ungraciously.

'I like your exhibition,' Tamsin said shyly, her wide, grey gaze briefly landing on mine. 'I'd like to buy the one of a cat up a tree when I get paid, if no one else does.'

'Oh god, no, they're not for sale.' I was horrified by the thought.

'Why not?' said the customer who'd been shamelessly eavesdropping while paying his bill. 'Isn't that the point of an exhibition?'

'It's not really an exhibition.' *It's a motley collection of drawings and paintings that have been stuffed in my grandmother's attic for years.*

'My wife's got her eye on the stormy one,' the man said, turning to point it out. 'She likes a good storm, does Evelyn. Says it reminds her of the year our son was born.'

'How lovely.' A swell of emotion rose in my chest. Someone wanted to *buy* it?

Trying to look at the pictures as though they were nothing to do with me, I decided that maybe they didn't look too bad – even quite professional – from a distance. With my eyes half closed.

'How much?' the man said, cocking a bushy white eyebrow.

'Sorry?'

'For the storm?'

Flustered, I pulled up my sleeves, then tugged them down when I remembered the rash on my wrist. 'I, er, well… I…' *haven't got a clue.* What did artists (was I really calling myself an artist?) charge for their work? I could hardly whip out my phone and google it. 'Ummmm…' Scrunching up my face, I tried to remember whether I'd seen any prices on Vicky Burton's website, but drew a blank. I remembered that one of Connor Daley's paintings would have set me back £750, but there was no way I could even think about charging half that much.

'I think that one's a hundred and twenty.' Gwen's gravelly voice brought my tortured musing to an end. 'We 'ain't got round to putting the prices on yet. They only went up this morning, mate.'

'I suppose.' Mum sounded resigned now, but no longer tearful. 'It's just so much harder than I thought it would be.'

I scratched at my wrist, which only made the itch worse, and was about to go into the office and say something – though I had no idea what – when the door opened fully and Mum and Dad came out.

'Cassie, love!' Mum looked so delighted to see me I was momentarily taken aback. 'What are you doing out here?'

Eavesdropping. 'Just, erm…' I indicated vaguely in the direction of the store room.

'Did you see your paintings?' Dad joined her, placing a solid arm around her shoulders. 'Don't they look lovely?'

'You don't mind, do you?' Mum's voice had tensed up. 'I did wonder whether we should have asked you first.'

'Well…'

'Danny thought you'd say no if we did, so we let him go ahead.' Dad was smiling genially, and they both looked and sounded so normal I could almost believe I'd imagined the conversation in the office. 'He brought them from your nan's house.'

'I didn't realise she had them.' Mum's (unthreaded) eyebrows rose a fraction. 'We'd have loved to have hung them up at home.'

'You would?'

'Of course,' said Dad, his forehead wrinkling, as if it was perfectly obvious. 'You just never seemed that bothered, back then.'

'She never showed us her paintings, did she?' Mum said to Dad, but not in a way that indicated she was upset about it – just puzzled.

'Hardly ever,' Dad agreed.

It was true, I'd been secretive about my art. It wasn't that I'd been ashamed, it just felt private somehow, and showing people – apart from Nan – too revealing in a way I hadn't really understood. Also, although

I'd loved painting and drawing at the time, I didn't really believe I was any good. Not good enough to *become* an artist, like Vicky Burton and Connor Daley. It had never even occurred to me.

'I've sold one,' I said, trying not to look as if I was checking Mum's eyes. It was hard to see properly in the passageway, but there was no sign of any redness, and Dad's face was arranged in a pleasantly relaxed expression that looked totally natural.

'Already?' He exchanged happy looks with Mum. 'Cassie, that's wonderful!'

'I know,' I said, deciding that now wasn't the moment to confront them. I had a feeling they'd be embarrassed if they knew I'd been listening, and if they had something to tell me and Rob, or Nan, they'd do it in their own time. 'I've put one aside for Tamsin.'

'You're so clever.' Mum reached out to press her palms against my cheeks. They were slightly damp – the only hint that perhaps she wasn't as OK as she seemed on the surface. 'We're *so* proud of you.'

It was what she always said, and although it was good to hear, it felt a bit off somehow. Like when she'd praise a particularly wonky sandcastle when I young, or the burnt-round-the-edges fairy cakes I'd made at school. *I'm so proud of you, love, you're so clever.* Was she still humouring me? Being kind, just as she'd been back then, because it's what mums did?

Before I could ponder it any further, Gwen hollered Mum's name.

'Oops, duty calls,' Dad sang, and they bolted into the café as if suddenly remembering they had jobs there. I followed behind with the nagging feeling that things weren't what they seemed.

Chapter 20

A couple of hours later, another picture had sold (a still life of eggs, a mixing bowl and a bag of flour on Nan's worktop) and I'd had a couple of commissions – another dog painting, and a 'sunrise with lots of yellows' to hang in a newly built conservatory.

Slightly giddy – *when was I going to fit it all in?* – and mindful of my real purpose at the café, I made a point of subtly mentioning my real job now and then, but people seemed more interested in my artwork than whether or not I could arrange a party or event, so I quickly stopped bothering, happy to chat about my pictures. Several people wanted to know why I'd given up.

'If I could paint like that, I wouldn't be working in the post office,' one woman said rather crossly, as if the fact that she couldn't was somehow my fault.

'It was just a hobby, back then,' I found myself saying, as though I'd recently taken it up professionally. 'I've kept my hand in though.'

When things were quieter, I finally sat down with my slice of cake and a fresh cup of coffee, and discreetly spied on Mum and Dad. It seemed to be business as usual, Mum gossiping with a couple of regulars, while Dad trained Tamsin how to use the coffee machine. Gwen circled the tables with a cloth, hunting down stray crumbs, and I had to grab hold of my cup to stop her clearing it away.

Buzzing with adrenaline and caffeine I took out my pad, and, drawn by the sun now warming the windows, was about to slip out onto the terrace and do some sketching – I could always network at the games night this evening – when a boy came over and said, 'Can you do one of those of me?'

He swung his arm round to indicate the caricature of the horsey customer on the wall, in all her toothy magnificence. 'It's funny,' he said with a throaty giggle. He looked about seven, his rosy-cheeked face topped off with a sandy-coloured bowl-cut.

'My mum said I could ask.' He looked to where a woman with an almost identical hairstyle was approaching, pulling on a long, multicoloured garment like a blanket.

'Sorry,' she said, holding her hand out to the boy. 'I told him not to bother you.'

'No, you didn't,' he said, standing his ground. 'You said I could do what I wanted for the rest of the day, because I didn't bite the dentist this time.'

Through a crimson-faced smile, his mum said, 'Don't be silly, Jonty.'

'I want a funny picture.' He stamped his foot and wrapped his arms across his chest, tears welling in his conker-brown eyes.

People were staring and, keen to avert a full-scale meltdown, I nudged out the chair opposite with my foot. 'I don't mind,' I said to his mum. 'It won't take long, if you'd like to sit down, Jonty.'

His mum's blotchy face was washed with relief as Jonty obediently sat, all smiles now he'd got his own way. 'Thank you,' she said, dragging another chair over and arranging herself to watch. 'There wasn't much point taking him back to school after his dental appointment, and he's a bit bored.'

Nan used to say 'boredom's the mother of invention' if Rob and I had ever complained we had nothing to do – which wasn't often as we'd been good at amusing ourselves.

'No problem,' I said, choosing a 5B pencil for dark lines with an air of assurance that surprised me, considering I hadn't done this type of drawing for a while. 'Do you like school?' I asked Jonty, as I started to outline his features. He was sitting stiffly, head cocked – a bit like a ventriloquist's dummy with his unnatural grin – and I wanted to get a feel for his personality.

'I don't like sums, but I like writing stories the best,' he said, his features relaxing. He laced plump fingers in his lap. 'My teacher says to write my own, but it's easier if I copy from my Roald Dahl books, because they're proper.'

'Jonty hasn't quite grasped the concept, yet,' murmured his mum, craning her neck for a glimpse of my page, and I had to resist an urge to cover it with my forearm. 'His latest title, "James and the Giant Peach", was a bit of a giveaway.'

Hiding a smile, I drew quickly, picking out his hamster cheeks and slightly bulbous eyes, exaggerating his thatch of hair and widening his smile, while he chatted about his best friend's pet parrot, who made a noise like a ringing phone.

I'd never been sure whether caricatures were cruel, highlighting what might be deemed to be faults – a big nose, or jug-ears – but most people seemed to be flattered or find them hilarious.

'Oh, I love it,' his mum said, clapping her hands when I'd finished, scribbling my name in the corner with a flourish. I ripped out the sheet and handed it to her, and Jonty studied it and giggled with his hand over his mouth.

'Ooh, that's good,' said a passing woman. 'Will you do me?'

'How much?' asked Jonty's mum, rummaging out her purse. I was about to wave her away, when Gwen shouted from behind the counter, 'Special price for one day only, ten pounds, cash,' and, within the hour, I'd earned a handful of notes.

'You can do me for free if you like,' Gwen offered, as another satisfied customer departed, but not before showing the drawing to her partner, who laughed rather meanly and told me I'd captured her 'witchy' nose.

Gwen plonked herself on the vacated seat, sturdy legs akimbo, face mangled by a forbidding frown. 'Do your worst,' she said, placing her hands on meaty thighs that strained at the material of her trousers. 'I already look like a cartoon.'

Mum whirled past, a proud little smile on her face, and for a second I imagined that this was my career: tucked away in a corner of the café, drawing people for money.

'Is that it?' said Gwen when I'd finished, her mouth tugged down at the corners. I'd more or less drawn her straight, worried she'd lamp me if I exaggerated what was already pretty scary. 'Coward.'

But she took it anyway, and flashed it at Dad when he asked to see it.

'Wow, you really went to town there,' he chortled, stopping abruptly when he realised his mistake. 'It's almost four if you want to go and catch your bus,' he said, looking chastened, and Gwen vanished without another word.

By the time I got home, I felt as though I'd done a day's work, which was odd when I'd been sitting down for most of it, while Mum and Dad ran rings around me at the café.

When they arrived home half an hour later, I was on my laptop at the kitchen table, ordering a set of watercolour pencils, unusually energised. By contrast, they seemed tired, their usual cheerful banter noticeable by its absence.

'Everything OK?' I ventured, looking up as I completed my purchase. Mum had her head in the fridge, as if hoping a meal might magically assemble itself, while Dad was fiddling with the dials on the radio on the windowsill, flipping between stations. They both still had their coats on, and even their hair seemed less buoyant than usual.

'Fine,' Mum said, turning to flash me a smile that didn't quite reach her eyes.

'All good, Pumpkin.' Dad switched the radio off, and stared out of the window before moving across the kitchen and slapping the light on.

'What did you do that for?' Mum slammed the fridge and stamped over to turn the light off.

'Sorry, love, I thought it was a bit dark in here,' Dad said.

The sun had been swallowed by a tumble of grey clouds and, for the first time in hours, I remembered it was games night.

'Why don't you go and get ready and I'll cook something quick,' I suggested.

'Ready?' Poised by the doorway, they turned simultaneously to stare. I was reminded of a spooky film I'd once seen, about androids who looked like people, but didn't react normally.

'Ready for what?' Dad said blankly.

A ripple of apprehension ran down my spine. 'The games night?'

'Oh god, I'd forgotten about that.' Mum's expression morphed into dismay. 'I just can't face it, love.'

'What?' Shaken, it was my turn to stare. Mum always faced things. She'd been facing things for decades. 'It's only a few board games for a couple of hours,' I said, aware of a weakness around my knees, even though I was sitting down. 'I thought you were looking forward to it.'

'We did tell you that we liked our evenings in,' Dad said quietly, resting a hand on Mum's shoulder as if to stop her fleeing. 'Apart from quiz nights at the pub.'

'But...' I'd been going to say it was only one measly night, but they were looking at me almost timidly now, as if I might go ballistic and start chucking things around. 'Are you ill?' The words burst through my lips before I could stop them.

'Ill?' Dad looked at Mum, as though verifying he had the right word.

'Why would we be ill?' Mum's face crumpled. 'Do we look ill?' She rushed to the toaster and studied herself in the chrome surface. 'I don't think I look any different, do I?' She pulled at the skin on her cheeks. 'Maybe I should get my eyebrows done again, but it was *so* painful.'

'You're both being really weird,' I said, wondering whether to mention overhearing their earlier conversation. 'Is it Nan?'

'Nan?'

'Getting rid of her stuff and going environmental.' I decided not to mention the bit about her preparing to meet her maker, in case they didn't know.

'You know we fully support your nan,' Mum said, and Dad nodded his agreement.

'Why are you being off, then?'

'Oh, love, I'm sorry.' Mum rushed over and hugged me from behind. 'It's just that we were kept awake last night by... a noise, like an alarm going off somewhere outside, weren't we, Ed?' I sensed her looking at Dad for confirmation.

'That's right.' He nodded slowly, finally removing his anorak. 'Quite piercing.'

'I didn't hear it,' I said, not adding that I'd been awake half the night too.

'It was out the front of the house, maybe a car alarm.' It didn't stack up, but I was too relieved that neither of them appeared to be ill to contradict him. 'We're absolutely fine,' he added, nodding for emphasis. 'Aren't we, Lydia?'

Mum gave me a final squeeze before straightening up. 'Nothing a nice hot shower won't solve.'

'And of course we'll be there tonight.' Dad became jaunty, tossing his coat into the hall, but it missed the hook and crumpled onto the floor. 'It'll be fun.'

Mum nodded, but her smile had a slightly pinched quality and I was overcome with guilt. They'd been on their feet for most of the day and were clearly tired out. It wasn't fair to expect them to go back to work.

'You don't have to,' I said firmly. 'I'm sure we'll be able to manage on our own. Won't we Robbie Robot?' I said, as he came in, whistling.

'Manage what?' He threw his rucksack down and scanned our faces, and I guessed he was wondering whether I'd spilt his secret.

I threw him my best 'I promised I wouldn't tell and I meant it' look and, seeming to understand, he gave a little nod. 'The café, for a couple of hours this evening, so the parents can do whatever it is they do when they're alone.'

'Thanks for that image,' Rob said.

'Cassie,' Mum scolded. 'We certainly won't be doing anything lewd.'

'Lewd,' Rob repeated and sniggered.

'That's a disappointment,' Dad said, playfully tapping Mum's bottom as she went into the hall, and Rob made a grossed out face that made me giggle. I kept forgetting how nice it was, us all being together. How much I'd missed the in-jokes and shorthand of family life.

'Anyway, I can't,' he said. 'I'm seeing Emma tonight.' The look he gave me was loaded with significance. They must have baby stuff to moon about, and I could hardly argue with that.

'I've told you, we'll be there,' Dad said, rubbing his hands together. 'We want to support you.'

'No.' I'd made up my mind. It would be easier to network if they weren't around. 'Will Meg be coming in?'

'Yes, and Tamsin,' Mum said. 'She was keen for a couple of extra hours' work.'

'Then we'll be fine.'

'But—'

'Mum, I've helped in the café before, I can do it again.'

'But not for years, and you're supposed to be in charge of the event.'

'The event will take care of itself,' I said. I was beginning to wish I hadn't arranged the event in the first place. It would have been nice to crash out in front of the television and have a think about my painting commissions – Evelyn's daughter had already emailed a photo of Boo-Boo, a sad-eyed greyhound wearing a diamanté collar – but it was out of the question.

After a dinner of reheated macaroni cheese, I donned a work outfit of narrow black trousers and an ivory blouse with a pussy bow, and once I'd retrieved all the board games from the cupboard under the stairs and reassured Mum and Dad that I wouldn't set the café alight or let any burglars in, they handed over the keys with surprising ease. Rob had borrowed their car to drive to Emma's, and, as it was raining again, I took Sir Lancelot. I cursed the weather, worried that no one would bother turning out.

Meg and Tamsin were waiting when I arrived, and Meg gave a squeal of pleasure. 'Just you?' she said, when I'd let us in, and we'd put down our cake tins and board games.

'I've relieved my parents of their duties,' I said, and she gripped me in a Sumo-wrestler hug that felt nice. 'Thanks for coming in.' I included Tamsin, who gave a pleased little smile and a tiny wave, before going to hang up her silky bomber jacket.

'Don't be silly, it's nice to have an excuse to get out in the evening.' Meg let go of me. 'It was either this, or looking at possible wedding venues again.'

'You don't sound too excited.' I put my bag down, admiring the way her hair always behaved itself, while mine wouldn't stay put for more than ten minutes. And I couldn't carry off a fitted dress the way she did. 'Aren't you supposed to have turned into Bridezilla?'

'God, no.' She pursed her lips. 'Is there such a thing as Mumzilla? If so, Sam's mother's it.'

'Scary,' I said, casting a critical eye around the café, unable to help a squeeze of pleasure when I spotted my artwork again.

'I still can't believe they're yours.' Meg had seen me looking. 'I told Tilly, and she's coming to have a look.'

'Honestly, they're nothing special,' I said, but it was still nice to hear. 'I might be doing some new stuff.' I told her what had happened earlier, and she clasped her hands, the way she used to when she was really excited about something. 'That's amazing, Cassie,' she said. 'But should you be accepting commissions if you're going back to London, soon?'

London. She might as well have said the moon. 'I might be staying a while longer, I haven't decided yet.'

'Oh!' Her eyes flicked wide. 'I mean, that's brilliant, but… this place?' She scouted the room. 'It's not exactly what you're used to, is it?'

'No,' I said, feeling something building inside me, but before I could say anything silly like 'It's better', there was the sound of knuckles rapping on glass, and I turned to see a familiar figure, waving a Scrabble box in a plastic bag, and my heart did a triple somersault.

'It's Danny Fleetwood,' said Meg, peering over the counter.

'So it is.' I smoothed back the annoying bit of hair that never went into my ponytail. 'And it looks like he's brought his mum.'

Chapter 21

'I told you I was good,' said Danny, adding up his score.

'I can't believe that quetzal is a word.' I was embarrassed that the best I'd come up with was 'lame'.

'It's a tropical bird from Mexico,' said Danny, pronouncing it Me'hico. 'Look it up if you like.'

'I will.' I got my phone out and jabbed the word into a search engine. Of course, he was right. 'It's pretty,' I said, admiring its green and red plumage and yellow crest.

'He saves up a new word for when we play at Christmas,' said Maggie, giving Danny an affectionate shove. His mum was nice. Quietly spoken, with eyes the same shade as her son's, and short blonde hair shot through with highlights. There was a wariness in her gaze, dispelled whenever a smile bloomed over her face, which was often. It was obvious she thought the world of Danny and that they had an easy relationship.

'I'll go and order more refreshments and be back to thrash you again.' He bowed deeply, before heading over to the counter, and I realised I still hadn't thanked him for hanging my paintings, and he hadn't mentioned them either. There hadn't really been time, as his arrival had been followed by the arrival of several more, and I'd found myself herding people to tables, and taking orders for drinks and cakes.

The café was almost full once again, couples and families playing everything from Monopoly to backgammon. A large group of students had corralled some tables and were indulging in a noisy but friendly game of dominoes, and opposite them were a handful of pensioners, playing whist.

Meg and Tamsin were rushed off their feet, but didn't seem to mind. Meg's cakes had almost sold out, and Tamsin had definitely got the hang of the coffee machine, her cheeks flushed candy-pink with pleasure.

I realised I was having a genuinely nice time. Usually, I'd be too busy checking and double-checking that everything was running according to plan, knowing the success of the event would impact on future business, and that even a tiny disruption would spoil everyone's enjoyment.

Admittedly, I hadn't done any networking, and people might assume that Mum and Dad had organised the evening, but it was too late now. I'd look like an idiot if I started going round saying, 'Oh, by the way, if you've enjoyed this evening's event and would like me to arrange something similar, preferably within the next fortnight, maybe you could give me a call.' Which reminded me... I really, really needed to order some business cards.

'Danny says he knew you at school,' Maggie was saying, and I realised I'd been watching him as he chatted easily to Meg. He had his hands in both his pockets so his jeans pulled tight across his buttocks.

'That's right.' I turned to meet her inquisitive gaze, which was unnervingly similar to Danny's. 'Though I didn't actually know him that well. We only shared art classes during our final year.'

'It was a difficult time for him, back then.' Maggie's fingers twisted a delicate gold chain just visible beneath the neck of her navy-blue jumper. 'He'd had quite a lot of time off school.'

'Oh?' My focus sharpened. 'Was he ill?' I tried to imagine him pale-faced in a hospital bed, but it wouldn't stick. A fractured leg, maybe. I could imagine him leaping out of a tree, or falling off his bike. Now I was picturing him as a little boy, pedalling along a street in hazy sunshine.

Maggie gave a sad little smile. 'No, he's been lucky that way, but his father… ' She paused. 'He'd been in the army for years, and was discharged with post-traumatic stress disorder. It was a bad time. Danny helped to take care of him, once we'd settled in Kingsbridge.'

'Right,' I said easily, reeling a little. 'That must have been really tough.'

'It was.' Her eyes grew shadowy. 'We did get help, but it wasn't always enough. Danny was an absolute rock. I probably shouldn't have relied on him so much, but his sister was away at university, so it was just the three of us. His dad's much better now, but it had a big impact on Danny.'

'I can imagine,' I said, trying to picture it. Mum and Dad had never involved Rob and me in their problems, if they'd had any, and I realised how lucky we'd been. 'You're obviously very close.'

Maggie smiled. 'He's an absolute diamond, but unfortunately his school work suffered a bit,' she said, just as Danny returned with tea for three and a plate of buttery shortbread. 'Not that it's done him any harm.'

'Talking about me?' Danny switched seats so he was next to me instead of Maggie, and I tried not to sneak looks at his Scrabble tiles. His proximity was having an odd effect, as if I'd drunk a few glasses of wine, instead of a cup of weak coffee and a peppermint tea. He smelt like outdoors after a rainstorm – *Why was I going all poetic?* – undercut with something like moss and old leather. His boots maybe, which looked enormous next to my size four feet. I experienced a surge of tenderness, thinking of him helping to take care of his father, and how hard – and frightening – it must have been.

'Cassie?'

I snapped my gaze away from his feet. 'Hmmm?'

'Do you want to play another game?'

I knew I shouldn't. I hadn't intended to get sucked in in the first place, but once Danny had introduced me to Maggie and slung his jacket, which I'd remembered to bring with me, over the back of a chair and opened the Scrabble box, I'd found myself chatting about the weather, and accepting Danny's offer to buy coffee and cake.

'Fine,' I said, watching him sort out the tiles for another game, smiling when I caught Maggie's eye. I hoped she didn't think we were on some sort of date, and wondered what he'd told her about me, other than we'd been at school together.

'I admire what your grandmother's doing,' she said, taking a sip of her drink. 'Danny's been telling me all about it.'

'She certainly knows her own mind,' was all I could think to say. 'It's just a shame that she thinks she's a burden to my dad, and won't ask for his help with anything, because she feels guilty.' I wasn't sure why I'd blurted that out, but Maggie nodded with an empathetic smile. I flushed, wishing I hadn't used the word 'burden' after what she'd told me about Danny helping out when his father was ill.

'If you're worried, talk to your dad,' said Danny, shifting his cup away from the Scrabble board. 'Does he know how she feels?'

'He just thinks she's happy with her fads, which she is, but I can't help thinking this latest one's a bit drastic, and that she's actually a bit lonely.'

'Sometimes, people need to hear that they're cared about,' he said. Guessing his family were the sort that discussed their feelings, I felt a beat of envy. 'When they're gone, it doesn't matter how loud you shout, they won't hear you.'

'Is that a quote?' I did a little eye-roll. 'I know someone else who lives her life by them.'

'There's nothing wrong with living by certain codes,' said Maggie, a light rebuke in her voice. 'Danny knows his own mind.'

He was biting his bottom lip, as if regretting what he'd said, and a rush of guilt engulfed me. 'Sorry, I didn't mean… it's just a bit of a cliché, that's all.'

He'd turned his attention to the wall. 'I see you sold some of your paintings.' Was that a subtle hint that I should be thanking him, not criticising?

'You shouldn't have hung them without asking me.' It was meant to sound lightly scolding, but came out as 'ungrateful brat'.

'He didn't mean any harm.' Maggie put down her chunk of shortbread and gave a protective bristle. 'My son always acts with the very best of intentions. Surely you can see that he would never knowingly hurt anyone?'

Danny's smile had fled and he was drumming the table with his fingers. 'Cassie's right, Mum,' he said, before I could react. 'I should have asked first.' His gaze met mine and I was shocked again by how full on it was. He was the sort of person who gave you his full attention, whether you'd asked for it or not. 'I'm sorry,' he said, with apparent sincerity.

I felt a creep of shame. 'No, I'm sorry.' I pushed at my itchy wrist with my fingertips, trying to hold his gaze. 'You actually did me a favour. It's just a bit embarrassing, seeing them there, that's all.'

'Were you like that boy on a programme we watched the other Sunday?' Maggie picked up her shortbread and took a generous bite, apparently prepared to forgive me for insulting her son. 'He's only thirteen and has been painting since the age of six, and is some sort of genius,' she said, wiping her fingers on a napkin. 'He's got his own website and his work sells for thousands, all over the world. His parents work for him, framing and packing his paintings, and he's already a millionaire.'

'Oh god, no, I was nowhere near that good,' I said, rearranging the tiles I'd drawn out of the bag to spell *wankers*. I quickly jumbled them up and placed an 'e' at the end of Danny's 'hat' to spell 'hate'. *Brilliant.* 'It was just a hobby, like my brother was into computers.' *And now he was going to be teaching other people about them. As well as being a father.* It still made my head a bit swimmy to think about that. 'I'm actually an event planner,' I said. 'I worked for a big company in London, and now I'm hoping to set up on my own.'

'In London?'

'Um, yes.' I tried to pull up the image I'd had in my parents' kitchen, of myself as an understanding boss, being interviewed for a magazine, living in an apartment near a park. 'I've been looking at some properties online,' I fibbed.

Maggie looked impressed. 'I expect it costs a lot more to live there now than it did when I was training to be a nurse at King's, before I met Danny's dad.'

Crap. 'Oh, er, yes, it's *ridiculously* pricey. I'll probably share too, with… someone.' Adam flew into my head. Maybe he could help me find somewhere. He might even let me stay at his Canary Wharf apartment, while I found my feet!

The thought died as quickly as it had flared. Even if he wasn't seeing someone else by now, it would be far too embarrassing to get in touch after the way I'd cut him out of my life.

'What about New York?' Danny said silkily, and I remembered too late what I'd said the night before.

'Possibly.' I concentrated hard on the board in front of me. 'I haven't decided yet.'

'Your job sounds like hard work,' said Maggie. 'But rewarding.'

'Actually, it can be a bit shallow.' The words had leapt out without warning, as I thought about the clients with more money than sense, spending hundreds, sometimes hundreds of thousands, on having a good time, when people were starving in the world. 'Well, not always,' I amended, aware of their curious gazes. There'd been plenty of occasions – the fundraising events – that were immensely satisfying, and I'd loved seeing someone's face light up when they realised all the stops had been pulled out to create an experience they'd never forget. 'It's fun, but a lot of responsibility,' I said at last, when I realised Maggie was looking at me with interest. 'Not as worthwhile as, say, being a nurse.'

'Oh, I don't know,' Maggie said darkly. 'It wasn't a barrel of laughs.'

'No, I guess not.'

'And there's no reason why you can't change career, if you don't like it,' she added.

'I *do* like it.' I wondered what Danny had said. Probably something to do with my paintings. 'I couldn't become an artist,' I said, though neither had suggested I should. 'It takes years to get to a level where you can make a living, and there are plenty of artists around already, especially in this neck of the woods.' I was thinking of the long list I'd seen online, and Connor Daley's furious face. 'Loads of them probably don't make it, and I can't afford to be one of those. Not that I was considering it.'

Still, no one spoke, and I started when Danny's fingers skimmed my hand as he stretched out to change 'hate' into 'chateau'. 'Not a bad score,' he said, licking the tip of his pencil before writing it down. It was as if I hadn't spoken.

Maggie pushed back her chair. 'Too much coffee,' she said with a little smile as she rose, smoothing her hands down her jeans. 'Can you point me in the direction of the ladies' room?'

When she'd gone, I cast my eyes around, surprised to find it was gone eight thirty, already. People were laughing and chatting, absorbed in their games, and Meg and Tamsin were engrossed in conversation behind the counter.

'I should take some photos for the website,' I said.

'The rain's stopped.' Danny spoke at the same time. 'Would you like to go for a walk?'

'What?' I paused in the act of diving for my bag and looked at him. 'Now?'

'When you've finished here.'

A list of excuses ran through my head: *I'm tired, I need to get home, I have to order some new business cards*, but all that came out was, 'Where?'

'Along the coastal path.' His eyes crinkled into a smile. 'I want to show you something that—'

'Will win me over?'

His smile widened. 'Maybe.'

'It's getting dark.'

'There's a full moon tonight.'

'How do you even know that?'

He gave a modest shrug. 'I wanted to time it right.'

'Can't you just tell me what it is?'

'Hardly,' he said. 'Where would be the drama in that?'

It was a fair point, and I was intrigued, in spite of myself. 'I'll think about it,' I said, adopting a lofty tone. 'But, business first.' I fished my phone out of my bag. 'Photos!'

He grinned. 'Make sure you get my best side.'

As I moved around the café, checking no one minded me taking their picture, I snapped away, careful to get everyone's heads in, laughing when Meg and Tamsin each picked up a pair of iced cherry buns and held them in front of their chests in a parody of the Calendar Girls.

'That won't make the website,' I warned, turning to take a shot of Danny and Maggie, heads touching as they leaned across the table and grinned for the camera. Maggie's teeth were as white and straight as her son's, and I found myself wondering what his dad looked like.

As I quickly scrolled through the photos, checking everything was in focus, I felt a draught stir my hair as the door opened, and heard a female voice, say, 'There she is.'

'Tilly! You're late.' I turned to see her coming towards me, casual as ever in ripped skinny jeans and trainers, her cropped hair hidden beneath the hood of a grey zip-up top. 'I found him wandering outside,' she said, doing something funny with her face that seemed to imply intense sexual excitement. A man had followed her in. She must have acquired a boyfriend, which seemed unlikely, given how vociferous she'd been about being single just two days ago. But… stranger things had happened.

'I know you said it was early days, but I didn't realise you hadn't even told him where you lived,' she was saying.

'What?' I couldn't get the gist of her words – or why she'd stepped aside like a hostess introducing a guest. My gaze slid to the man behind her, waiting patiently for me to speak, his dark-chocolate eyes glimmering with suppressed amusement… my hand flew to my throat.

It was Adam.

Chapter 22

'What are you doing here?' I stuttered, a smile breaking over my face. 'I was literally thinking about you just minutes ago!'

'I'm pleased to hear it.' He raised an eyebrow, channelling James Bond. 'I came to find you,' he said.

'That's so romantic.' Behind me, Meg didn't bother lowering her voice.

'You mean, he didn't know where you lived?' Tilly was flicking glances back and forth, as if trying her best to see us as a couple. Adam looked too polished for the café, like a visiting Hollywood actor in his heavy, double-breasted coat and well-cut suit. His dark hair waved neatly back from his forehead, and a thick, gold watch peeked out from beneath his cuff. He exuded money and good breeding, and the part of my brain still functioning was impressed that I'd chosen someone so clearly out of my league.

'It's quite a story,' he said. I'd forgotten how lovely his voice was – deep and warm, and just the right side of authoritative. It sent a little shudder down my spine. 'Shall we sit down?'

'Aren't you going to introduce us?' Tilly clearly wasn't letting us off the hook.

'Adam Conway,' he said to her, switching on his charming smile.

'Good to meet you, Adam.' Her hand disappeared inside his. 'Tilly Campbell.'

When he'd let go, she smiled demurely and said, 'I've come to have a look at some paintings.' Her eyes grew wide as she looked past Adam's broad shoulder to the wall behind him. 'I want to know *everything*,' she said to me in a whisper as she passed.

Left alone with Adam, I began to panic sweat, as the enormity of him turning up out of the blue began to sink in. 'Would you like a drink?'

'I'd love a beer, but I'm guessing that's not on the menu.' He pulled at the knot of a grey-and-blue striped tie that was probably silk.

'No, I'm sorry,' I said. 'We could go to the pub.' I cringed, recalling what Tilly and Meg had said about the state of the Smugglers Inn but, luckily, Adam was shaking his head.

'Actually, I've been cooped up in the car for hours and wouldn't mind some fresh air,' he said. 'Shall we take a walk? There's a full moon, it's quite spectacular.'

Suddenly reminded of Danny, I spun round to see him clearing away the board game, while Maggie stared at her phone. He didn't look over and I couldn't tell whether or not he was deliberately avoiding my eye. 'I'd love to,' I said. 'But why are you here, Adam?' Remembering I'd blocked his number, nerves rushed to the surface. 'I thought we'd broken up.'

'Well, you broke up with me, if I remember correctly.' He thrust his hands in his coat pockets and tilted his head. 'Thing is, I can't stop thinking about you.' It was a line straight out of a romance novel, but somehow didn't sound corny. 'How about we go for that walk, and have a chat?'

I still couldn't quite believe he was there, but my racing pulse, throbbing cheeks and madly itchy wrist said it was true. 'Give me a second,' I said, and quickly crossed to the counter.

'He wants me to go for a walk,' I said urgently to Meg.

'That's… nice?' She looked unsure of my tone. 'He's gorgeous, Cassie. You've chosen well.'

'Shouldn't I stay and help you close the café?'

'Don't be silly, we can manage, and Tilly will help.' She shot me a smile. 'He's obviously dying to spend some time with you.'

As her eyes danced over him, I knew I couldn't tell her I'd broken up with him – not when I'd implied a couple of days ago that we were dating. And, now I thought about it, I didn't want to tell her. 'Right. Well, I'll see you tomorrow,' I said, aware of Adam waiting, and that he'd driven for hours to see me.

'Oh, Cassie, I can't come in tomorrow.' Meg pulled a regretful face. 'Remember, I'm allergic to cats.'

'Oh god, Meg, I'd totally forgotten, I'm sorry.' She'd once picked up a stray tabby on the school playing field, and was sent home when her eyes swelled shut.

'Don't worry.' She waved a hand. 'I've earned overtime this evening, and I'm working some extra hours on Friday.'

More money I would have to cover, so Mum and Dad wouldn't be out of pocket. It was a good job I'd earned some today, from my paintings. 'Thanks, Meg,' I said. 'I'll see you some time on Friday, then.'

Grabbing my bag and coat, I started making my way over to Adam, who watched my approach with a look of such open pleasure that I had to refrain from looking over my shoulder to check that Scarlett Johansson hadn't wandered in. Danny was helping Maggie on with her leather jacket, and finally caught my eye.

'I'm… sorry,' I said, slowing down. 'I didn't know Adam was coming, and…' My voice petered out.

'You should have told me you were seeing someone.' As direct as ever, only this time his gaze was sharper, as though seeking something he'd missed. Maggie didn't look at me.

'I'm not seeing him, I… he's just… someone I met.'

'Right.' He picked up the Scrabble board and tucked it under his arm. 'Thanks for a nice evening.'

'We can go for that walk tomorrow, if you like.' I wondered why I was bothering when I'd already stressed that he was wasting his time with me, and Adam was here in the flesh, clearly keen to rekindle our fledgling relationship.

'No worries,' Danny said, handing Maggie her bag. 'I'll see you in the morning when I drop off the cats.'

'Cats?' Suddenly, Adam was beside me, his expensive cologne filling my senses, making my head spin.

'Oh, I've been organising some events for the café while I'm here, for my parents, remember I told you they run a café,' I said, zipping into professional mode – if professional meant babbling like an idiot. 'I'm turning it into a cat café for a day, though it may happen more often if it's a success, which I hope it is, as that's what I do for a living, ha, ha.'

'Hey, that's a great idea.' His openly appraising glance sent a heatwave through my body. He was so big and shiny, I couldn't help comparing him with Danny, who seemed smaller somehow, though they were more or less the same height. Danny was watching me closely, a small smile tilting his mouth, and I wondered what he was thinking. 'You ready?' Adam offered me his elbow, like an old-fashioned gentleman, and I took it self-consciously, aware of at least four pairs of eyes tracking our steps to the door.

It felt blissfully cool after the heat in the café, and letting go of Adam's gym-hardened arm – I'd felt his muscles flexing through his coat – I led the way round to the coastal path, which was bathed in silvery moonlight.

'Isn't it beautiful?' Adam said, pausing to tip back his head. 'You don't see a sky like this very often in the city.'

'It's lovely,' I agreed, aware of him in a new way. Going out in London, we'd always been surrounded by other people: in a restaurant, where the waiters had known him by name; the exclusive bar, where he'd ordered a bottle of champagne that cost more than a month's rent on my flat; the Italian bistro, where the overly attentive waiters had barely left our table. Even cloaked in darkness at a preview of the latest James Bond – Adam was a massive fan – we hadn't been alone.

Leaning my head back, too, I gazed at the inky sky, which was littered with stars that dazzled my eyes like sequins, and wished we were back in London and knew each other a lot better.

'How did you find me?' I said, as we walked a little way down the path. His leather shoes were made for pavements, not rain-slippery paths close to the edge of a drop that, while not high enough to kill, might at least result in a broken limb.

'It would have been easier if you hadn't blocked my number.' I glanced up to see a smile touch his eyes. They looked almost black in the moonlight, while the rest of his face was cast in a ghostly glow. I could only imagine what I must look like. 'I wondered why you didn't reply to my text messages,' he said. 'But I didn't realise you'd blocked me until I tried to call you.'

'I'm sorry about that.' My whole body cringed, even as I absorbed the fact that he'd kept trying to contact me. 'I've had a lot going on,' I said, lamely.

'I remembered you saying you'd been raised in Devon, but that was all. I called your work number in the end, and your colleague told me you were staying up here for a while, with your parents.'

Nina. 'She'd shouldn't really have given you my address.'

'I promised her I wasn't a psychopath.' There was a smile in his voice. 'She explained you'd left the company and were looking for a new challenge.' I mentally thanked her for not telling him I'd been fired. 'I just wish you'd talked to me about it.'

'I didn't think it was fair for us to get in any deeper when I was in, a, er, a state of, um… of flux,' I said, though 'in a state' would have been more accurate.

'You never even let on that you were thinking of leaving. I had no idea.'

Oh god, this was awful. 'It had been in the back of my mind for a while,' I lied. 'I'd gone as far as I could at Five Star.' I really needed to stop saying that – especially as it wasn't even true.

'So, it wasn't that you didn't like me?' His tone was warmly teasing.

'Oh, no, I mean yes, no, of course it wasn't… I mean, I really do.' I was wildly overcompensating.

'Well, that's a relief, because I really like you.'

'Oh,' was the only word my racing mind seemed capable of producing.

'Your parents seemed to like me, too.'

My head jolted round. 'You spoke to them?'

'Well, obviously I went to the address I'd been given, and they told me you were working this evening.'

I tried to imagine him rocking up on my parents' doorstep, and the look on their faces when they answered the door. An actual man, asking to speak to their daughter. A film-star handsome man, wearing a coat and suit that probably cost more than the combined contents of their wardrobes. I imagined they'd been suitably awestruck. I hoped they'd been fully clothed.

'Hey, you are OK with this, aren't you?' He rested a hand on my arm, his fingers long and elegant. *Piano player's fingers*, Nan would have said. When I didn't reply right away, he added, 'It just felt like there was unfinished business between us.'

His sentiments echoed the feelings I'd had while looking at his picture on my phone, and it was as if my thoughts had transmitted themselves to him. 'Of course it's fine, it's just a surprise, that's all.' It was starting to feel as if I was starring in my own rom-com, or creating a 'how we met' story to tell our children one day. Incredibly good-looking children, providing they took after him. Things like this just didn't happen to people like me.

'I don't normally do this sort of thing.' Slowing, Adam pushed his palm over his hair. 'To tell you the truth, I feel a bit of an idiot.'

His honesty was endearing. 'You're not.' I touched his sleeve. 'I'm glad you're here.'

We stopped walking and looked at each other, then burst out laughing. His laugh was nice, confident sounding, and revealed his straight, white teeth. I hoped I didn't have cake crumbs stuck between mine.

'Shall we walk on a bit further, or go back?' he said. 'It's chillier than I thought.'

I remembered Danny giving me his jacket the evening before, but although I was a bit shivery – from nerves and excitement more than anything – I wouldn't have expected Adam to hand over his designer coat.

'We could walk a bit more, if you like.' I felt suddenly shy – almost as if we were meeting for the first time, and that I hadn't once imagined us locking lips (and more) in his apartment to mellow music. 'Are you driving home?'

'God no, I've booked into a hotel in Kingsbridge.'

'Ah.' Sensible, really. And at least I didn't have to offer him a bed at home. That would have been a bit awkward.

He cast his eyes around, and I was wondering whether he was building up to asking me back to his room, and what I would say if he did, when he said, 'Once I retire, I'd quite like to move to the seaside. Somewhere with clean air.' He breathed deeply, inflating his lungs to maximum capacity.

'That won't be for a while yet,' I said, shivering slightly.

'I'm hoping it'll be when I'm forty-five, so not that far away.'

I'd almost forgotten he earned the sort of salary most people only dreamt of. 'Wouldn't you be bored?'

'I'm sure I'd find plenty do, with the right person by my side.' His light-hearted tone was undercut with sincerity.

Was he talking about me? Rubbing my upper arms, I said quickly, 'That unfinished business you mentioned. What if it's actually finished?'

'I guess that's what I'm here to find out.' He stopped, and we turned to face each other once more. The breeze tugged at my hair, and the tip of my nose felt frozen. Behind Adam, the sea glittered like mercury beneath the moonlight. 'I never said it before, but when you pushed your card in my pocket that day and asked me to call you, and gave me that cute little wink, it was like a breath of fresh air.'

Wow! I'd never been called a breath of fresh air before. Or cute.

'No one does things like that, especially on the Underground. And I only took the train that day because the Alfa was in for a service.' He was talking about his Alfa Romeo, which he'd seemed inordinately fond of. 'It felt then like it might mean something, and I know you felt it too.' His gaze sought mine. 'You're not like anyone I've ever met before.'

My mind flashed back to our first date.

It isn't only old men who carry wallets, he'd said, rummaging in his jacket pocket and pulling one out.

Nice, I'd said, hoping the pinkish lighting in the restaurant would hide the worst of my blushes. *I bet you own some sheepskin slippers too.*

He'd laughed at that. *Seriously*, he'd said. *Don't ever become a pickpocket, you'd be terrible at it.*

He was smiling affectionately at me now, as if reliving the same moment.

'We don't really know each other,' I said. 'Not properly.'

He spread his arms wide, his coat gaping to reveal his crisp white shirt underneath. 'Like I said, that's why I'm here. Oh, and to tell you about a job you might be interested in.'

My head jerked up. 'What?'

He planted his hands in his pockets. 'My sister has this friend, she's a luxury wedding planner, expanding into corporate and private events, and she's looking for someone to take over the wedding side of things.' He paused. 'I know you've said you'd like to be your own boss, but you'd have an assistant, and you'd be the one in charge,' he said, as if that might be the reason I hadn't already snapped his arm off or started doing star jumps.

The truth was, I'd always found weddings the most stressful of all events. Nina had enjoyed them, but being responsible for arranging the happiest day of someone's life had given me violent headaches. I'd even thrown up on a couple of occasions.

'You'd be earning fifty grand a year, at least, though obviously you'd need to discuss that with Grace, but I've told her you'd be perfect for the job.'

Fifty grand a year? I felt like my heart was going to fly out of my throat.

'And there's an apartment that goes with the job; it's above the premises in Mayfair so you'd be on site, as it were.'

Accommodation? I must be dreaming. 'I'm, er, that's... that's a very generous offer.'

'The company's doing incredibly well,' said Adam. 'It's been featured in *Bride* and *Hello* magazine and the *Sunday Times*.'

'Gosh, that's amazing.' I'd never said gosh before. But then, I'd never had such an extraordinary offer. On that salary, I'd be able to afford my own place, never mind live in an 'on site' apartment. And I'd have an assistant, so I could take time off now and then. Go on holiday. A proper holiday, that didn't involve work, so I could sightsee properly and not have to keep my phone switched on. I'd be able to update my wardrobe, and buy a new Kindle and smartphone. Treat my family. Buy tons of baby things for my unborn niece or nephew.

'She specialises in destination weddings, so there'd be plenty of opportunities to travel abroad.'

A thought sliced through a swirling image of me in Tahiti, beaming with pride as a beautiful bride swayed down a petal-strewn aisle. 'Your sister's friend is Grace Dewsbury?'

He nodded. 'You've met her?'

'No, but we lost a client to her once,' I said. 'My boss was furious.' I didn't add it was because of me. That I hadn't been able to secure the venue the client had wanted, because it was private property and not available for weddings.

'I'll take my business elsewhere then,' she'd said, as if we hadn't already sourced loads of suppliers, which I'd had to cancel, creating a tidal wave of venom from Carlotta.

'She's gone straight to the competition,' she'd spat. 'Grace whatsername in Mayfair.' I had no idea how she'd found out. 'You're on a final warning, Cassie, I mean it this time.' Even Nina had tried to tell her it wasn't my fault, but she hadn't listened.

I realised I was staring at Adam, who was looking at me with his nicely shaped eyebrows up, clearly wondering when the hugging and you over' nonsense, he wasn't the type to get all jealous because a man had turned up out of the blue and whisked me on a moonlit walk. Not that he had any right to be jealous. Or anything to be jealous of. *Yet.*

Wondering what time Adam was going to turn up, I felt a prickle of anticipation, and, as if sensing my attention had wandered, Danny backed away. 'Remember the rules and you'll be fine,' he said. 'I'll be back to pick them up around four.' I watched as he jogged to his van and drove off, feeling as if I'd lost something without knowing what it was.

Sighing, I approached the office, which already had a tang of litter trays – probably because there were several of them lined up – and anticipation gave way to a more familiar feeling of panic and apprehension.

The rules.

What were they again?

'He's a little coochy-coochy-coo, isn't he? Yes he *is.* He's mummy's little fluffy, wuffy darling boy. He's wuvverily, yes he *is,* he wants cuddles and snuggles and he's going to get them, if I don't gobble him up, 'cos he's gorgeous, yes he *is.*'

Mum and I gaped in astonishment as Gwen babbled baby talk to a one-eyed, black and white tomcat, pausing only to lavish him with noisy, wet kisses. He was clearly loving the attention, purring like a generator in her arms, where he lay like a furry baby while Gwen's glowering face transformed into one of gooey-eyed adoration.

'I had no idea she was so fond of cats,' Mum whispered.

'Fond?' I whispered back. 'She looks like she's just birthed him.'

Mum stifled a snorting laugh with the back of her hand, but Gwen didn't even look up. She was so rapt by Dickens (strange choice of name for a cat) that she wouldn't have noticed if we'd burst into song.

'I think she's in love,' Mum murmured, and I was suddenly grateful to Gwen for creating a welcome diversion. It was obvious, from the moment we'd arrived at the café, that Mum wasn't sure about the cats, viewing them gingerly, as though they were ancient artefacts that might be cursed. 'Maybe she'll adopt one.'

'Oh, I think that's a given.' I reached for the checklist that Danny had left on top of one of the carriers, and we crept out of the office and through to the café, leaving Gwen in her elevated state – probably making the other cats wild with jealousy. 'It's mostly common sense,' I said, skimming the list of rules. At the top the words THERE ARE NO OFFICIAL GUIDELINES SO USE COMMON SENSE had been typed in big, bold capitals. 'Make sure they've access to food and water, which the shelter has supplied, make sure they don't escape, supervise the animals around children, etc. etc.' They'd also listed the cats by name, as well as their breed 'where known', or their colours and markings, and reiterated that they were all 'well-trained and friendly'.

I glanced around. It was still early, so not very busy yet, just a few people reading newspapers with toast and coffee, and several more on the terrace, enjoying the sunshine. 'We should keep the doors closed, just in case,' I said. 'The cats might smell fresh air and make a bid for freedom.'

The image of them bolting out was inexplicably funny, and Mum joined in when I started giggling.

'I think this might be fun,' she said, wiping her eyes, and relief made me feel giddy. She kept glancing at the entrance, and I guessed she wasn't so much checking it for safety as wondering when Adam would appear – just as I was. I could tell she was dying to ask more about him. She'd held back over breakfast, flashing a warning look at Dad when

'Mum, can you shut the passage door, so no more cats can get in?'
I called, but she was serving several people at once, and didn't hear.

A bundle of fur fired past me and dived on a chair, where it stretched
out a dainty paw to swipe at a cup. It fell, as if in slow motion, and as
I watched it smash in a puddle of foamy coffee, I wondered whether
it was too late to cancel the event.

Chapter 24

After swiftly clearing up the mess and assuring Mum it wouldn't happen again ('How do you know, they're unpredictable?' she argued), I shot into the passageway after Dickens, almost tripping over a tortoiseshell cat that was weeing against the skirting board.

'Oh, no,' I groaned, rushing back for a cloth and some disinfectant spray, relieved that Mum was too preoccupied to ask what I was doing. 'Why didn't you use a litter tray, you little… pussycat?' It wasn't his (or her) fault, I reminded myself, as it rubbed its purring face against my arm. It was probably just marking its territory.

The floor seemed to be swarming with furry bodies, all appearing as startled to see me as I was to see them.

'Cruel, leaving them in their carriers all this time.' Gwen came out of the office and stormed past like the Pied Piper, but with cats instead of rats streaming after her into the café.

I followed, bellowing, 'Keep the entrance door shut, or the cats will get out!'

I managed to scoop up an attractive long-haired blonde one, and ferried it awkwardly to the office, to match it with its name. 'Queenie,' I read, which seemed appropriate, somehow. She squirmed in my hands and I dropped her on the floor, where she promptly shot out a paw and clawed my ankle.

'OW!' I collapsed on the chair behind me, and a terrible yowl brought me back to my feet. 'Oh, god, I'm so sorry,' I said. I'd almost sat on a cat the same shade as the chair, and attempted to stroke its back – surreptitiously checking for damage – but it drew back its head and hissed at me through bared teeth.

Christ! It looked feral. Or maybe it just didn't like being sat on.

Deciding to leave it alone – after checking the back door was shut – I grabbed hold of Queenie and dashed back into the café with her clamped to my shoulder. Literally. Her claws were in so deep my eyes flooded with tears.

The amount of customers seemed to have trebled. Word had clearly spread and while part of me was pleased, my overwhelming feeling was one of fright. I was responsible for a dozen rescue cats, with no 'real guidelines' and not enough staff to help.

I couldn't even ask Tilly to stick around, as she was ushering her reluctant walkers through the door, turning to give me a quick wave.

I looked around, scenes leaping out at me. There were mums with pre-schoolers, their toddlers' chubby hands reaching for twitching tails, and an old man was stuffing a writhing tabby into his shopping bag.

'Hey, you can't take them,' I said, finally unhooking Queenie's claws and putting her down, before wrestling the cat out of the shopping bag and trying not to scream when it sank razor-sharp teeth into my finger.

'I was just keeping it warm,' the man said sadly. He had the look of a retired colonel and reeked of loneliness. I was briefly tempted to give the cat back and turn a blind eye. 'If you call the shelter, you might be able to adopt him,' I said, more gently. 'Or they do a fostering scheme, if you can't commit to looking after one full time.'

'They're a delicacy in China you know.' The man brightened. 'I ate one when I lived out there. Tasted just like chicken.'

Hastily backing away, I tried to do a quick head count, to make sure they were all still there – apart from the big cat, Tabitha, who hadn't materialised yet. One was using a table leg as a scratching post, and another was perched on top, lapping tea from a saucer in a genteel fashion, while a woman wearing an eye-catching leopard-print scarf took photos on her phone. I realised I'd forgotten once more to invite someone from the local paper to cover the event, but it wasn't too late. About to reach for my phone, I hesitated. The event was horribly reminiscent of the petting-zoo party that had led to me being unceremoniously fired. Perhaps it was best not to have it on record, judging by the way things were going so far.

Shooting forward, I managed to scoop a clump of banana loaf from Dickens' jaws just before he started to choke. 'Don't feed them,' I said to a sweetly startled girl of about four. Her mother was too busy taking pictures to notice. 'He has to have special biscuits.'

Gwen swooped down and bundled up Dickens, and the little girl burst into tears.

'W-w-w-w-want a c-a-a-a-t!' she wailed. 'Want that cat, now, *ple-e-e-e-ase*, Mummy, *NOW!*'

'This one's mine,' said Gwen. I could tell she was trying to be calm and friendly, but it didn't transfer to her face. The girl emitted an ear-piercing shriek, as though she'd encountered the witch from *Hansel and Gretel*.

'*MUMM-I-I-I-I-I-E!*'

Three of the cats flew past me, ears flattened.

'What are you doing?' Finally, the girl had her mother's attention. She spotted Gwen backing away with Dickens, as though taking him hostage. 'Hey, I wanted a picture of Lucy with that cat.'

'They're not photo opportunities,' I snapped, even though everyone else was taking pictures. 'They're damaged, and looking for homes.'

My gut twisted with embarrassment. 'Right.'

'Bit too literal, and I've always found caricatures rather crude.' He was still looking over, eyes scrunched in contemplation. 'I prefer more abstract stuff myself, and am partial to a bit of sculpture.'

I nodded, not trusting myself to speak.

'Local artist?'

'Yep.' I gulped the rest of my coffee, praying no one would come over and ask me to draw a 'funny picture'.

'Maybe your parents would be better off sticking with the cats.' He smiled, as if we were sharing a joke, but my mouth wouldn't cooperate.

'So, about this evening,' he said, but before he could continue, the door flew open and a police officer strode in, carrying an enormous cat I realised was Tabitha. Panic swelled. I'd assumed she was still in her carrier.

'Looks like one of your cats got out,' said the officer, into the pin-drop silence that had fallen. 'Someone called the police to say they'd seen a lynx.'

'She does have unusual markings,' said one of the customers.

I scraped my chair back and stood up. 'How did she get out?' My eyes sought Gwen's.

'She didn't get past me.' Gwen puffed out her body to fill her five-foot frame, looking ready to throw a punch. 'I think I'd have noticed if she had.' She looked at Tabitha, who really was scarily massive. 'Poor thing could have got run over.' Gwen was giving me daggers, as though it was all my fault – which, to be fair, it probably was. I mustn't have closed the back door properly.

'We found her digging up a flowerbed,' said the officer, a reproving look on his oblong face. 'The home owner remembered seeing the sign outside the café yesterday, so I thought I'd bring her here.'

'That's very kind of you.' I stepped forward, aware that Adam was watching with slight amusement, clearly expecting me to take control. 'As you can see, we're quite busy and it's been difficult to keep an eye—'

'You do have a licence?' He looked around, adjusting his truncheon belt around his rather womanly hips. 'You're serving food.'

Licence?

Adam stood up, as if to intervene – but I didn't want a man stepping in to settle things for me – especially one who'd offered me up for the job of a lifetime, on the assumption I was capable of doing it.

'It's a one-off event, officer, to raise awareness of the plight of homeless cats,' I said, a hot, tight feeling racing across my chest, as the responsibility of it hit me. One of the cats could have been killed and the others deeply traumatised. They hadn't asked for their lives to be messed about with. And I could do without being arrested and thrown in prison.

The officer looked at Mum. 'You OK with this, Mrs Maitland?'

'Oh, yes,' Mum said, ignoring the cat directly in front of her, its paws resting on a glass dome as if about to help itself to a scone. 'My daughter organises things like this in her sleep. And Liz Fairbrother at the cat shelter gave us her blessing.'

'Oh, I know Liz.' The officer swung over to the counter and scanned the cakes, one hand absently fondling the placid cat. 'Could I have a latte and a slice of chocolate fudge cake, please? Actually, make that two slices.'

As Mum bobbed about, getting him a takeaway coffee, the noise levels in the café returned to normal, and my shoulders sagged as I let out the breath I'd been holding. I felt as if I'd got away with murder. In fact, if anything had happened to Tabitha, that's what I'd be – a murderer. I wanted to pick her up and hug her, but she was so large,

I had no idea how to go about it. I settled for giving her ginormous head a pat.

I felt Adam's eyes on me, and wondered whether he was wondering how to retract his job offer, and how quickly he could flee back to London. I straightened, discreetly scratching my wrist, which felt as if it was on fire.

'That was well handled,' he said, hands in his trouser pockets, eyeing me with a look of such flattering admiration that I wondered whether I was missing something.

Or, maybe he was.

Chapter 25

Keeping tabs on the customers, making sure no one fed the cats cake, advising youngsters to be careful of claws and to not pull the cats' ears or whiskers, and explaining why they couldn't just take one home 'for a bit' was exhausting.

Once it became obvious that I couldn't sit and chat with Adam, we arranged to meet that evening at the Smugglers Inn and he took off to explore the area. 'It's a while since I've been near the sea, so I'm going to make the most of it.' He rested his hands on my shoulders and searched my eyes, before grazing my cheek with his lips. 'I'll leave you to it,' he said, his breath tickling my nose. It smelt of coffee, and the peppermint he'd popped in his mouth from a tube he'd pulled from his pocket.

Tamsin returned in time for the lunchtime rush and there was a lull before schools kicked out, so I sat and did some sketches of the cats and customers, keeping an eye on the door in case Adam returned, and wondered what I was doing. Each time I remembered his comments about my paintings, I shrank with embarrassment, and had to remind myself we were all entitled to our opinions. I should probably have mentioned the artwork was mine, and that I didn't like sculpture, but the moment had passed too quickly.

I wondered whether Adam was scoping out somewhere to live in his early retirement. Perhaps he'd want to build his own place, like those people on *Grand Designs* – a glass-and- metal construction, like an office space – or maybe snap up a listed building, set in several acres, with a pond and an orchard, and a paddock for a pony. I realised I'd drawn out the image in my head, and decided to paint it later, in watercolours.

No, not later. Maybe never. As a future 'bespoke' wedding planner, there'd be no time for painting, never mind sketching.

By the time the café flooded with schoolchildren and mums and dads, the cats were starting to look jaded, scooting here and there or hiding, and Mum was looking frazzled from constantly shooing them out from behind the counter. At three thirty, Gwen helped me round them up. Docilely, they followed her back to the office, where they clambered into their carriers, looking relieved. It must be hard being the focus of so much attention, no matter how desperate you were to find a new home. And I was certain that most of them had. In fact, a fight had almost broken out over a rather smug-looking Tabitha, with two families claiming they loved her the most, and that she 'obviously' preferred them.

'Reckon it worked out all right in the end,' Gwen said, almost flattening Dickens with the force of her stroking. 'Still a bit much though, pimping them out like this.' She gave me a sly look. 'I saw that bloke of yours, picking hairs off his trousers. Don't seem like much of an animal person.'

'You've just got it in for him because he didn't want any cake.' I tried to sound teasing, but didn't quite pull it off. 'He's into healthy eating, that's all, there's nothing wrong with that.' Actually, I'd felt a bit put out that I couldn't tuck into a wedge of carrot cake, in case he judged me.

'I've got it in for 'im, 'cos of what 'e said about your paintings.'

'You heard that?'

'I'd have told 'im to do one,' she said. 'Cheeky bar steward.'

'He's entitled to his opinion.'

'As long as it 'ain't the wrong one.' I didn't know whether to be flattered that she rated my art, or annoyed that she was judging Adam without even knowing him. 'Not that I know anythink about paintings, mind. Only thing I can draw is me curtains, know what I mean?'

In a surprisingly swift movement, she bent to pack Dickens in his carrier, and I concentrated on making sure that all the carriers were securely fastened, with their cargo safely inside. Most of the cats were fast asleep already.

Danny arrived dead on time, bits of leaf in his hair, his stubble like gorse round his jaw. His jeans were covered in mud stains, as though he'd rolled down a hill, but as usual he radiated health and goodwill.

'All present and correct?' he said, as Gwen backed out of the office blowing kisses to Dickens. The cat's face was pressed to the grill of his carrier, and I could have sworn there were tears in his eyes.

'There's been plenty of bonding, let's put it that way.' I watched Gwen pass her arm over her face as she vanished into the café. 'I reckon all of them will have new homes by the end of the week.'

'That's great.' A smile broke through the grime on Danny's face. 'It'll take a load off at the shelter. They're full at the moment.'

'I'm glad to have helped.' I felt a flush of pride, now the day was over and had gone without a hitch... apart from one cat escaping, a police officer turning up, and every health and hygiene rule being shattered. 'Thanks for all this.' I handed him Tabitha's carrier, which was significantly heavier than the others, and decided not to mention her little adventure.

'I hear she escaped,' Danny said, peering inside and pulling a funny face. I didn't ask how he knew. The police officer was probably

did. Not until things were over, and even then I'd replay everything
back in my head, wondering what could have gone better. 'Just as
well, or I'd be a basket case,' he added. His hair was stiff with product,
sticking up at weird angles. Comedy hair, I'd thought, the last time I'd
seen him perform. 'But they come back every time. Good job I love
what I do.' He made jazz hands. 'It wouldn't be worth it otherwise.'

'No,' I said, a hollow feeling in my stomach. I should have eaten
before coming out. 'It probably wouldn't be.'

'Really, thanks for booking me,' he said, unexpectedly. 'Work's been
a bit thin on the ground since I was dropped from *Mock the Week*.'

'Dropped?' My insides rolled over. So, that's why he'd been available
at short notice.

'I did a couple of bad-taste jokes.' Seeing my face, he added, 'Don't
worry, Cassie, I'll keep it as clean as a whistle, I've learnt my lesson.
People don't want experimental, and I'll make sure I steer clear of
Trump.'

'Who wouldn't?' I joked, despite the knot in my throat.

He let out a high-pitched laugh and clapped his hands. 'Nice one,'
he said. 'You should go into comedy.'

Not if my life depended on it. 'Well, I just wanted to wish you good
luck.' I prayed he wouldn't need it. 'They look like a good crowd.'

'I've been booed off stage in seven seconds, been told I'm as funny
as piles, had beer chucked over me, and had a heckler who turned out
to be my next-door neighbour so, whatever happens, I'll cope,' he said,
which I found only marginally reassuring.

'I'll leave you to your preparations.'

He was pacing again before I'd left the room, and I was relieved to
see Adam by the bar, looking out of place in the well-worn surroundings, like a politician at a homeless shelter. 'You look amazing,' he said,

eyes lingering around my chest. 'I like the dress.' If he was puzzled by the plain grey cardigan I'd pulled on to cover my wrists – the other one had broken out in a rash, now – he didn't show it. 'What would you like to drink?'

Imagining a tussle between Andy Farrington and someone who'd taken offence at one of his jokes, I knew I should stick to soft drinks. 'A glass of white wine, please,' I heard myself say, and Adam nodded his approval.

We'd just settled at a table, facing a scuffed area of wooden flooring, where I assumed karaoke night took place, when Meg and Tilly turned up, bright-faced with anticipation.

'I've been looking forward to this all day,' Meg said, when we'd all greeted each other, and I'd introduced Meg to Adam. 'Sam's training for a cycling event, so he can't make it.' I noticed Tilly's eyebrows arch, and wondered what she was thinking.

'Can I get you both a drink?' Adam asked, and when they'd given their orders and he'd gone back to the bar, which was three-deep now – people must be coming from neighbouring villages – they hunched forward with eager expressions.

'So?' said Meg, which I knew from old meant *tell us everything*.

'He seems nice,' said Tilly. She was wearing an army-style jacket with the sleeves pushed up, and I wished I could do the same. It was roasting in the pub, but I couldn't bear to expose my rash.

'He *is* nice,' I said, and quickly told them about the job in London.

'It sounds amazing,' sighed Meg, sounding a little bit sad. 'It's just a shame you've got to go away again, now we're back in touch.'

She presented it as a fait accompli. It didn't occur to her that I might not want the job.

Wait. Did I want the job? *Fifty grand a year.* Of *course* I did.

'You and Sam should come and visit,' I said, helping myself to a handful of crisps from a china bowl on the table. All the tables had them, I'd noticed. Bill had pushed the boat out. 'And you,' I said to Tilly. 'I'll give you both my new address, once I'm settled in.'

'Or you could visit us,' she said. 'It's not like you can't ever leave London.'

'Of course, if I get the chance. I'll be busy though.' I told them about the destination weddings and Meg pulled a face. 'Sam wants to hire a barn owl for our ceremony.'

'An *owl?* Even at Five Star we'd never had such a bizarre request.

'To be the ring bearer. Honestly,' she said, seeing Tilly's disbelieving face. 'It's a thing, you can look it up.' We were silent for a moment, imagining it, and when Adam returned with drinks we were in fits of laughter.

'What have I missed?' he said, which only made us laugh harder.

He gave a low-level chuckle which turned into a frown as an operatic aria floated from the pocket of his brown suede jacket, which he'd draped over the back of his chair.

'I bet they've never heard that sound in here before,' Tilly said.

'I'd better get this.' Adam took out his phone. 'Sorry to be rude.'

He moved away with it pressed to his ear and disappeared outside, just as Mum and Dad came in, swiftly followed by Rob. The next few minutes were a flurry of greetings and jacket-shedding and drinks orders, and Rob telling Meg that one of his mates in Year Seven had fancied her at school because he 'liked older women'.

I kept an eye on the door for Adam. When he came back in he looked distracted. 'I'm sorry, but there's a crisis at the bank I need to deal with,' he said, pulling his jacket back on.

'You're going back to London, now?' I stood up, almost sending the table flying, and he reached out a hand and curled it around my wrist.

'I need to make some important calls,' he said, bringing his head close to mine so I could hear him. 'But I can do it back at the hotel.' He glanced at the bar, where Mum and Dad were chatting to Bill, and made a regretful face. 'I'm so sorry to abandon you, Cassie, I was looking forward to spending the evening with you. Can I call you in the morning?'

'Of course,' I said, disappointment rising like acid. 'I hope you manage to sort out whatever it is.'

'Something incredibly dull that would make your eyes roll back in your head.' He squeezed my wrist. I desperately wanted to have a good scratch, but couldn't think of a polite way to do it, so endured another few seconds as he placed his mouth unexpectedly on mine. It was the briefest of kisses – more of a peck – but held the promise of more to come. As he said goodbye to Meg and Tilly, who were pretending they weren't watching, I touched my lips with my fingertips and realised I was smiling. The smile stayed as he left and I'd sat back down, and it only died when I looked across to Mum and Dad and saw Danny Fleetwood pulling a pint behind the bar.

Chapter 26

'Is there anywhere you don't work?' I reached for the wine I'd ordered, having drunk the one Adam had bought me. 'I'm surprised there are enough hours in the day.'

'I knew it would be busy tonight, so I offered to lend a hand.' Danny leaned across the bar and raised his voice above the swell of noise. At least everyone seemed in high spirits, and hopefully wouldn't heckle an anxious comedian. 'I did some gardening work for Bill earlier this year.'

Of course he did. 'When are you getting your knighthood?'

'Funny you should ask. The Queen called me this afternoon.'

'You'll have to smarten up before going to the palace,' I said, seeing he was in the same clothes he'd had on earlier. He must have come straight from work.

'I'm not the suited and booted type, in case you hadn't noticed.'

I wondered whether he was having a dig at Adam. 'I can't imagine you wearing a suit.'

'As it happens, I wore one to my uncle's funeral when I was six, and at a wedding when I was eleven.' His eyes crinkled. 'And then there's my birthday suit…'

'I'd rather not imagine that, thank you.' And yet, I was. I slurped my drink and turned away, pausing for a moment when I glimpsed my friends and family, gathered around two tables they'd pushed together.

Their faces were lively with chat and laughter, and when I joined them, squeezing between Meg and Mum, I was overwhelmed with a feeling of rightness, as if I was exactly where I was supposed to be.

'Where's Adam?' Mum asked, brushing a speck of fluff off my dress.

'He had a work emergency.' I thought of him in his hotel room again, and wondered whether he often had work emergencies that had to be dealt with immediately.

'Is he a surgeon?' Rob asked, overhearing. His cheeks were rosy, and some curls had stuck to his forehead like a toddler's. I could suddenly see what his baby was going to look like, and was certain it was going to be a boy.

'He's an investment banker,' I said.

Rob gave a hammy gasp. 'You'll be forever taking his suits to the dry-cleaners.'

I gave him a beady stare. 'Sorry, Sandra, I'm sure he's a good chap, though I can't see the Clooney resemblance.'

Mum nudged me with her elbow. 'Meg said you might have a job lined up in London.' She looked at me as if to say 'Well?' but I was saved from answering by a squeal of microphone static.

'That was my friend, Mike,' said Andy Farrington. 'He always was a noisy bugger.'

A shot of laughter spread around the pub, and I quickly finished my wine.

'Did you hear about the megabytes who formed a rock group? They haven't had a gig in ages.' Another rumble of laughter, as everyone caught on.

'Nice one,' said Rob. 'I'll have to remember that.'

'Shush,' said Dad, with an expression of suppressed mirth I recognised as him preparing to enjoy himself. He was wearing a dapper waistcoat over his 'going out' shirt, and I was pleased that he and Mum had made an effort.

'A pirate walks into a bar with a steering wheel in his pants and the bartender says, "Sir, you have a steering wheel in your pants." "I know," says the pirate.' Andy paused. '"It's driving me nuts."'

Everyone laughed – Bill making an odd honking noise – and Dad almost choked on his beer. There was no sign of Andy's earlier nerves, even though a woman standing close by was wearing a blue-and-green stripy top.

'I bet you do karaoke here,' he said. There was an appreciative roar. 'I went to a karaoke bar once, that didn't play any Seventies music.' His eyes surfed the crowd. 'At first I was afraid. Oh, I was petrified.'

More giggles were generated. I glanced over to see Danny leaning on the bar, mouth curved in a smile. As if sensing my gaze he turned and gave me a thumbs-up.

'Adam's missing out,' Meg said, close to my ear.

I jerked my gaze back. 'Probably not his cup of tea.' I had nothing to base the opinion on, but when I tried to picture Adam at the table with us, shoulders shaking with laughter, it wouldn't come into focus.

Bill came over with a tray of drinks. 'On the house,' he said, and I gave him a grateful smile before taking a slug of wine.

'My gran started walking five miles a day when she was sixty. She's eighty now, and we don't know where the bloody hell she is.' The laughter grew. 'Hey, does anyone know how to fix broken hinges?' Several hands flew up. 'Well, my door's always open.' Mum snorted some Guinness onto the table, and Tilly buckled with laughter.

I pushed my shoulders down, trying to release the ache across my back. I wanted to laugh along, but was growing tenser, waiting for the moment Andy would say the wrong thing – mention Hitler, or use the 'c' word – or break wind into the microphone, and for the laughs to turn to outrage and disgust, and everyone to turn on me.

My wrist was throbbing and burning and I realised that I'd been scratching without being aware of it. I sipped some more of my drink to distract myself.

'You OK?' Meg laid a hand on my knee, her face knitted with concern.

'Fine,' I said, and she studied me for a moment, before turning as Andy said, 'Did you hear about the bloke who drowned in his muesli? He was pulled under by a strong current.'

That one elicited a few groans and I quickly finished my wine. No one had touched Adam's drinks, so I finished those too, even though red wine gave me a headache.

The room had begun to rotate. I'd barely eaten all day, and the crisp bowl had long since been emptied.

'I've heard about this new restaurant on the moon. Great food, but no atmosphere.'

Laughter again. *Thank god.*

I carefully monitored the audience's reaction for the next half-hour or so, scanning faces to make sure they were laughing and not angry, and that no one looked offended. I also surreptitiously finished off Mum's glass of Guinness while she wasn't looking.

'Sometimes, I wish I was an octopus, so I could slap eight people at once.'

There has a hiss of indrawn breath and a few titters, though Dad found that one hilarious. As if sensing he might have misjudged things, Andy launched into a story about his mother-in-law that had everyone roaring again, but suddenly I couldn't bear it any more and stood up, swaying slightly. 'Need some air,' I said, to nobody in particular. I saw

Danny straighten and look over, then his face was blocked by someone approaching the bar. I pushed through the crowd to the door and burst out onto the pavement, gulping as though I'd been locked in a basement for months.

Instead of clearing my head, the fresh air increased my dizziness, and I staggered round to the garden at the back of the pub, hands out to balance myself. I collapsed on the nearest bench and shut my eyes to stop the spinning, but that made it worse, so I opened them again, and blinked when I saw that Meg and Tilly were sat opposite.

'Where d'you come from?' My words weren't working properly. 'S'like you were in there a second ago,' I waved an arm. 'Now, you're here.' My hand dropped limply to my lap and I scraped at my wrist.

'She's trollied.' Meg's voice sounded a long way off.

'And she's crying,' said Tilly.

'No, 'm not.' I dabbed my face with my fingers, surprised when they came away wet. 'S'not crying,' I slurred. 'My eyes are running.'

'That's called crying,' Meg said, so kindly that something in me came loose, sending more tears storming down my face.

'Cassie, what is it?' said Tilly. She and Meg were suddenly either side of me, like bookends. Meg placed an arm around my shoulders, and Tilly took hold of my hand. 'You can talk to us,' she said gently.

I tried to speak, but forgot what to say, and made an odd whining noise instead, like a distressed bobcat.

'What's happened to your wrist?'

My head drooped down. I'd tugged my sleeve up to scratch more efficiently, and even in the low light it was obvious my wrist was a splodgy mess.

'It looks like eczema,' said Meg, lifting my arm to look more closely. 'My mum gets it, especially when she's stressed.'

I lifted my head, which seemed to take ages, and caught them trading looks. 'Are you stressed, Cassie?' Tilly's voice sounded weird and I realised she was being assertive.

''Course I'm bloody stressed,' I said, and the feeling of release was instant, like taking pressure off a bruise. ''ve been fired from my job, which I was *good* at, by the way.' I stabbed the air with my finger. 'My boss was a massive bitch, and I don't know what to do, 'cos 've got no money, and m'parents are *soooooooooooooooo* so proud, so bloody, bloody, *proud* of me, 'cos 've lied, see?' I nodded hard, even though it hurt my brain. 'I've told them I'm here on holiday, Meg and Tilly, 'cos I didn't want them to know I'd lost my brilliant job, because they're so proud of me, they're very, very *proud,* they tell everyone how clever I am, and I was going to be a good boss on my own, but now I don't have to be, because I'm going back to London to do weddings for Grace, and will probably end up living with Adam because he likes me a LOT.' I stopped, unsure where I was heading. 'He's very handsome, isn't he?' Meg's face zoomed in and out, as if I was fiddling with a telescope. 'Why you lookin' at me like that for?'

'Oh, Cassie,' said Tilly, tightening her grip on my hand. 'Your parents aren't going to be angry, or stop being proud of you because you've been fired, and you don't have to go back to London if you don't want to.'

'Of course I want to, I'm going to do weddings, and I'll be in charge this time,' I promised. 'Can't stay in Devon, not really, 'cos then I'll be a failure. Just wish I wasn't tense all the bloody time, it's like I'm waiting for something to go wrong, even when it doesn't go wrong, so I can't bloody enjoy anything, ever.' I snuggled against Meg. She was the perfect shape and consistency for cuddling. 'Sam's a lucky man,' I murmured, sleepy now I'd vomited out the words in my head. 'Sorry for swearing.'

'We had no idea you felt like this.' Meg enfolded me into her. 'You seem so in control. You've done brilliantly at organising tonight, and your Mum said the cats were a real hit at the café, and people are still talking about games night. They're going to try it weekly at the pub.'

'Really?' I tried to look up, but my eyes had shut.

'And my mum's friend has booked Rodney's Dad to play at her sixtieth in August.'

'Oh, that's good.' My head cleared a little. I pushed away from Meg, my hair flowing with static from the sleeve of her tunic top. 'Think I need water.'

'Cassie, we should talk about this some more, maybe tomorrow,' said Tilly, motioning to Meg to help me stand up, but the world had finally stopped spinning like a fairground ride and I shouldered them away.

'Take no notice of me,' I said, brushing my hands on my dress, which was creased from where I'd been sitting. 'I was being a silly sausage.' A bit giggly now, I trailed back to the front of the pub, Meg and Tilly close by as if I might topple over.

The door was propped open, and a wave of laughter flowed out.

'I got a photo in the mail this morning from a speed camera,' Andy boomed down the microphone. 'I sent it back. Terrible quality and too expensive.'

I gave a squawk of laughter and was nearly sick.

'Cassie, I'm glad your chap talked me round,' Bill said, after I'd weaved my way to the bar to ask for some water. Meg and Tilly hovered like nannies with a fractious toddler.

'Adam?' I looked around to see if he'd reappeared, wishing he was there so I could snog him. I needed a snog. I hadn't properly snogged anyone for absolutely ages.

Bill was frowning. 'Fleetwood Mac.' He jutted his head to where Danny was clearing tables. He looked round, but things had gone a bit hazy, and I couldn't make out the expression on his handsome face. 'That's what I call him.' Bill chuckled. 'Fleetwood Mac. Or Danny boy. Or Dan the Man.'

'What do you mean, he talked you round?'

Loud laughter erupted at Andy's next joke – something about a spaceman – and I had to strain to hear Bill's answer.

'Well, you know I wasn't keen, because we try to keep things local, but Danny sent me a clip of his nibs and I fell about laughing. He was right, booking Andy's been great for business.'

Fabulous. So Danny had secured the venue for Andy, not me. *Brilliant.*

I marched over to Danny, Meg and Tilly at my heels like mother hens.

'Hang on, Cass.' Meg tried to grab my arm, but I swung away from her.

'Why don't you stay out of my life?' I said to Danny, prodding him hard on the shoulder. He put down the glasses he'd been holding and wiped his hands on his jeans.

'Now what have I done?'

'Look at the bloody state of you.' I bunched the front of his shirt in my hands, and almost laughed at his shocked expression as I yanked him towards me and squashed my mouth against his.

Chapter 27

I woke to a wraithlike figure at the end of my bed and screamed.

'Cassie, for heaven's sake, it's only me.'

Moving closer, Mum placed a mug of coffee on my bedside table.

'I thought you were a ghost,' I said, peering at her white waffle bathrobe. 'Why are you creeping about?'

'I'm not, I was just checking you were OK.'

As soon as she'd said it, I realised I wasn't. Apart from my heart palpitating with fright, my tongue was sticky and my head felt like it had been crushed into a cube.

'Your hair looks like purple silk fanned out on the pillow,' Mum said, fancifully.

I scrunched one eye shut and looked at her with the other. 'It's not purple, it's Plumberry.'

'Do you remember last night?' she said.

'Of *course* I do.' Memories rolled in. 'The comedy night...' Too much wine. Crying in the garden. *Snogging Danny Fleetwood.* I dragged the duvet over my face. How could I have done that? Especially when I was supposed to have been tearing a strip off him for interfering in my life.

Helping he'd called it, when I'd finally peeled my lips away from his. He hadn't resisted one little bit. In fact, he'd joined in after the initial shock, and it had felt like there was a Catherine wheel twirling in my stomach. 'I was helping, that's all,' he said, when I'd shoved him away and gone back to being cross. 'The idea of a comedy night was yours; you made the booking. I hardly did anything.'

I'd flounced away in disgust, tripped over someone's bag and gone flying, and the next thing I remembered was Mum and Dad hustling me into the car, and Rob threatening to push me out if I was sick.

'I didn't thank Andy, or even say good night,' I wailed now, from my cocoon.

'I'm sure he won't mind, after the reception he got,' Mum said. 'You can always email him, can't you?'

I peeped out, to see Mum looming over me.

'Please, open the curtains,' I begged. 'It's too green in here.'

She did, but the light was like daggers in my eyes, so I covered my face again.

'I'm going to make some breakfast.' I sensed Mum's stare through the duvet, but didn't budge. 'It'll be ready in ten minutes,' she said, rather tersely. 'You need to line your stomach, Cassie.'

I heard her slippered feet leave the room, and the door clicked softly closed.

Shoving the bedding off, I dangled an arm to the floor and felt for my bag.

It was on the chair, which meant I had to get out of bed.

Everything swung and tipped, so I crawled across the floor and took out my phone, hoping Adam hadn't tried to call already. Unlikely as it was only 7.30 a.m. I whimpered, wishing Mum hadn't woken me so early, hovering about like a spirit.

About to crawl back to bed, I noticed a couple of texts:

Sorry to rush off like that. Job done now. If you fancy coming over for a nightcap, I'm in room 73 A x

He'd sent it at ten o'clock. Right about the time I'd locked lips with Danny bloody Fleetwood. I rocked back against the dressing table and closed my eyes. What the hell was wrong with me? Had I really been so desperate for a snog that I couldn't wait until I saw Adam again? Had it been the press of Adam's lips in the first place that had fired me up? *Ugh.* What a revolting thought. It was the stress of the comedy night, and drinking on an empty stomach, that was all.

He'd sent another text at midnight:

Guess you've been busy! I'll call you AM X

At first, I thought he'd got his initials wrong, then realised he meant in the morning.

Suppressing an urge to cry, I plugged my phone in to charge and sniffed the air. A delicious smell of frying bacon was drifting under the door, sending a flood of saliva to my mouth. I was officially starving.

'You look pale,' Dad observed as I entered the kitchen and dropped down at the table.

'She's doing too much, that's why.' Mum threw two rashers of crispy bacon onto a plate, slapped on a heap of mushrooms and crashed the plate in front of me. Her lips were pressed together and her eyes were too bright. Or maybe it was the effect of her dazzling white bathrobe.

'You look like you're at a spa,' I said, falling on the food as if I hadn't eaten for a month. It wasn't until I'd nearly cleared the plate that I realised neither parent had spoken since Mum's outburst. Which, now I thought about it, was so out of character, I couldn't believe I hadn't reacted immediately.

'Are you OK?' I pushed my plate aside, feeling slightly restored. Mum was washing up noisily, crashing plates into the drainer, while Dad – in his work trousers and shirt – leaned against the worktop, staring into his mug as though there was something more than coffee inside. I suddenly noticed his hair was receding more quickly than I'd realised ('It's not that my hair's receding, just that my head's getting bigger,' Andy Farrington had joked), and the sight of it made me sad. 'I'm sorry if I showed you up, last night.' I wondered whether that was the root of Mum's apparent annoyance. My behaviour hardly reflected the brilliant daughter she loved to boast about. 'I shouldn't have kissed Danny Fleetwood, I don't what came over me,' I said, when neither of them responded. 'I think I was high on the success of the evening.' I attempted a little laugh that sounded fake.

'High?' Mum's head whipped round, curls flying sideways. 'You looked to be on the verge of a nervous breakdown!'

'What?' I stared as two red patches bloomed across her cheeks.

'Lydia,' Dad warned, putting his mug too close to the edge of the worktop. It teetered before dropping to the floor where it smashed into three large pieces.

'*Now* look what you've done.' Doubling over, her bathrobe gaping to reveal two slices of bosom, Mum snatched up the segments and hurled them into the bin. 'Things are turning to crap around here and I've just about had ENOUGH!'

The last word was evicted so violently, Dad and I jumped as though she'd fired a gun. 'Lydia,' he tried again, a hand outstretched as though calming a volatile dog.

'Don't Lydia me,' she growled. Literally growled. She looked feral, fingers clawing the air, as though she longed to drag her nails down his face. 'And you!' She spun round, eyes flashing like lasers. 'You need to sort yourself out.'

'Mum!' I cowered, but the part of me that wasn't scared was rather impressed. I'd never seen her properly lose her temper, and the sight was riveting. She seemed to have swelled in size, like Jigglypuff from the Pokémon series. 'What are you *talking* about?'

'I'm talking about… about *everything*.' Flinging her arms wide she tipped her head back, as if trying to encompass the world. 'Nothing feels RIGHT any more.'

'Lydia, come and sit down.' Firmer now, Dad took her elbow and she visibly deflated and let him steer her to a chair, where she plopped down and burst into tears.

'I knew something was up,' I said, scooting round to sit beside her, while Dad stood like a centurion, one hand on her shoulder. 'What's going on?'

'Oh, I'm just bloody fed up.' She threw off the arm I'd placed round her and clamped her head between her hands. 'I'm sick of working all hours at the bloody café, I miss you and Rob like crazy when you're not here, and I think you might be messing up your lives and I don't know what to do.'

Her words exploded in my head like a stick of dynamite. I flicked a look at Dad, who was staring at the table, lips pursed, and I knew this must have been the core of the conversation at the café I'd partly overheard. They weren't ill, they were worried sick. About Rob and me. And Mum was fed up with working at the café. That was almost more shocking than anything else. The café was their lifeblood – or so I'd thought.

'Do you feel the same way?' I said to Dad. My voice sounded hoarse, as though I'd been the one shouting.

'Not all the time, love, no, of course not,' he said, meeting my eyes at last with a pained expression. 'It would be nice to have a break from it for a while though.'

'But when I said about getting a manager in, you weren't interested.'

'We thought it would look bad if we handed over the café to a complete stranger and swanned off somewhere for six months.'

Six months sounded oddly precise. They'd obviously discussed it; taking a sabbatical, which they totally deserved.

'Bad to whom?'

'You and your brother,' Mum said, as though it was glaringly obvious. 'We're supposed to set a good example, not give up as soon as things get a bit much.'

'But you *have* set a good example.' My mind was spinning. 'So, it's all been a front, you pretending to love your job, so Rob and I wouldn't think you were massive failures?'

'We *do* love the café.' Releasing Mum's shoulder, Dad shuffled round the table and sat opposite. His posture was one of defeat – as though he'd confessed to a murder he thought they'd got away with for years. 'But it's got so much busier lately, since the makeover, which is great, but it's bloody hard work.'

They were swearing a lot for people who didn't usually swear.

'It's a pain in the bloody beehive,' Mum said, wiping her nose on the back of her hand. 'I think I liked it better before. And now it's going to be even busier, thanks to your... *events*.'

I reeled back in shock. 'Why didn't you say, if you didn't want my help?'

'Because,' Dad said, holding up a hand, presumably sensing another eruption from Mum. 'Our roles are to support you and Rob, whatever you want to do. We could see how much you wanted to help us, and it's been wonderful seeing you in action.'

'But you didn't really need my help,' I said in a mechanical voice.

Mum dried her face on the sleeve of her bathrobe. 'It's not that,' she said with a sniff. 'It's just that it's reminded us how hard you work all the time, how you can never just... *be*.'

I stared. 'Where's all this coming from?'

'Oh, it's just that sometimes, I wish you didn't live so far away,' she said on a sob. 'I wish we saw more of you, or you came to stay more often, and we could go shopping together like Meg does with her mum. I know it's not very exciting here for you, but we bloody well miss you.' Her voice was muffled by the back of her hand. 'If you must know, we're *glad* Rob's back. I know it sounds selfish, but there it is.'

'Oh, Mum...' I tried desperately to sift through this startling new information. I'd never for one moment guessed they'd worried about Rob and me, or that they'd missed us so badly. I remembered what Sid Turner had said. *I don't know how your parents coped with the pair of you off goodness knows where from such a young age.* 'But you seemed so keen to get rid of us,' I said, amending my words when they started to protest. 'OK, not get *rid* of us, but you acted as though us leaving was the right thing to do, and you were happy to be left to your own devices, because you had the café. And each other.'

'We wanted you to have the opportunities we didn't,' Mum said, sniffing.

'And now you begrudge us taking them?'

'No, god, no.' Dad's hands stretched across the table. He looked grey, with crescents under his eyes. 'We were delighted when your careers took off, we couldn't have been happier for you and your brother. If you were happy, it meant we'd done our job, but, yes, we missed you both terribly, especially when Rob started touring and you got so busy you never had time to come home. But we could see how much you loved your jobs.'

Guilt twisted my insides. I recalled how I'd thrived on their pride; enjoyed them boasting about me – their brilliant, clever daughter – it had made me push harder to do better. Maybe I'd liked who I was in their eyes just a smidge too much. Being so busy all the time – too busy to visit – meant I really was the career-driven high-flyer with the exciting lifestyle, who they bragged about back home.

'And the point of this is?' I said, because there had to be one. Something had been building, maybe even before Rob and I had returned.

'The point is, I suppose we're tired of putting on a front now that it's obvious things aren't going right for either of you, or for us. Or for Sylvia, come to that.'

'Nan?' I looked at Dad.

'We don't want her getting rid of all her things and killing chickens, or weeing in her garden, and refusing to come for Sunday lunch because our beef might not be organic.'

'She's trying not to be a burden,' I said.

'Not that again.' Dad gave a heavy sigh. 'She's *not* a burden.'

I could see a pattern emerging. 'Then you'd better tell her,' I said. 'How are any of us supposed to know how you feel if you don't ever say it?' *That's a laugh, coming from you,* piped a voice in my head. 'I reckon Nan's been waiting for ages to know what you really think of her latest fad. That's why it's gone so far. She's pushing the boundaries.' There, I'd finally said what had been lurking at the back of my mind since I'd seen her packing her life away. 'We need to feel our loved ones give a shit about what we're doing. Pardon my French,' I added, when Dad automatically lowered his brow, aware of my rampant hypocrisy, considering I hadn't known what the hell was going on at home. How much of a shit had *I* given about what they were doing? 'It doesn't mean you're being controlling or putting us under pressure to say that you don't always agree with our choices.'

'So, you think we don't give a shit?' Mum went screechy again. 'We give a *massive* amount of shit.' She banged her fist on the table, and Dad and I jolted upright like startled meerkats. 'That's why we're *in* this state, from giving too *much* of a shit, but not telling you about it. And now you're in a mess, judging by the state of your wrists, and I've *no* idea what's going on with Rob. He's been acting so weird I think he might be on drugs.'

'Who's on drugs?' Rob entered the kitchen in tartan pyjama shorts and a baggy T-shirt and headed straight for the Cheerios, seeming oblivious to the tension swilling about. I'd forgotten he was even in the house, and couldn't believe that he'd slept through Mum's shouting and Dad's mug smashing on the floor. 'What have you been up to, Sandra?'

'It's not *my* fault,' I said. Or was it? I'd clearly had a role to play, because I hadn't been behaving like part of this family for ages. I'd been too busy living up to their supposed expectations, scared to admit I'd cocked up and wasn't the success story they believed I was. 'Mum and Dad are fed up with the café, they think I'm having a breakdown, they don't want Nan killing chickens, and they think you're a drug addict.'

'Oh, is that all?' Abandoning the cereal, he turned to look at us properly; Mum, supporting her head as though it might fall off, Dad slumped over the table studying his hands, and me, bolt upright, fingernails raking my wrist.

His look said *this is weird*.

He came over and crouched next to Mum. 'I thought we'd already talked about me switching jobs, and making a go of things with Emma, and you were fine with it. You seemed really glad that I was back.'

'We think you might be slipping off the rails,' Mum said tearily, letting him take her hands in both of his. 'We were so upset when you told us you'd been drinking too much, because we weren't there for you.'

He looked at me, but all I could offer was a helpless shrug. 'Like I said, Mum, I didn't want to let you down.' He jumped at her wail of protest. 'It's not your fault, I'm a grown-up,' he said earnestly. 'I just wasn't coping, that's all.'

'But you should have felt you could talk to us, or your sister, and you didn't.'

He glanced at me, and I looked away from his open gaze, hot-cheeked.

'But now I have talked to you.' He tried to get Mum to face him properly. 'We can't change the past, so let's not go on about it. And anyway, I'm fine now. Brilliant, in fact.' He bounced her hands up and down. 'I didn't have any alcohol at the pub last night, did I?'

'But your eyes always look funny, as if you're on something.'

'And you've been smiling too much.' Dad sounded certain he was on to something, his fingertip prodding the table. 'No one smiles that much unless they're hiding something.'

'I don't think that's true,' I said. 'I've been beaming as well and so have you, but...' I trailed off, remembering we'd all been hiding quite a lot, but they didn't notice.

'Are you really doing a teaching course, Rob?' Mum's eyes explored his with unusual intensity, and he blinked a couple of times, but held her gaze and nodded.

'And I can't be a drug addict, Mum,' he said, with a grin. 'Not when I'm going to be a dad in six months' time.'

Chapter 28

The effect of Rob's words was transformative. Mum had him hooked in a bear hug before he could move, almost snapping his neck, while Dad leapt up and switched on the kettle, his smile so wide it almost swallowed his ears.

'Why didn't you *say?*' Mum kept repeating, rocking Rob from side to side, until he managed to wriggle free, adjust his glasses, and explain why he'd kept it a secret.

'We're going to be grandparents!' Mum practically leapt into Dad's arms and they jigged around the kitchen like teenagers. Rob caught my eye and smiled sentimentally. I grinned back, a golf-ball-sized lump in my throat.

'Congratulations, son,' Dad said, slapping Rob's shoulder, the rims of his eyes suspiciously pink. 'You'll be a brilliant father, and I'm sure that Emma will be a wonderful mother.'

'She'll be able to channel her bossiness into our child,' he said, slipping Mum and me a look that said he'd always known our secret nickname for her.

'Of course she will,' Mum said, oblivious.

'You just need to get to know her properly.' Rob's words were directed at me this time.

'I will,' I said, defensively. Maybe Emma's bossiness was a manifestation of how much she cared about Rob. I guessed I'd find out, in time, but as long as Rob was happy… I could see now that this was all that mattered.

'I'm so glad you're OK, Rob,' said Mum, cradling his face between her palms, the subtext being, *I'm glad we haven't messed you up too much.* 'We're a proper family again.'

Don't take your family for granted, Cassie, they're part of your history, of who you are. As Danny's words came back to me, tears flew to my eyes. I'd taken them totally for granted.

'We're going to be completely open with you and your sister from now on, even if it means we might not always agree, and you must be honest too. Isn't that right, Ed?' Mum looked at Dad, who nodded eagerly.

'Does that mean you'll take on a manager at the café and go on your cruise, or whatever it is you want to do?' I said.

'Oh, I doubt we'll be going anywhere if there's a baby on the horizon.' Mum glanced out at the sunny garden, as if she could see it hovering by the hedge. 'But maybe…' She glanced at Dad. 'We could always ask Gwen, she'd love to do it.'

'Good choice,' I said, realising it was true. Gwen worked hard and was obviously reliable, and I was sure a warm heart lurked beneath the bluff exterior that the customers inexplicably loved. 'And the baby's six months away, so you could still take a break.' I felt an ache around my heart as I said it. All this time, they'd been longing for a little escape, but had stayed put because they'd thought that's where they should be.

'I can just see them lying stiffly on a beach in their Maitland's Café shirts,' Rob said, finally tipping some Cheerios into a bowl.

I gave a hiccupy giggle. 'Or offering to do the washing up at a hotel.'

'You sit down, we'll make our own cappuccinos,' Rob said, mimicking Mum, but she and Dad were gazing at each other wide-eyed, as if hardly daring to believe it could actually happen.

'Maybe a tour of the Greek islands?' Mum said, and Dad held her close and buried his head in her hair, while Rob and I traded smiles.

Mum sat back down, hands clasped in front her, only a slight redness around her nose suggesting she'd been bawling her eyes out fifteen minutes ago. Even Dad looked like he'd had a blood transfusion.

'So, it looks like we're all setting off in new directions.' Mum's eyes shone like polished glass. 'Rob's going to be a dad, and you've got a wonderful job lined up in London, so you don't have to be self-employed, which I'm so glad about, Cassie, because it's very, very hard work, being your own boss.' She blinked a few times. 'We should have said that as soon as you told us your plans, but we didn't want to—'

'Influence me, I know,' I said, remembering their secret conversation at the café. How had I not guessed they were talking about me?

'And you're painting again.' Dad picked up the picture of Meg's cake still lying on the table where I'd left it to dry. 'No reason why you can't keep it up,' he said, ruffling my hair. 'You must make sure you get some time off work so you can relax.' As if that was going to be possible, flying back and forth to Hawaii or Singapore, finding waterfalls, and elephants and whatever else a bride required to make her day super-special. The groom was usually last on the list.

'And what about that rash?' Mum turned over my wrist, where the itchy patch was horribly inflamed and sore.

'Ouch,' said Rob. 'Looks like you've been trying to escape a pair of handcuffs.'

'Ha, ha, not funny.' I pulled away and hid my hands in my lap. 'Like I said, it's just an allergic reaction to something.' *It looks like eczema.* Meg's voice rang in my mind. *My mum gets it when she's stressed.*

A knock at the front door made us jump like scalded cats, and as Rob went to answer it, unembarrassed by being in his nightwear, Mum said, 'It's a shame in a way about the job, well, not a shame, of course it's not, it's a wonderful opportunity, and we're very, very proud—'

'Mum.'

'Sorry, love, I was going to say that there've been a few enquires at the café about those menus you did, and people asking about the drawings, wanting me to pass on their details, but I said you'd be leaving soon.' Her eyes moved past me and widened, and then she was on her feet, smoothing her curls and checking her boobs were covered. 'Adam, how lovely to see you again, we're not usually in our dressing gowns at this time of day.'

'Not at all, I'm sorry for dropping in unannounced,' said Adam, as I swivelled in my chair. He looked tanned and rugged in a black shirt and fawn trousers and I was acutely aware of my ancient Quidditch nightdress, which Mum must have helped me into as I couldn't remember putting it on. It was riding up, revealing my pasty thighs and bony knees. His dark eyes ran over me, and I shivered as if he'd touched me with his hands. ''Morning, Cassie.'

'Hi!' I stood up, hoping he couldn't smell my breath from where he was standing. 'This is…' I scooped one arm round. 'My family!' I said, talking like a children's TV presenter.

'Yes, we met briefly.' Adam gave an all-encompassing smile, seeming unfazed that only Dad was fully dressed. 'I wondered, if you were free, whether you'd like to go for a spin in the Alfa?' he said to me.

'Ooh, the Alfa,' Rob mouthed behind him.

I shot him a warning look. 'Sounds great!' I beamed. 'If you wouldn't mind giving me ten minutes to get ready?'

'Of course.' He glanced at the table and, following his gaze, I saw my sketch pad open on a drawing of Dickens, strolling along the counter at the café as though he owned the place. 'Cute,' he said.

I froze, wondering whether Mum might tell him I'd drawn it, followed by a speech about how clever I was, and braced myself to admit that the artwork he'd seen at the café was mine, but he was already backing towards the door.

'I'll wait in the car,' he said, raising a hand.

'Good idea.' I hadn't meant to sound relieved.

Mum gave me a scandalised look. 'Won't you stay for coffee?' she said. 'I have to get ready for work, but Ed will make some.'

Dad was heading for the coffee maker as she spoke, but Adam shook his head. 'Thanks, but no,' he said affably. 'I have some paperwork to catch up on.'

He gave me a lingering look, which I knew Rob had picked up on, and sure enough, once the door had closed, he stuck a model-like pose and made sexy-eyes at me.

'Hey, Miss Moneypenny, let's go for a ride in my *Alfa*.'

'Bond drives an Aston Martin, and why do you sound like a sex pest?'

Rob reverted to normal. 'He's a bit smooth for you, isn't he?'

'What's that supposed to mean?'

'I thought you were into Danny Fleetwood,' he said. 'He's obviously into you.'

My heart fluttered. 'He's playing games with me, that's all.' *Danny likes Cassie.* 'I'm his latest challenge.'

'Not the impression I got.'

'Leave her alone, Rob,' said Dad, pouring himself some coffee. 'Adam's quite a catch.'

'A catch,' Rob sniggered. 'This isn't *The Great Gatsby*.'

'He's *very* good-looking,' Mum said, winding a curl around her finger. 'I wouldn't kick him out of bed.'

'*Mum!*'

'Lydia!'

I raced upstairs and left them to it.

The sun was out, and the view of Salcombe estuary was as stunning as I remembered, but I felt nauseous as we wound through the narrow streets and around the yacht-packed harbour. Adam had been swinging the car round every bend as though training for the Grand Prix. He was clearly at home behind the wheel, and I'd done my best to appreciate the 'twin-scroll turbos', silky smooth gearbox and low, red leather seats, but the best I'd managed was a prosaic, 'It's very comfy.'

I'd also discovered we had very different tastes in music when Guns N' Roses had blasted out of the speakers. 'Helps me unwind,' he'd said, smiling as he turned it down, and I told myself we didn't have to like the same things to be a good match, just tolerate each other's differences.

'Have you thought any more about the job I mentioned?' he said, as we strolled through the pretty town, which was full of trendy clothes shops, and past the Maritime Museum. Adam wanted an ice cream and, although my stomach felt unsettled, I didn't want to spoil his seaside adventure. 'I have to let Grace know by tomorrow so she can advertise it, if you're not interested.'

'Oh, I am,' I said, because no one in their right mind would say anything else. He smiled and took hold of my hand, which felt small and delicate in his.

'Here we are.' I stopped outside Salcombe Dairy, which I remembered sold the tastiest ice creams I'd ever eaten. 'They use farm-fresh milk,' I said, leading him inside, where he swiftly chose a chocolate peppermint flake flavour and I picked the stem ginger – wasn't ginger good for nausea? – but as soon as we were back on the pavement, a series of musical notes heralded a phone call.

'Sorry about this.' He winced, handing me his ice cream. 'I'm afraid I have to take it.'

He wandered off, while I held his cone, licking the edges of mine before the ice cream started melting, catching odd words floating back – *acquisition, status report, all-nighter.*

He came back, pushing a hand through his hair, his brows drawn down. 'Cassie, I'm sorry about this, but something's come up and I have to pop down to London.'

'Pop down?'

'I'll be back tonight.' He took his ice cream and wound his tongue around the soft, creamy mound. 'I've booked us a table at a restaurant called The Brook for eight o'clock,' he said. 'The owner of the hotel recommended it.'

My heart juddered. It was the restaurant where Danny worked. The one he'd invited me to for a meal. Tonight.

'It's much too far to go and come back, if you've work to do as well. Let's leave it,' I suggested.

But Adam was shaking his head before I'd finished speaking. 'No way.' He took a big bite of his ice cream and swallowed. 'I came here for a reason, and I'm not going let a cock-up at the office stand in the way. It'll only take half an hour to sort out, but I have to deal with it in person.'

'Does this sort of thing happen often?' I darted my tongue at my ice cream, which was starting to run down my hand. 'Dashing off at a minute's notice.'

'Well, usually, I wouldn't be so far away,' he said, not really answering the question. 'I imagine it's the same in your line of work.'

For a second, I imagined someone calling at 3 a.m. to say the picture I'd painted wasn't quite accurate, and would I come round and dab on a bit more blue. 'I guess,' I said, remembering how I'd carried my phone everywhere at Five Star, even into the toilet.

'Hey, it's not a deal-breaker, is it?' It was clearly a rhetorical question. He looked at his massive watch, while efficiently finishing his ice cream, and I could tell he wasn't tasting it, not properly. In his mind, he was already in his office, brokering a deal, or whatever it was that investment bankers did.

'Is it like *The Wolf on Wall Street* where you work?' I said, as we set off back to the car at a pace too brisk for eating ice cream. I tossed mine in a bin as we passed, and surreptitiously wiped my hand on my jeans.

'You wouldn't believe how many people think that.' I had a sense that my comment had annoyed him slightly, but I might have imagined it, because in his car he leaned over to help me with my seat belt, and pushed his lips against mine, his dark eyes serious.

'We'll make a night of it tonight,' he murmured, brushing the back of his hand down my cheek. I gave a little shiver. 'I want to know everything there is to know about you. The *real* you,' he added, as though he'd just kissed an imposter.

'That won't take long,' I said.

He laughed, as though he didn't believe me, and didn't speak again on the short journey back, as if saving up all his words for later.

Chapter 29

At a loose end after Adam had dropped me home, having pressed a kiss on my fingers before driving off, I called Andy Farrington's agent.

'Worth every penny, was he?' Her voice was ripe with sarcasm.

'Definitely,' I said, taking it on the chin. I could have found a local comedian for a lot less than Andy's fee, if I'd really tried, but the fact that he'd been on TV – and was a bit risqué – had undoubtedly added to his appeal. 'Please pass on my thanks.'

I brushed off the overwhelming temptation to go back to bed, and decided to make the most of the day by taking my sketch pad and pencils to the beach. It wasn't as if I needed to think about my career any more, other than what to wear to impress Grace Dewsbury, and I had plenty of outfits that should do the trick.

As I strolled to the beach, I wondered whether I should phone The Brook to check whether Danny was working later. Had he meant us to eat there together tonight, or to cook me a meal? Either way, in spite of my drunken pass the night before, I doubted his invitation still stood. But it would be awkward if he was there, and saw Adam and me.

I'd half expected him to call, to gloat about our snog, then remembered he didn't have my number. It wouldn't have been hard to get hold of though, and I fished my phone out of my bag to check, but there were no missed calls. No message from Adam either. Not that

I'd expected one. He'd be on the motorway now, foot down, singing along to 'Sweet Child o' Mine', while Danny would be working at one of his many jobs.

I remembered what Bill had said about Danny sending him the clip of Andy Farrington, and wondered why Danny had gone out on a limb like that. He couldn't have been trying to win me over if he hadn't even bothered to tell me about it, so maybe he was just being... *nice.*

My mind felt full of sharp edges, so I focused on putting one foot in front of the other, careful to steer clear of the café, because I didn't want to be spotted, knowing it would lead to questions about Adam's whereabouts.

Down on the beach, I walked past the fortresses of windbreaks and tartan blankets and sat on a smooth-topped rock, out of sight of the café, and angled my head to the sun to warm my face. There wouldn't be any of this once I was back in London. And even in Thailand or Fiji, or wherever I was required to arrange a wedding, there wouldn't be time to relax and soak up the atmosphere.

My shoulders tightened as I took out my phone and googled Grace Dewsbury. Her website was exquisite; all pastel colours and tasteful fonts, and dramatic shots of brides and grooms in stunning surroundings. Prices ranged from outrageous to unbelievable. Surely roses dipped in gold were a step too far, and was it really necessary for a bride to arrive by elephant, or to fly in a world-class tap-dancing troupe for the wedding reception?

Grace's profile picture was intimidatingly beautiful. Couldn't she have had scraped back mousy hair and a bad complexion, instead of softly cascading blonde waves around a flawless heart-shaped face? I'd have to get my hair re-done. The Plumberry was growing out, leaving behind a sludge-coloured strip at the roots. Maybe I could go lighter, this time – marmalade, perhaps. Or very dark. Midnight black, or maybe a tawny colour, with lighter stripes… I realised I was thinking in cat colours, just as my phone rang. It was Liz from the shelter, calling to apologise for not making it to the café.

'Danny said you did a great job of looking after the cats,' she said, while I bit my lip in an agony of guilt, wondering what he'd have made of everything that had happened before he'd turned up to collect them. 'And it's not the first time Tabitha's escaped,' she went on. 'That's why it's been hard to find her forever home. But we've had so many queries today, we don't think she'll be here much longer.'

When she didn't suggest a repeat of the event, I was flushed with guilty relief. I was pleased it had worked out well for the cats, but it had been a strain being responsible for all those feline futures. Better to stick with people, who could at least voice a criticism (and frequently did) and say if they weren't having a nice time.

I'd just pulled out my sketch pad, when I heard familiar female voices. Using my pad as a visor, I saw Meg and Tilly approaching, shoes dangling from their fingers. 'How did you know I was here?' I said, when they'd thrown themselves down on the sand in front of me, faces brimming with smiles. Tilly had an emerald scarf wound around her hair, fastened in a bow on top, and Meg's Maitland's shirt was the exact same shade as the sea.

'I saw you walking down the path,' Meg said, brushing at her sandy feet. 'It's my lunch break and I was having coffee on the terrace with Tilly.'

'Today's walk was cancelled,' said Tilly, sifting sand through her fingers, squinting her eyes against the sun's glare. 'I was celebrating with cake.'

'I thought you liked walking.'

'I do, but it's nice to not do anything too.' I couldn't help smiling. That just about summed up the Tilly I remembered. 'What are you doing here?' she said.

'I was with Adam, but he got a call and had to drive back to London.'

I couldn't miss the little look she exchanged with Meg.

'He's coming back,' I said, with a bristle. 'We're going out for a meal this evening.'

Meg's eyes grew round. 'Isn't it something like a four-hour journey?'

'More.' I suddenly realised how big a deal it was. All that way – for me.

'Wow,' said Tilly, resting her chin on her drawn-up knees. 'No one's ever made an eight-hour round trip to take me out to dinner.'

'If they did, you'd have forgotten and gone out with someone else,' I said, amazed by how comfortable I felt in their presence. 'Or you wouldn't be in the mood.'

'True.' Her smile was accompanied by a gentle prod at my shin. 'I couldn't cope with that sort of intensity.'

'Most women would love some intensity like that.'

'Including you?'

I half laughed, but the truth was, I didn't know. Nothing like it had ever happened to me before. It didn't feel *wrong*, I knew that much. It was lovely knowing someone was willing to go the extra mile – or hundreds of miles, in Adam's case.

Eager to change the subject, I said, 'I was going to pop into the café when I was done here,' even though I hadn't planned to. I still hadn't fully processed everything that had happened that morning, and wanted to avoid Mum and Dad for a bit longer. I knew they'd be anxious to reassure themselves that they hadn't done the wrong thing by revealing their true feelings, and I wasn't ready to face them when mine were still such a tangle. 'Listen, I'm sorry about last night.'

'That's why we're here, actually.' Meg looked at Tilly as if for confirmation before continuing, and Tilly gave a little nod. 'We're staging an intervention.'

'What?' I stared at Meg, half wondering what product she used to make her hair so impossibly shiny. 'I don't think a few glasses of wine on an empty stomach warrants an intervention.'

'I'm sure Danny Fleetwood would agree with you.' Seeing Tilly's saucy pout, I went hot all over. 'And it's not that sort of intervention,' she said, before I could produce a coherent response.

She plucked my pad from my lap and started flicking through it. 'These are great,' she said, showing Meg. 'Can I have the one of the cat washing its face?'

'If you want.' I stroked a strand of hair off my cheek. 'It's not very good.'

'You have to stop that.' Meg wagged a mum-like finger. 'Making out you're not very good, when you quite clearly are.'

'I'd pay for one,' agreed Tilly. 'Top dollar.'

Not knowing how to handle their compliments, I said, 'Look, what's this about?'

Tilly put down the pad and knelt up, tugging her phone from the pocket of her jeans. 'We were looking up all the qualities you need to be a successful event planner.'

It was the last thing I'd expected her to say, and I felt a cold plunge of dread. 'And?'

Still on her knees, she read aloud from her screen. 'Good interpersonal and people skills.'

'I *like* talking to people. If I'm in the mood.' *People I actually like.* Thinking back, there hadn't been too many of those during my time at Five Star.

'Creative.'

'I'm *definitely* creative.'

Meg held up a finger. 'Listen, Cassie, it's important.'

I folded over and ran my fingers through the sand between my feet. 'Go on.'

'Tech savvy,' Tilly continued, in a schoolmarm voice. 'Flexible, good organisational skills, great eye for details, natural leader, enthusiastic and passionate about your role.'

'OK, I get it.' I straightened, brushing sand from my hands, wondering whether the hurt I felt was written all over my face. 'You're saying I'm none of those things.'

'Hang on.' Tilly held up a finger, and carried on reading. 'Event coordinating is one of the top ten most stressful professions, up there with being a fire fighter or pilot. For the second consecutive year it's been ranked number five, behind police officer.'

'That's just silly,' I said.

Meg laid a hand on my knee, the jewels in her engagement ring winking in the sun. 'Last night, you looked terrified,' she said. 'Even though it was going really well. And when you were telling us about your job the first day we saw you at the café, you got this sort of glazed expression – like you were trying to remember what it was you actually liked about it.'

'We didn't see it at first,' Tilly said, sitting back. 'It just felt like something was off.' I could feel perspiration gathering on my brow. 'Then, last night, when you were in the garden – those things you said, about being fired from your job. You looked relieved.'

'That's rubbish, I was gutted—'

'It all made sense,' Meg broke in, her hand cupping my knee. 'All this time, you've been trying to be something you're not, and wearing yourself out in the process by the look of it.'

I jerked away from her touch. 'Sounds like you've been having a good old bitch about me behind my back.'

Meg's face fell. 'Oh, Cassie, we'd never do that. We're worried about you.'

'We don't think you should take that job in London.' Tilly gave me her steadiest look. 'It won't make you happy.'

Tears formed in my eyes, and I tilted my head back so they wouldn't see. 'I had a bit too much to drink last night, that's all. We all say stuff when we're drunk.'

'Yeah, stuff we usually mean,' said Tilly. 'Are you saying you *didn't* get fired?'

'No, but that doesn't mean I'm *glad* about it.' Blinking furiously, I began stuffing my things back into my bag.

'Do you love your job?' Tilly pushed.

'*You can learn to love something, if you do it long enough.*' I was talking in Nina's quotes again.

'You can learn to get *used* to it,' Tilly countered. 'Not the same thing.'

'*Do the same thing, day after day, year after year, and good things will come your way.* And they have.' I was becoming high-pitched in the face of Tilly's unnatural scepticism. 'There's a job in London I wouldn't have dreamed could be mine a couple of months ago.'

'That doesn't mean you have to take it.'

I stood up, lungs tight. 'Look, you think you know me, but you don't,' I said, striving to stay calm. 'We haven't seen each other for years. You've no idea how I feel about anything.'

'We do, because we've got eyes and ears, and it's obvious that something's not right.' Meg's voice was gentle.

'Mum and Dad don't see it.' I realised too late that my words were a sort of admission, and dumped myself back on the rock.

'Parents often see what they want to.' Tilly's smile stayed in place but her entire face looked troubled, and I felt as if I'd jumped into icy water.

'If they knew I'd been fired…' I gulped back tears, and Meg raised her eyebrows just a fraction, like someone encouraging a toddler to tell the truth. 'They'd be so disappointed,' I blurted. 'They love having a daughter they can boast about, and, to be honest, I liked *being* that daughter. Even if things weren't always as exciting as I made out.' I swiped a hand over my face. 'I worked so bloody hard, I was certain Carlotta – that was my boss – would eventually promote me, and I'd be able to move out of my flat – which was tiny, by the way, because it was all I could afford – and buy somewhere more glamorous. And maybe I'd get an assistant and be able to cut down on my hours a bit, but it didn't happen because I was *so* tired all the time that I messed up a couple of jobs. But Mum and Dad are so proud of me, I couldn't bear to let them down and tell them the truth, especially after Rob had announced he was back for good.' The words tore in my throat. 'I still can't.'

'Oh, Cassie.' Meg sounded on the verge of tears. 'If they'd known, they'd have understood, and asked you to come home straight away.'

My head shook, fiercely. 'They've always stuck to their policy of non-interference, you know what they're like,' I said. 'And I didn't *want* to come home. I mean, I did – I really missed this place at times – but not because I had no choice.'

Tilly's mouth turned down. 'They wouldn't want you to be unhappy.'

'I'm not,' I said. 'At least, not any more. I was worried about becoming my own boss, and not having any money, but now I've been offered this amazing job and I'd be mad to turn it down.' I was gabbling, in my effort to make them see it through my eyes. 'I'll be in charge this time, so I can set my own hours, and I can put into place everything I've learnt.'

'I s'pose.' Meg looked doubtful.

'I don't know,' said Tilly. 'It might be even more stressful than working for a horrible boss.'

'I'll have an assistant,' I said, because that seemed like the most important part. 'It'll be like *The Devil Wears Prada.*'

'What, you being a bitch?' Tilly's frown cut a line between her brows. 'We can't make you change your mind, but I'm telling you, Cassie, you've got a future here if you want it.'

'Not one where I can earn fifty thousand a year.'

'Good point.' Meg was making an effort to match my tone. 'I'd do the job for that salary.'

'No, you wouldn't,' Tilly scoffed. 'Sam wouldn't want you to.'

Meg scooped up a handful of sand and threw it in Tilly's lap. 'He would if it stopped his mum sending links to wedding venues.'

'I could do that,' I said, my mood miraculously lifting. 'If you don't mind selling your grandmother to pay for it.'

'When do you have to go?' Tilly's question had an air of resignation.

'Soon,' I said. 'I'll need to travel to London next week to talk to Grace Dewsbury.'

Tilly's face cleared. 'Hey, there's a barbecue at the Smugglers Inn on Saturday afternoon. We should do our routine there.'

'*Yes!*' Meg punched the air with both hands. 'We're long overdue a Legal Mystics reunion.'

'Oh god.' I buried my face in my hands. 'We can't.'

'We can,' said Tilly, pulling my hands away. I was relieved to see her smiling. 'And we will.'

'I'm not sure the world is ready for my vocals.'

'No, but I reckon the locals are.' Meg's eyes danced. 'They loved us the first time round.'

'That was a long time ago,' I said. 'They could forgive us when we were teenagers.'

Meg was already jigging her shoulders and humming the tune we'd belted out.

'I've still got my outfit.' Tilly gave an impish grin. 'I found it when I was packing to come back from Canada. Even those awful trainers. I've no idea why I took them with me.'

'I've kept mine too,' Meg confessed. 'I can just about fit into the combat trousers.' Seeing our quizzical looks she said airily, 'I might have tried them on.'

'I bet mine are still in my wardrobe,' I said. 'I'll check when I get home.'

We exchanged little smiles, a feeling of warm relief flowing between us, and I was suddenly overcome with gratitude that they'd cared enough to find me and tell me how they felt – even if I didn't agree. For a moment we gazed at the sea, which the breeze had tossed into white-capped peaks, and a feeling of peace descended.

'I suppose I ought to get back to work,' Meg said, but didn't move.

'Just five more minutes.' Tilly reached for her jacket and bundled it into a pillow. 'Let's lie down like we used to and imagine we're sixteen again.'

'That'll be a bit of a stretch,' said Meg, but she shuffled onto her back, lacing her hands behind her head, and I slipped between her and Tilly, resting my head on my bag as I stared at the sky. It was so big, and blue, and vast, that my worries shrank instantly. A couple of seabirds dipped and turned, caught on a current of air, and distant childish squeals took me back to all the happy times I'd spent on this beach.

'What would you say to your sixteen-year-old self?' said Tilly, lazily.

Meg shifted, lowering her arm so it brushed against mine. 'I'd say, cutting your own hair's a big mistake.' We snorted, remembering the time she'd tried to layer it to look like Rachel's from *Friends*, only it kept on getting shorter.

'You looked like Austin Powers in the end,' I said, giggling.

'Hey, it wasn't *that* short!'

'I'd tell myself to leave my eyebrows alone,' said Tilly. 'I spent a year looking permanently surprised and no one told me.'

'That's because all the girls looked the same,' I said. 'Apart from me.'

'You were trying to start a new trend.' Meg's shoulder bumped mine. 'Strong, bushy brows.'

'I was way ahead of my time.'

Tilly's voice held a trace of laughter when she said, 'So what would you say, Cassie?'

Her hand nudged mine and I caught hold of it, pushing my fingers through Meg's on the other side, feeling warmth spreading across my chest. 'That's easy,' I said. 'I'd tell myself to never lose touch with my friends.'

Chapter 30

I arrived at The Brook, nerves jumping, to find the car park was full. Unwilling to leave Sir Lancelot on the road outside, I parked by the kerb, hoping someone might be about to leave.

I'd vastly overestimated how long it would take to get to Kingsbridge and was half an hour early, but figured sitting in the car was better than sitting at home with Mum and Dad. I'd avoided the café in the end, after waving off Meg and Tilly, and stayed on the beach until the breeze picked up and the sun went in, then wandered home, head swirling with seismic thoughts. Once there, I'd distracted myself by making a list of the commissions I'd accepted, and organising a time frame in which to complete them. Grace might want me to start work right away, but I intended to honour them all – even if it meant painting or drawing right through the night.

Adam had texted at three thirty to say he was on his way back, and when Mum and Dad returned home I'd stayed upstairs, getting ready.

'You look lovely,' Mum had gushed when I came down, self-conscious in a stretchy, metal-grey dress with long sleeves and cut-out shoulders. 'Your boobs are coming back.'

'It's all the cake I've been putting away.' I'd discreetly made sure my rash was covered and subdued the itching with a liberal coating of antiseptic cream, disguising the smell with some of Mum's 'Evening in Paris' perfume.

'You look like your mum,' Dad had said, nodding to their honey-moon picture on the wall with a whimsical smile on his face. 'Except for your purple hair.'

'It's Plumberry,' I'd said, checking myself in the mirror to make sure the loose curls I'd fashioned hadn't dropped out already. I was pleased to see that the eyeliner I'd applied had made my eyes look bigger.

Sensing Mum was about to ask me something I wouldn't be able to answer, I'd made my escape, certain I'd spotted Dad unbuttoning his shirt before I even made it out of the door.

Sighing, I checked my phone to see if there was an update from Adam, wishing we were at the stage where I felt comfortable calling him, but there was nothing. Maybe he was here already. I scanned the car park again, but couldn't see his Alfa.

At least the restaurant looked like the sort of place he'd feel at home in. The building had an attractive, honey-stone exterior and a low, thatched roof with fairy lights strung around the edges. It used to be a pub, according to TripAdvisor, and overlooked a brook at the back, hence its name. I'd had a quick peek on the website to see whether Danny's name appeared, but although there were plenty of flattering references to the quality of the food, the chef wasn't mentioned by name.

I wondered whether to drive around and come back, but, on a wave of recklessness, decided to text Nina instead.

Might be working with Grace Dewsbury!!

I deleted the exclamation marks. They weren't really me. Or Nina.

Worried she'll ask C for a reference X

Her reply was instant:

*Thought you were going it alone??!!!! Am jealous, would love to work
with G. Ask her to contact me, I'll lie through my teeth, tell her you
were an asset (jokes) x*

Jokes? And what was with all the punctuation marks? I wondered
whether she'd been drinking, but knew she kept a tight rein on her
alcohol intake, because of work. Another text pinged in:

*Jokes, about lying, I mean. You WERE an asset, even if C didn't think
so, moody cow ha ha. PT just proposed, bit squiffy on champers,
we're going to elope on New Year's Eve!!!!!!*

Definitely drunk. Which meant, when she'd sobered up, she might
tell Carlotta, and Carlotta might contact Grace.

*Don't worry, won't tell C. Everyone deserves a second chance to be
an events manager – said no one, ever!!! HAHAHAHA!!!!*

It sounded almost as if Nina wasn't enjoying her job, though she'd
never once given that impression when we'd worked together.

Why didn't C like me? Might as well take advantage of her inebriated
state. *Never did find out! XX*

*Probably saw you as a threat – all those hours you put in, you crazy
cow!!! You should have legged it ages ago, you'll fly now, Cazzzie, I'm
jealous as fuck (s'cuse my language) HUGS XXX*

She might be drunk, but Nina wouldn't have said it if she didn't truly believe it.

Thanks and CONGRATULATIONS!!! I texted back, carried away on a soaring sense of hope. *Let me know if you'd like me to plan your wedding :) XX*

Lifting my head, I saw that the car park had miraculously emptied and swung Sir Lancelot into the nearest bay.

It was almost eight o'clock. Outside, the sky was smudged with gold and lilac, and a tiny moon had risen above a row of conifers, reminding me of Danny's message in the sand. I rubbed my finger between my eyebrows to erase the image, but another instantly replaced it: his face coming closer to mine, his lips slightly parted, his eyes hazy with lust…

I shouldered the car door open and almost fell out, taking a few deep breaths that did nothing to steady my pulse. Tucking my bag underneath my arm, I adopted what I hoped was the stance of a successful woman, before walking round to the entrance. Hopefully, no one noticed me stumble on the gravel.

Inside was warm and softly lit, all nooks and beams, and gleaming cutlery set on soft white napkins, but I was surprised to see that all the tables were empty, considering it was a Friday night and the place had a good reputation.

'I'm supposed to be meeting Adam Conway,' I said to the waist-coated waiter approaching with a smiling welcome, holding my breath in case there'd been a mistake and the restaurant was closed for a private party that hadn't yet materialised.

'Mr Conway hasn't arrived, but if you'd like to follow me.'

He led me to a table set for two in the centre of the restaurant, a fat candle flickering in a jar in between the place settings. 'This is nice,' I said, glancing around me. 'How come it's so quiet?'

'Mr Conway booked the whole restaurant for the rest of the evening,' the waiter said, as he pulled out a high-backed chair for me to sit on. 'You have the place to yourselves.'

Dumbfounded, I looked at him. 'But… surely he can't do that.'

'If the price is right, he most certainly can,' he said, inclining his head. I sat, feeling suddenly breathless. Adam had booked the whole restaurant, just for the two of us? I didn't know whether to be flattered or embarrassed. It seemed so… *extravagant.* Romantic, though.

Piano music piped through the room, light and delicate. I flapped out my napkin and tried to look like this sort of thing happened to me all the time.

'What can I get you to drink?'

'I'll, er… just some sparkling water, please,' I said, recalling my behaviour the night before. The waiter bowed his head and, as he hurried away, my phone bleated.

Stuck in traffic, running late. Have a drink on me! X

Bugger.

How late? X

Could be an hour. Sorry. Have a drink on me! X

Sighing, I smoothed a tendril of hair behind my ear and picked up the menu, but I couldn't focus and put it down again. It felt a bit spooky being the only one there. The atmosphere was oddly flat. I glanced at the empty tables and thought they looked a bit sad. I'd have preferred the friendly hum of conversation and the musical scrape of crockery to the tinkly piano music.

The waiter came back with my water. 'Mr Conway's running a bit late,' I said.

'Ah.' He made a sympathetic face. 'Would you like me to fetch you something? Some olives, perhaps, or bread?'

'Mmm… maybe some bread, please.' Apart from the ice cream that morning, which I hadn't finished, I'd stuck to fruit and coffee all day – partly through nerves, and partly because I wanted to save myself for the meal. 'And some olives. Please.' I felt awful ordering him about, even if he looked perfectly happy as he scuttled off to the kitchen. Fancy having to work tonight, just for Adam and me.

Thank god Danny wasn't there. How mortifying, if he saw me waiting for the handsome hero to turn up, like a character in a film.

'Are you planning to make an olive sandwich?'

I almost spat out my mouthful of sparkling water. 'Danny!' Heat rose and pushed to my cheeks. 'I didn't think you'd be here tonight.'

'I usually work on Fridays.' He had a bread basket in one hand, a bowl of olives in the other, and a smile plastered to his face.

'What are you smiling at?'

'You,' he said. 'You look… wow.' He mimed eyes popping out on stalks. 'Stunning.'

'Oh. Thanks.' I stroked my hair and tugged the hem of my dress over my knees, even though it was already over my knees. 'You don't look so bad yourself.'

I couldn't believe I'd said it. I mean, he did look good – he particularly suited chef's whites, which made everything about him – hair, skin, eyes – more vivid, but I'd sounded almost… *flirty*. I never flirted;

had assumed I was physically incapable of it, like doing more than one push-up, or licking my elbow. 'Where's the waiter?'

'Having a sit down, he's been run off his feet,' Danny quipped, placing the bread and the olives in front of me, before bowing with great solemnity. 'I thought I'd recommend the chef's special, but I see your paramour hasn't arrived.'

'He's stuck in traffic,' I said, thinking how lame it sounded. The opposite of romantic. 'He won't be long.' I wondered whether Danny had thought about our kiss last night, or whether women threw themselves at him so often it had barely registered. Or maybe it had been really awful and he couldn't bring himself to mention it.

'Why are you looking at my mouth?' he said, eyes glinting. 'Fancy a replay of last night?'

'Oh, shut up.' I slumped back in my chair. 'I thought you'd forgotten.'

'Hardly.' His eyes caught hold of mine. 'I've wanted to kiss you since the second I saw you at Sylvia's.'

'Well done for holding back,' I said, switching from flirty to outrage. He knew I was waiting for a date, and had chosen now to tell me he'd wanted to kiss me for ages? I wished my heart would stop flapping around in my chest like a startled hen. 'You need to stop playing games with me.'

'Me, playing games?' He pointed to his chest with pantomime astonishment, before pulling out the chair opposite and sitting down. 'I don't play games. I think I made it clear from day one that I liked you.'

'You said you were going to win me over, not that it means anything, coming from you.'

His smile lost some of its power. 'What's that supposed to mean?'

'You said it once before, remember, when you invited me to the school leavers' dance?' *Why the hell had I brought that up?*

Danny's eyebrows jolted in surprise. 'I tried to explain about that, and you told me you'd got off with someone else.'

Heat settled in my face. 'I saw you with another girl as I was leaving.' As soon as I'd said it, I wanted to take it back, but Danny's gaze turned inward, as if he was trying to remember.

'I was asking where you were, because I thought you might have already left,' he said slowly. 'Jennifer Hartwell stopped me on the way in. I can't even remember now what she was talking about, but she was pretty drunk.' That made sense. I'd seen her earlier that night with her gaggle of friends, swigging from a bottle she'd smuggled in in her bag. 'By the time I got away from her, you must have gone. Probably to snog Lennie Jamieson.' The warmth in my face intensified. 'My dad hadn't been very well,' he went on, and my stomach clenched, remembering what his mum had told me. 'Mum was on her way back from visiting my sister at uni and Dad wasn't very good at being on his own, so I stayed with him until she got home.'

'I didn't snog Lennie Jamieson,' I blurted. 'I couldn't stand him, actually.'

'You know he's wanted by the police now, for embezzlement?' The corners of Danny's mouth twitched upwards. 'He swindled a lot of money from the company where he worked, and fled to Brazil a couple of years ago. I bumped into an old friend, who's in the police force, and he told me all about it.'

'Oh god.' I laughed softly, wondering whether Meg and Tilly knew. Against her better judgement, Tilly had quite fancied Lennie. 'Sounds like I dodged a bullet.'

'He definitely took a wrong turn.'

A small silence fell, broken by a soft-rock ballad that had replaced the bland piano music and which made me think of Adam.

'I'm moving back to London soon.'

'With Mr Conway?' Danny popped an olive into his mouth. 'You mean, he's succeeded where I failed in winning you over?'

'He's doing a pretty good job.' I fiddled with the cutlery, swapping the knife and fork around. 'He's very romantic.'

'Ah, well, if romance is what you want…'

'Doesn't everyone?'

He propped his elbows on the table. 'I don't know, I'm not everyone.'

'You don't seem that bothered for someone who was desperate to win me over not long ago.' I did scratchy quote marks with my fingers.

'If I'm really not what you want, well…' He propped his stubbly chin on his hand and gave me a penetrating look. 'I want you to be happy,' he said, seriously. 'I happen to think you deserve it. I want you to do what you feel is right for *you*.' There was something about the way he said it… he sounded so genuine. As if he really did care, which was odd when I'd hardly made the best impression since crashing back into his life.

I snatched a wedge of seeded bread from the basket and took a bite, but it turned to dust in my mouth. He was watching me too closely for comfort, and the sound of my phone ringing came as a welcome relief.

'Cassie, I'm so sorry, but I'm not going to make it.'

'What?'

'The traffic's terrible, I've been on the same stretch of road for nearly an hour.'

'But I'm at the restaurant. Alone.' I gave Danny a pointed look, but he was gnawing a crust and pretending not to listen. 'I can wait.'

'No, don't,' he said, in his quietly authoritative way. 'I wanted it to be special, but I probably won't make it until ten, and I'll be tired from travelling. You deserve better than me yawning over the Bollinger.' I heard the smile in his voice and marvelled that he didn't seem fed up to have been in his car for most of the day, with no reward at the end of it. Maybe he just really loved his Alfa. Or, maybe in his world, this sort of thing happened a lot.

'I can't believe you booked the whole restaurant.' I sensed the evening and all its possibilities sliding out of my grasp, and wanted to hold on to them for a few moments longer.

'Stay and have something to eat, it's all paid for,' he said. 'Why don't you come down to London tomorrow, join me at the party I mentioned? I'd love you to meet my family, and Grace will be there. I can introduce you.'

'Oh.' Put on the spot, my mind began spinning in circles. We'd get to spend time together, I'd meet his parents (he'd already met mine) and I'd have the chance to impress Grace Dewsbury. And it wasn't as if I had any plans for tomorrow, other than a karaoke routine at the Smugglers Inn with Meg and Tilly.

'Sure,' I said, though it was more of a squeak. 'I'd love to.'

'Great!' Adam sounded gratifyingly pleased. 'I'll text you my address.'

'Great,' I echoed, and sat for a second when he'd hung up, staring at my phone.

'He's not coming,' said Danny. It wasn't a question.

'No.' I looked at him, wondering whether he'd heard Adam's side of the conversation. 'He's still stuck in traffic.'

'That's a shame.' Danny pushed his chair back and stood up. 'I had a lovely menu prepared. In fact, I prepared something of everything for you to try.'

'To try and win me over?' It was a poor attempt at a teasing tone that fell flat.

'Maybe. Before,' he said. 'When I thought I was in with a chance.' His smile was back, but not as convincing. 'Seems a shame to let it go to waste.'

'I don't really want to eat on my own.' My wrist tingled, and once again I fought the urge to scratch. 'I'm really sorry we've wasted your time, but I think I'll just go home.'

Danny folded his arms and gave me a disarming stare. 'Stay there,' he said at last. 'I've got an idea, if you can bear with me for half an hour.'

'What are you going to do?'

'Wait and see,' he said, and disappeared into the kitchen.

Chapter 31

I'd finished my water and the olives, visited the loo, checked my eyeliner wings hadn't smudged, and was trying to fashion a swan with my napkin, when there was a kerfuffle at the door and Mum and Dad came over, their faces wreathed in smiles.

My jaw dropped. 'What are you doing here?' I said, as the waiter shoved another table over to make more seating.

'Danny called and said you were here on your own, and would we like to come for dinner.' Mum bent to kiss my cheek and took off her coat, releasing a scent of 'Evening in Paris', before sitting beside me and smiling up at the waiter.

'But… haven't you eaten already?' I said, as Dad sat opposite Mum and unwound his scarf. They'd both put on smart tops and brushed their hair, and Mum was wearing lipstick.

'We hadn't actually got round to eating.' Dad tipped Mum a wink and a flush coloured her face.

'You two are disgusting.' Now the shock was wearing off, I realised how pleased I was to see them. I'd assumed that Danny had been planning to wheel out a series of dishes for me to sample, to impress me with, not invite my parents over for dinner. 'You didn't have to come.'

'We wanted to,' Mum said, pressing my knee.

'We don't see enough of you as it is, love.' Dad leaned over and gave my hand a squeeze.

'We're really sorry that Adam let you down though,' added Mum.

'It's fine,' I said – and it was. Maybe I could just relax and be myself. For a while, at least. We turned as voices signalled more arrivals, and I was stunned to see Rob saunter in with Nan on one arm, and a wide-eyed brunette with a wavy bob, cupid's bow lips, and a feline gaze on the other. I hadn't seen Emma for ages, and was surprised to see how soft she looked. In my mind, she'd morphed into a hard-faced harridan, fuelled by the memory of how she'd ordered Rob around last Christmas, not letting him drink more than a couple of beers, and whipping away the wine bottle whenever he reached for it. Now, I understood why.

'Look who we found,' Rob said, leading Nan over as though she was the Queen.

'I do like Emma's car.' She cast a gracious smile around. 'It's electric, very good for the environment.'

'I can't believe you're all here,' I said, as the waiter brought over a couple of extra chairs. Standing, I drew Nan into a hug, pleased to see she'd eschewed her bamboo robe in favour of a pleated skirt, and a sparkly, silver cardigan that complimented her coil of hair.

'I kept a few clothes back, just in case, *chérie*,' she said, seeing me looking, her face tinged pink with pleasure. She was wearing eyeshadow too.

'Hear you got stood up,' said Rob, flicking my bare shoulder. 'Looks like the moths have been at your frock.'

'No one says frock any more.' I punched his upper arm. 'Hi, Emma.'

'Hi, Cassie, you look lovely.' She gave Rob a reproving look, but her face quickly relaxed back into a friendly smile.

'I hear congratulations are in order.'

Her hands automatically shot to her still flat stomach, and her eyes had a gleam of happiness. 'Thanks,' she said. 'It's due in October.'

'Ooh, our wedding anniversary's in October,' Mum said, giving Emma's fingers an excited squeeze. 'Twenty fifth,' she added, helpfully.

'Maybe it'll come on that very day and we can have a double celebration.' Rob escorted Nan to the seat facing me, before he and Emma settled at opposite ends of the tables.

'The Maitlands, all together under one roof.' Dad looked round with a wide, satisfied smile. 'And none of you are glued to your rectangular sweethearts, either.' That's how he referred to mobile phones.

'I'm honoured to be included,' said Emma, and as if the tone had been set we all beamed at each other, until the waiter cleared his throat and asked, 'Shall I bring some champagne?'

Danny's food was a revelation; three courses of perfection, starting with a simple but delicious leek soup that we inhaled in about three seconds. My cod with chorizo on a 'tangle' of pea shoots tasted as good as Danny had promised it would, and Dad was chuffed to finally be cooked a steak exactly how he liked it – 'rare, but not still mooing'. Emma, who was vegetarian, praised the 'heritage' carrots; while Mum raved about her 'melt-in-the-mouth' scallops; and Nan, who appeared to have thrown her new environmentally friendly eating regime out of the window, declared her venison the best she'd eaten outside France, which Dad said was so long ago he was surprised she could still remember.

She tapped his arm with a spoon. 'There are lots of things I remember about living in France,' she said. 'We should take a trip there one day.' Immediately the words were out, she dropped her eyes to her plate as if she hadn't spoken.

The air pressure around the table seemed to change, apart from where Rob was shovelling braised hare into his mouth as though a famine was forecast.

I put down my knife and fork. 'Mum and Dad were saying they're a bit worried about your new lifestyle,' I said, in case they'd decided that being too honest with Nan might prove cataclysmic. 'It takes up so much of your time, they don't see as much of you as they'd like.'

Nan put down the glass of champagne she'd been about to knock back. 'You know I don't want to be a burden.' Her gaze slid to Dad. 'I've put you through too much as it is, Edmund.'

'You were never a burden,' Dad said quietly.

She stared at him with a tremulous expression of hope that was hard to look at. 'Really?'

He opened his mouth, closed it again, looked at Mum, then at his empty plate, and nodded. 'Never,' he said. 'And I don't like to think of you going without your comforts, Mum, especially at your age. Not that you're past it, far from it, but we'd like you to come down to the café sometimes, or over to ours for lunch. We know you're busy with your hobbies, and saving the planet, and we wouldn't want to discourage you, but it would be nice to make time for each other.'

Nan's face suffused with pleasure. 'But you've already done so much for me, Edmund. You shouldn't have to look out for me any more.'

'I know you can take care of yourself,' he said, looking at her sideways. 'But you're my mother, and I love you, and want to spend time with you while I still can.'

'I'm not at death's door,' she scolded gently. 'I'm very healthy these days, but thank you.' Smiling with watery eyes, she rested her veiny hand on his arm, and leaned in close so their heads were almost touching. '*La vie est une fleur*,' she said. 'Life is a flower,' and, for once, Dad didn't roll his eyes. Instead, he draped his arm around her shoulders and kissed the top of her hair. 'I have something for you, Edmund.' She tilted towards her handbag and pulled something out. It was the photo album she'd hurled across her living room and threatened to burn, looking a bit battered around the edges. 'I thought you might like this,' she said, briefly catching my eye as she pushed it in front of Dad. 'There are some lovely pictures in there, of you and your *papa*.'

Dad's face worked as he gazed at it for a moment – perhaps thinking about all the memories it contained – before resting a hand on Nan's and saying in a strangled voice, 'Thank you. I'll have a look through it, later.'

Mum sniffed and hiccupped, and said, 'Aw, now, isn't that lovely?' and I had to blink a few times to clear my vision.

'It's like a Hallmark movie,' said Rob, now he'd stopped eating, a big smile puffing up his cheeks. Then I realised it wasn't the smile; his cheeks were stuffed with food.

'Sylvia, we're not happy about you slaughtering chickens,' Mum burst out.

Nan reached over and patted her hand. 'Don't worry, Lydia,' she said. 'Danny's had no luck finding me a *coq*.' Rob sniggered. 'I'm going to stick with some laying hens, for eggs.'

After we'd finished dessert – I wanted to marry my melt-on-the-tongue chocolate fondant – Danny appeared, his face pink from the heat of the kitchen. 'Everything OK?'

Everyone spoke at once, about the deliciousness of the food and how clever he was ('Your parents must be *so* proud of you,' Mum gushed), and as he deflected their praise, saying, 'I'm sure any one of you could have thrown it together,' and 'Did you know the heritage carrots were from Sylvia's garden?' it hit me just how badly I'd underestimated him.

I'd presumed he was going to try to win me over with a flashy show of his cooking skills but, instead, he'd given me an evening to treasure with my family.

'How did you know they'd be hungry?' I said, when our plates had been cleared by the quietly efficient waiter, and Dad had been told to put his wallet away, and everyone was gathering up bags and jackets, ready to head home for a nightcap.

'I didn't,' he said with a relaxed grin, as if he hadn't been slaving in the kitchen for the past two hours. 'But I knew they'd want to see you.'

Not sure how to deal with the surge of clashing emotions his words had aroused, I stood up and said reached for my purse. 'I'd like to pay,' I said. 'I don't think it's right that Adam should foot the bill for my family's greed.'

'It's on the house.' Danny grabbed my credit card and pretended to snap it in two, before passing it back. 'I've been wanting to practise that hare recipe for ages, and I can't claim credit for the desserts. They were made by the chef I job share with.'

'Seems an odd kind of job share,' I said, when I should have been thanking him from the bottom of my heart, like any civilised person would have. 'Don't you ever think about doing it full time?'

He pulled his head back. 'I've already told you my work philosophy, Cassie.' His eyebrows rose. 'I can always pick up more hours if I need to, and I've got a good pension plan, if that's what you're worried about.'

'Why would I be worried?' I rubbed my wrist, which was starting to itch again. 'You can do whatever you like.'

'We all can,' he said, smoothing a hand around his jaw. 'It's not that difficult, really.' When I rolled my eyes, he grinned. 'Have a nice time at your party in London tomorrow night.'

So, he had been listening. 'Thanks,' I mumbled, bending to pick up my napkin which had slid to the floor.

'You coming, Cassie?' Mum called.

I straightened to see everyone waiting for me by the door. 'On my way,' I said, waving the napkin. 'Listen, Danny...' I turned, ready to thank him properly, but he'd already gone and the door to the kitchen was swinging softly shut.

Back home, we assembled in the living room. Dad, in a celebratory mood, opened the bottle of whisky that normally only came out at Christmas. 'I think a toast is in order,' he said, pouring out generous measures – and an orange juice for Emma and Rob – and we toasted the parents-to-be.

'I've said Rob can move in with me now,' she said. 'At least that way, I can keep an eye on him, and he gets to see what morning sickness really looks like.'

'Yay!' Rob, oddly delighted by this unsavoury scenario, cuffed her shoulder and she grabbed his hand and kissed it and, seeing them together, it suddenly made sense why he'd chosen to be with her. Emma was 'home', and that's what he'd craved more than anything while he was drinking in anonymous hotel rooms. It's what I'd craved at times, too, only I'd been far too busy working to do anything about it, and had ignored any pangs of loneliness I'd felt, putting it down to not having time for a relationship.

'Isn't this lovely?' Nan said, settling herself on the sofa where, a mere two weeks ago, I'd walked in on Mum and Dad... *smooching* was the only word my brain would allow. 'I'd like to invite you all to mine on Sunday for home-grown vegetable soup.'

'You haven't got any furniture,' I pointed out, easing my shoes off and raking my fingers through my hair. 'Where are we supposed to sit?' Then I remembered, I probably wouldn't be there. If I was going to Adam's party on Saturday night, there was no way I'd be back in Seashell Cove in time for Sunday lunch. 'Oh, I'll ask Danny to bring some of it back,' Nan said breezily, as though he was a genie she could summon with a rub of a lamp. '*Que sera, sera.*'

'Sounds good to me.' Dad smiled at Mum, who nodded.

'We'll be there.'

'I'll be using water from my butt,' Nan said.

A horrified silence rang out, which I allowed to stretch to snapping point, before saying, 'She means her water butt.'

'Thank Christ for that,' said Rob, through his fingers.

'Oh, Cassie, I had another enquiry at the café today, about your drawings,' Mum said. 'The vicar's wife is throwing a garden party on the May Bank Holiday, and wondered how much you'd charge to draw the guests. Not all of them, but some. Oh, and we sold another of your paintings. Gwen charged nearly two hundred pounds and they didn't even blink.'

'I'm not surprised, they're wonderful,' Nan cried, looking delighted as she raised her whisky glass again. 'I'm so glad I kept one,' she added. 'It was the one of your parents in the café.'

Dad's smile was a bit tearful and he cleared his throat a couple of times. I noticed the photo album on the arm of the chair, and guessed he would probably look through it later, with Mum. 'You're going to have to do some new ones, or the wall will be bare again,' he said.

'Will you be home by then?' Mum tugged me down next to her on the sofa, where she was squashed next to Nan.

'Sorry?'

'I was saying, you'll pop back for the May Bank Holiday, won't you?'

'Back?'

'From London?'

'Remember to take plenty of breaks in this new job of yours,' Dad said, going a bit red at his unaccustomed sternness. Or maybe it was the whisky. He'd already emptied his glass. 'You won't be able to do much painting, otherwise.'

Why were they all talking about painting, instead of asking me about my new job? I fixed my eyes on Emma's round-toed shoes, which would have made the feet of someone with less slender ankles look like hooves. 'I will,' I said, discreetly chafing my wrist against my thigh.

'Look at us, we're turning into the Waltons.' Rob leaned his head on Emma's shoulder. They were nestled so close in the armchair, they looked like they were zipped together. 'You're going to miss this, Sandra.'

There appeared to be a tennis ball lodged in my throat, blocking normal speech.

'She knows where we are, Rob, and I'm sure she'll be back whenever she can, won't you, love?' said Mum.

As I nodded mutely, my phone vibrated.

It was a text from Adam. *Home, at last. Can't wait to see you tomorrow, my little pickpocket. A X*

He had a nickname for me. One with criminal connotations, but still. I'd never had a nickname before (Sandra didn't count). Even Danny called me by my actual name.

I imagined Adam meeting me at King's Cross tomorrow, and us falling into each other's arms, and suddenly everything fell into place and I knew what I had to do.

'Excuse me,' I said, standing up. 'I just need to make a call.'

Chapter 32

Everything felt different when I woke the following morning. It took a moment to realise that the strange lightness in my body wasn't a sign of illness – it was a lack of tension. While I knew it wouldn't last (I wasn't insane) I prolonged the sensation by soaking in a bath piled high with bubbles, instead of taking my usual five-minute shower, and read a *Sweet Valley High* book of Meg's that I'd never got around to returning. The main characters, the Wakefield twins, were more her than me, with their 'shoulder-length blonde hair and green-blue eyes' and it was unlikely Scotland Yard would have taken them on as interns, but I found myself engrossed.

When a rap sounded on the door, the book slid through my fingers and plopped into the water. 'Just to say, there's a suitcase on top of our wardrobe if you want to take it,' Mum said, sticking her head round the door. 'Cassie, where are you?' I bobbed up, cradling a pulpy mass in my hands. 'Is it papier mâché?' She edged in for a closer look, smiling when I shook with laughter. 'You're in a good mood,' she approved, taking the soggy mess and depositing it in the bin. I resolved to order Meg a new copy – and maybe a couple more in the series for myself. 'Your wrist looks a bit better.'

'It's not itching,' I said, studying the livid patch. 'I'll keep using the cream though.'

'We'll miss you, you know.' Mum perched on the side of the bath. She'd pinned her hair at the sides, revealing her dainty ears, and her eyes had gone a bit misty. 'It's been so nice, having you here.'

I flicked some bubbles at her. 'It's not like I'll be a million miles away.'

'No, I suppose not.' Her smile bounced back. 'Your dad and I are off to the café now,' she said. 'We're going to talk to Gwen about, you know.' Her eyes expanded. 'Being our new manager.'

'That's great, Mum. Just make sure she knows she has to keep her cat in the office, and not in the café.'

'She doesn't have a cat.' Mum rose, brushing at a damp patch on her trousers.

'She will, soon.' I blew her a soapy kiss as she backed out of the bathroom, and she pretended to catch, then drop it, then pick it up and put in her cardigan pocket.

'Too much, Mum,' I said, laughing.

I looked at the door for a few seconds when she'd gone, glad that I'd decided not to come clean in the end. The temptation to confess that I'd been fired, and that my job hadn't always been the glamorous and exciting roller coaster I'd made it out to be had been overwhelming after I'd talked to Adam. But looking at their happy, expectant faces when I'd returned to the living room, I'd wondered what it would achieve; other than getting it off my chest. Things still felt a bit fragile between us, and I knew Mum and Dad would end up blaming themselves. They'd only just come to terms with Rob's full disclosure about how miserable he'd been. It would have felt selfish to tell them I hadn't been happy at Five Star, especially as I hadn't fully realised it myself. I had assumed that the stress and Carlotta's outbursts were simply part of the job. The sort of thing employees everywhere had to put up with. Maybe, one day, when everything had settled down – perhaps in twenty years – I'd tell them and we could laugh about it, and reflect how it didn't matter any more, because I'd eventually got to where I wanted to be.

I started when a fist pounded the door. 'Hurry up, Sandra, I need a sh—'

'God's sake Rob, I'll be out in a minute.'

'I was going to say shave.'

It was the first time I'd heard Emma giggle, and the sound was oddly encouraging. She'd stayed over in the end, after driving a tipsy Nan back to her cottage, and I'd fallen asleep to a soundtrack of her and Rob's low-voiced murmurs in the room next door.

'And Em might need to throw up.'

I clambered out and, swaddled in a towel, returned to my bedroom to dress and pack, which wouldn't take long, considering a lot of my stuff was still in my suitcase.

'Call us later, Cassie,' Dad shouted up the stairs. 'Love you.'

'Love you more,' I shouted back.

'Love you to the moon and back,' Rob called from the bathroom.

There was the sound of thundering feet on the landing and Emma's panicked voice yelled, 'Get out of the way, Rob, I'm going to be—'

I winced at the sounds that followed, and hoped Rob was holding her hair back. It was a far cry from his life as a musician, even though that had probably involved a fair bit of sick as well.

When I'd finished packing, I dressed in the outfit I'd left out, and loaded my hair in a messy bun before clunking my bags and suitcase downstairs.

There was a plate of fresh croissants in the kitchen, but my stomach was fluttering with nerves as I thought about what lay ahead, so I poured some coffee and sipped it slowly at the table, before pulling my sketch pad over and taking out my pencils.

'We're going to the café for breakfast,' Rob said, appearing freshly shaved, with his hair flattened down and a newly ironed T-shirt over his jeans. 'It's going to be our new Saturday-morning thing.'

'It's good to have a thing,' I said, smiling when Emma appeared at his side, pale but smiling, in her outfit from the night before. 'Try some ginger tea, Emma, it might settle your stomach.'

'It won't,' she said, not breaking her smile. 'But, thanks.'

'What are you drawing?' Rob strained to look, but I covered the sheet with my arm. 'Please yourself.' He tugged a strand of hair out of my bun.

'You're such a pain,' I said, trying to stuff it back in.

'And what the hell are you wearing?' He looked at my old trainers.

I jigged my feet at him. 'Shouldn't you be going?'

'Shouldn't you?'

I glanced at the clock, feeling my heart speed up. 'Soon,' I said.

'Do you want us all to wave you off, or something?'

'I think I'll be OK, thanks.' I made a shooing motion. 'No offence, but I'm busy.'

'Stop being a pain, Rob.' Emma rolled her eyes and dragged him away. I was warming to her by the minute.

Although my drawing was simple, I wanted it to be perfect, and spent ages going over the lines, taking care with the shading and detail, smudging in delicate colours here and there and, when I was satisfied, I rolled it up and slotted it carefully into my bag.

It was time to go.

♥

Nan was in her living room when I arrived, arranging some of her knick-knacks on the windowsill. 'I thought you were staying minimalist?' I said, looking at the boxes scattered around.

'That was before I knew I was going to have a great-grandchild.' She stepped nimbly over a bag to give me a hug. She was wearing one of her robes again, but her hair was in a neat chignon and her mouth bore a trace of lipstick. 'Everything outside is staying, after all Danny's hard work.'

'Even the compost toilet?'

'*Mon dieu.*' She closed her eyes and pressed a hand to her forehead. 'I only used it once and that was enough.' She shuddered. 'I'm all for being environmentally friendly, but I want to do my business where I won't get my bottom stung.'

'Who wouldn't?' I said. 'You can still do your bit for the environment, without peeing outdoors.'

'I'll carry on using recycled loo paper.'

'Good,' seemed to be the only response to that. A movement by the window caught my eye. 'Is Danny here?' I said, though it was obvious he was. I'd recognised his shape. 'I need a word, if you can spare him.'

'Have as many as you like, *chérie*. I told him he didn't need to stay once he'd dropped off this lot, but he insisted on fixing the wobbly hinge on the gate.' She pulled some thickly lined curtains from a bag. 'I don't like bare windows at night,' she announced, throwing them over her shoulder. 'They're going back up.'

Danny was putting his tools away when I entered the garden, and didn't look particularly surprised to see me. 'Couldn't stay away?' He grinned, and my heart tripped. 'Nice outfit,' he said, eyes sweeping my top and trousers.

'Wish I could say the same.' He was wearing a creased pink polo-shirt with the collar flicked up, his jeans were covered in oil stains, and his hair was all over the place. 'You're looking at my mouth again,' he observed. 'Is that why you're here and not in London?'

'Don't flatter yourself.' I hitched my bag onto my shoulder. 'I just wondered whether you'd like to come for a walk.'

He swiped his forearm across his forehead. 'Better late than never,' he said, eyes scrunched against the sun. April was going overboard on the sunny weather. 'As long as you're not going to try and kiss me again.'

My face felt like it had been microwaved. 'Are you coming, or not?'

'Yes, ma'am!' He saluted and leapt over his toolbox, pausing for a moment to give me a searching stare. 'Let me just say cheerio to Sylvia.'

We didn't say much on the way to the coastal path, where he'd invited me to walk with him the evening Adam had turned up. It was as if he sensed I had something important I was working up to saying, and was trying to make it easy by sticking to easy topics, like work – he had more gardening jobs than he could handle – and his sister, Louise, who was taking a trip to Japan with her partner, and how he was planning to watch *Breaking Bad* even though he was years behind everyone else.

'I hope you're not going to push me off,' he said, when we'd reached the spot where I'd stood with Adam on games night, and read Danny's message in the sand. 'It's not actually that high, so I'll probably land on my feet.' He turned to face me, eyes twinkling like the sea behind him, a quizzical smile on his handsome face.

I took a deep, quivering breath. 'I saw it,' I said, flinging my arm in the direction of the beach. 'What you wrote, that night.'

His smile faded like the sun going in. 'I did wonder.' He glanced over his shoulder, as if it might still be there. 'But when you didn't mention it…'

'I couldn't,' I said. 'I didn't know what to say.' His eyes moved back to mine. 'But now I do.' Before losing my nerve completely, I slid the rolled up picture out of my bag and handed it to him with trembling fingers. 'I wanted to write it in the sand like you did, but there isn't a full moon tonight, and I thought if I did it this morning the tide might come in and wash it away, or some kids would mess it up, so…' I ran out of steam. There was no option but to endure him studying my drawing, with no idea of how he would respond.

'*I like you too,*' he read out loud, turning the page for me to look at, even though I knew that the words were drawn inside a heart in golden sand, with the letters C and D at the top and bottom. I hadn't been able to resist adding some waves, a starfish, and a couple of seashells, but the message was loud and clear.

'It's my response,' I said. 'To your message.'

'I can see that.' His voice was soft and querying, his face packed with emotion. 'But… aren't you going back to London?'

'No,' I said. 'I'm not.' Adam had been more understanding than I deserved when I'd called him the night before, to explain why I wouldn't be applying for the job with Grace Dewsbury because I wanted to stay in Seashell Cove and become an artist. Not a Connor Daley or a Vicky Burton type, but one who drew whatever she fancied – sad-eyed greyhounds, seascapes, or caricatures like the ones he'd seen on the wall of the café and dismissed – and that I couldn't wait to start.

'That person who slipped her business card into your pocket on the train,' I'd said, trying not to cry. 'It wasn't me, Adam. I did it because I thought it was something I *should* do, because I wanted to be in a relationship. It was the same with my job. I was good at it, but I'd never really considered whether it was right for me. I was completely stressed all the time.'

'But you seemed so composed at the café, with all those cats.'

'Maybe on the surface.' It was clear he thrived on pressure, and probably couldn't understand what I was on about. 'I've got eczema.'

He hadn't responded to that but, instead, suggested I visit anyway, so we could talk face to face and he could take me out to dinner, but I'd made up my mind and knew I wouldn't be swayed.

'I know someone who'd love the job with Grace,' I'd said, and gave him Nina's number. 'I'm sorry for wasting your time.'

'I really hope you find what you're looking for, Cassie.' He'd sounded sad, but not heartbroken, and I knew he'd waste no time in moving on. 'I've enjoyed getting to know you.'

It was the nickname that had really clinched it. Adam had been so keen for romance he'd seen what he wanted to see. Only Danny had had an inkling that things weren't as they seemed, and he'd liked me anyway.

'I saw your bags in the car, back at Sylvia's,' he was saying, returning me to the moment.

'Oh, yes.' I smiled. 'I'm moving in with her for now. Mum and Dad really like their own routine, and Nan's got plenty of room. We can keep each other company, and there's space there for me to paint.'

He looked at the picture again, and back at me. 'You're going to be an artist?'

I laughed, because it sounded absurd, but also like the only thing I really wanted to do. 'Better late than never,' I said, feeling a rush of happiness. 'I was actually fired from my job in London but I'm glad now, because I've realised I'm not cut out for event planning.'

'I know,' he said gently. 'I heard you talking to your friends the other night, at the pub. I came out to see if you were OK.'

'You did?'

'It was obvious something wasn't right. Until the moment you kissed me,' he said. 'That felt very right indeed.' His tender smile made my heart soar. 'So, if you're staying, there's every possibility we might keep bumping into each other.'

'Maybe,' I said. 'I might even have hatched a plan to win you over.'

'I think you just did.' He pressed my picture against his chest, and the look in his eyes stole my breath. 'Come here, you.'

I stepped into the space between us, and his arm slid around my waist and pulled me closer. When our lips finally met, his response was instant and somehow familiar, as if I'd been dreaming about it for a very long time.

'Wow,' he said, when we pulled apart, his eyes smiling into mine. 'If you hadn't won me over before, you have now.' He slid the picture back into my bag with great delicacy, then slowly ran his hands down my arms and took my hands in his. 'Can we do it again?'

'Actually, that wasn't how I was planning to win you over.' My mouth wouldn't stop smiling. I hadn't thought it was possible to feel this good. 'I've something even better in mind.'

'Not possible,' he said, letting me lead him back along the path, his hand strong and sure around mine. 'Where are we going?'

'There's a barbecue later at the Smugglers Inn, and they're doing karaoke.' I looked over at the terrace outside the café. They were there, by the picket fence, waiting for me to join them; my friends, in strappy tops, combat trousers and ugly trainers. *Legal Mystics, reunited.*

'Is that why you're dressed like a nineties girl-band?'

'It is.' The look on Danny's face made me laugh. 'I'm going to win you over with the power of song,' I said. 'I hope you're ready, Danny Fleetwood.'

A Letter From Karen

I want to say a huge thank you for choosing to read *The Café at Seashell Cove*. If you did enjoy it, and want to keep up to date with all my latest releases, just sign up at the following link. Your email address will never be shared and you can unsubscribe at any time.

www.bookouture.com/karen-clarke/

Being a lover of cake and coffee, the idea of basing my new book around a family-owned café felt very natural. A lot of the book was written in cafés, as I find the atmosphere both relaxing and inspiring – the busier the better. Obviously, they're handy for refuelling, too, though I have to be careful I don't only eat cake when I'm writing! I've had some happy holidays in Devon, an area I find beautiful and inviting all year round, so having the café overlook a pretty cove seemed like the perfect setting. I've never visited a cat café, but I couldn't resist adding cute animals to the story. From my research, cat cafés are becoming more popular, but it's probably best I stay away, or I'd never get any writing done!

I hope you loved *The Café at Seashell Cove* and if you did I would be very grateful if you could write a review. I'd love to hear what you think, and it makes such a difference helping new readers to discover one of my books for the first time.

I love hearing from my readers – you can get in touch on my Facebook page, through Twitter, Goodreads or my website.

Thanks,
Karen

[facebook icon] karen.clarke.5682

[twitter icon] karenclarke123

[globe icon] www.writewritingwritten.blogspot.com

Acknowledgements

A lot of people are involved in making a book, and I would like to thank the brilliant team at Bookouture for making it happen. Particular thanks to my wonderful editor, Abi, for her clever and insightful comments, to Anne for her seamless copy-editing, Emma for the gorgeous cover, Claire for her eagle-eyed proofreading, and Kim and Noelle for spreading the word.

As ever, I owe my lovely readers a massive thank you, as well as the blogging community, whose reviews are a labour of love, and Amanda Brittany for her tireless feedback and friendship.

And last, but never least, thank you to all my family and friends for their constant encouragement, my children, Amy, Martin and Liam for their unwavering support, and my husband Tim for everything – I couldn't do it without you.

25272732R00181

Printed in Poland
by Amazon Fulfillment
Poland Sp. z o.o., Wrocław